Mint Juleps and Justice

Center Point
Large Print

Also by Nancy Naigle and available from
Center Point Large Print:

The Adams Grove Novels
  Sweet Tea and Secrets
  Out of Focus
  Wedding Cake and Big Mistakes
  Pecan Pie and Deadly Lies

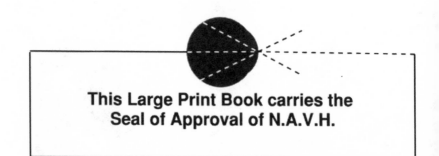

**This Large Print Book carries the
Seal of Approval of N.A.V.H.**

Mint Juleps and Justice

An Adams Grove Novel

NANCY NAIGLE

CENTER POINT LARGE PRINT
THORNDIKE, MAINE

This Center Point Large Print edition
is published in the year 2016 by arrangement with
Amazon Publishing, www.apub.com.

Originally published in the United States
by Amazon Publishing, 2014.

The text of this Large Print edition is unabridged.
In other aspects, this book may vary
from the original edition.
Printed in the United States of America
on permanent paper.
Set in 16-point Times New Roman type.

ISBN: 978-1-68324-039-6

Library of Congress Cataloging-in-Publication Data

Names: Naigle, Nancy, author.
Title: Mint juleps and justice : an Adams Grove novel / Nancy Naigle.
Description: Center Point Large Print edition. | Thorndike, Maine :
Center Point Large Print, 2016. | ©2014 | Series: Adams Grove series
Identifiers: LCCN 2016014680 | ISBN 9781683240396
    (hardcover : alk. paper)
Subjects: LCSH: Divorced women—Fiction. | Private investigators—
Fiction. | Large type books. | GSAFD: Romantic suspense fiction.
Classification: LCC PS3614.A545 M56 2016 | DDC 813/.6—dc23
LC record available at http://lccn.loc.gov/2016014680

To all of the new friends I've made
through the small town of Adams Grove.
Thanks for reading the series and
allowing me to live out a lifelong dream.
May our connections remain small-town strong.

❖ Chapter One ❖

Who would have thought there'd be more excitement in the little town of Adams Grove than in the resort city of Virginia Beach? Okay, maybe not on any given day, but today for sure.

It was eight o'clock sharp when Brooke Justice breezed into the Cooperative Extension office to grab her things and get on the road. She had a string of farm visits scheduled, and even though the temperatures were going to be in the high nineties with humidity to match, she was looking forward to them. Meeting with local producers was her favorite part of the job, and the last visit on her list today was one she'd been looking forward to all week. Country superstar Cody Tuggle had recently announced his engagement to local photographer Kasey Phillips, and they planned to set up a new facility for racehorses on her property here in Adams Grove. It was Brooke's job, as the county extension agent, to help them put together a pasture-management and grazing plan specific to their needs.

When she transferred from Virginia Beach to the position here in Holland County, she never dreamed she might get to mingle with the rich and famous in such a little town.

Just the remote possibility of getting to see

Cody Tuggle in person was going to make the rest of this day drag. Her best friend, Jenny, would flat-out lose it if she knew there was a chance of her meeting Cody today on the farm visit, which was exactly why she hadn't mentioned this assignment to her yet. Cody probably had "people" to talk to her about the land, but it was still a possibility he might be there. She crossed her fingers. *Never hurts to add a little luck.*

Transferring from her old position had been one of the hardest decisions she'd faced. Those farmers back in Virginia Beach had taught her as much as she had them in the beginning. College hadn't prepared her for the real-life problems farmers faced, but she'd been a quick study and they'd taken her under their wing. She loved that job, but her separation from Keith had gotten out of control, and putting some miles between them and their broken marriage seemed like the right thing to do when the opportunity arose.

Brooke gathered a stack of soil-sample kits and a notebook with the list of her appointments for the day, then grabbed the keys to the truck the county provided for her use. She headed out the back door of the Main Street office where the truck was parked.

The little white four-wheel-drive pickup was much more suitable to the roads than her own car. Many of the roads were still unpaved in this county. In Virginia Beach they'd provided her with a vehicle too, only it was a big twelve-seater passenger van. It was a bear to maneuver and forget about parking it.

The first stop on her list of appointments was to check in with the farmer who would be supplying the market lambs and goats for the 4-H'ers. They'd weigh and tag the animals in preparation for the nominations next week. She worked her way through the next three farm visits, a mix of crop and livestock farmers, and then tapped in the address on the GPS for the farm on Nickel Creek Road. It was less than eight miles away. Nervous excitement built as she got closer to Kasey Phillips's farm.

Just one turn off Route 58 and she was there. She pulled into the driveway of the sprawling white ranch with the red metal roof. A nice barn and lots of high-dollar fencing were already in place. Goats lay chewing their cud under the shade of a huge pecan tree in the front pasture. From here it looked like mostly clover and weeds, fine for goats, but the horses would go hungry in that field. There was tall fescue too—that could spell disaster for a horse farm that planned any type of breeding program.

A bright red cardinal fluttered by as Brooke got out of the truck. *Cardinal, good luck.* Seeing the good-luck sign calmed her. The lucky signs might have started as a fun diversion when she was just a kid hunting for four-leaf clovers with her brother, but over the years luck had become kind of like a second religion for Brooke. She believed in it, and it could make or break her day.

The front door opened and, at first glance, the height of the man sent her heart racing. For that one fleeting moment she thought it *was* Cody Tuggle, but then she caught the brown hair peeking from beneath the cap and realized it wasn't. *Wishful thinking.* At least the ball cap didn't bear a tractor company theme and it wasn't camo like those of ninety percent of the guys she met during these visits.

He met her on the driveway, extending his hand as he approached. "Hey there, I'm Mike."

"You're the farm manager?" Brooke asked.

He raised his brow slightly, and then smiled. "Yeah, I guess that's me. For now."

Nice voice and good-looking too. He might even be better-looking than the music man. His eyes were almost too blue for a dark-haired man, and his tan showed them off just right.

It was hard to not stare into those baby blues. "I'm Brooke Justice." She shook his hand, feeling tiny in his presence. He stood a good foot taller than her, with broad shoulders that pulled his T-shirt taut and biceps . . . *well, let's just stop this gawking right here.* "I was told y'all wanted to work on a pasture and grazing rotation plan. Want to show me around?"

"That's right. We do." He motioned her to

follow. When they got to the back of the house he jumped behind the wheel of a Polaris Ranger, and she climbed into the seat next to him. He hit the gas pedal on the utility vehicle and it lurched forward.

She sucked in a breath as his arm flung across her midsection with lightning speed as she ricocheted back in the seat. His softball-size bicep didn't go unnoticed, nor did the way it flexed when he repositioned his hand on the steering wheel. She knew she'd need to check out the rest of him as they sped through the smooth terrain.

They rode the entire property line first, then backtracked, stopping to talk about each area that was fenced off.

Brooke listened and took a few notes. "Y'all are in really great shape here as far as the fencing goes. Whoever set this up had some experience. It's already cross-fenced, so you'll be able to rotate to get the most from your pastures."

"I can't take credit for that. Guy that remodeled this place had been a farmer his whole life. Horses, cattle, goats. He remodeled this place for his wife as a surprise. He died. She's finally moving on."

"Is she the one who's engaged to Cody Tuggle?" She wished the words hadn't tumbled from her mouth, but there they were. Daddy had always said he'd named her right because words rushed right out of her like water over the rocks, and there was no stopping them.

"Sure is," he said with no hint of emotion either way.

She tilted her head. "That bother you?"

"That Kasey has moved on? No. Cody is a nice guy. They're good together."

"You've met him? And he's nice?" she said with a little too much enthusiasm. *Hello, mouth, quit going all fangirl on me.*

"Sure." He leaned forward on the steering wheel. "Why do you look so surprised? Famous people can't be nice?"

"No. Not that, I just never met a star before. It's kind of cool that he's going to be moving here."

Mike tugged on his hat. "Well, not right here. He and Kasey are building a place on the acreage on the other side of that fence line. They bought the adjacent land all the way to the next curve. About four hundred acres."

"They bought the cut-over from the timber company?"

Mike nodded. "They did, but I think they're actually building on the far end. That land is still cropland right now."

"The old Doyle farm. I know of it. Nice piece of land." Too bad it wouldn't be farmed, though. She didn't like to see cropland lose its purpose. Once that cycle was broken, it just didn't come back. More and more of it was being repurposed for nonagricultural use. A bad thing for the county.

Brooke wondered if she'd get the chance to

meet Cody Tuggle when they got ready to do something with that land. Probably not. He probably had "people" who would handle those conversations too. When she looked up, Mike was staring at her like he was waiting on a response. Just how long had she been standing there daydreaming?

"Cody's mother is going to be using this property. She's the one who's into racehorses."

Hugging her notebook to her chest, she asked, "How long have you been working with race-horses?"

"Me?" Mike chuckled. "I don't have any experience with racehorses . . . with the exception of a few lousy bets."

"I'm sorry, I'd just assumed you—"

"Of course you would, but no, I'm just doing a favor for Kasey, the one who is engaged to your favorite singer. She asked me if I'd take care of things for her while they are away. It was a win-win since I wasn't sure where I was going to put down roots when I got out of the military. This kind of helped me make the decision."

"Nice town to put down roots. I just moved here myself. I'm a Virginia Beach native."

"I've been here for a while now. Was your dad in the Navy?" he asked.

She nodded. "A pilot."

"How are you adjusting to Adams Grove?"

"I like it. I never realized just how loud it was

out there near Oceana until I moved here. What a difference."

"The quiet is nice. When my parents split up, my brother lived in Virginia Beach with my mom. I stayed up this way with Dad. I kind of prefer the wide-open spaces."

"Well, welcome home then."

"Thanks."

He looked like he was going to ask her something else, but chickened out. "I won't be actually managing the farm. I'm just helping coordinate things that need to happen before all that, but I'll be your guy for a little while."

My guy? In another lifetime that would have thrilled her. "Got it. Well, I appreciate you giving me the tour, and look forward to working with you for a little while, Mike." She should be done with this appointment by now, but she was still curious about him. Another few minutes wouldn't put her too far behind schedule. Usually she was meeting with married couples wanting to give the country life a try in their second half of life or lifetime farmers with big guts. It wasn't often she got to visit with young, hot, available men. Not that she was in the market for one. "What branch of the service were you in?"

He pulled off his sunglasses. White squint lines framed his eyes against his very tanned skin. "Marine Corps."

"Of course you were." He had Marine written

all over him: muscles, confidence, and blue eyes just plain begging her to get lost in them so he could rescue her. "How long have you been out?"

"Not long enough."

There was more to that story. Was that a no-trespassing sign hanging on that expression? "Were you in Iraq?"

He nodded, but it was clear she wasn't going to get any other details.

After an hour of riding the fence line, walking the land, pulling soil samples, and discussing land use, Brooke knew a lot about the property and still only a little about the guy who had given her the tour, other than he'd grown up in the area. She wasn't sure how being a Marine was going to translate into his hanging around a farm for a while, but then that wasn't her call and it would be a nice addition to her schedule, so she wasn't going to complain. She hoped he'd have lots of questions along the way. That would suit her just fine.

He walked her back to her truck, and opened the door for her to get in. "You wouldn't want to get some dinner one night, would you?"

"I'm a big fan of dinner." *Why didn't I just say no? I haven't even gotten rid of Keith yet. The last thing I need is another guy causing havoc in my life.* And there was that smile again.

"Me too."

"You've got my card. My cell number is on it." *Hello, brain . . . just who is the boss of my mouth? I hope he doesn't call. Please don't call.*

He slammed the truck door wearing a big smile that showed off perfect white teeth and a slight dimple . . . right on the left side of that grin. He glanced down at her card. "Brooke Justice. Nice name."

"Thanks. I didn't even ask your last name."

"Hartman."

Of course it was. Why couldn't she quit looking at him? She forced herself to look in the rearview mirror as she backed out of the driveway. When she pulled onto the road and looked back toward the house, the image of him walking away made her smile too.

I take it back . . . a call would be nice. I may have to hand-deliver the soil-sample reports.

❖ Chapter Two ❖

Even with being sidetracked by Mike Hartman on the Nickel Creek Road farm, Brooke had finished the long list of farm visits with time to spare. She pressed the speed dial on her phone to tell Jenny about her last appointment. Maybe she hadn't actually met the superstar, but meeting someone who knew Cody Tuggle was noteworthy among friends, right?

"Happy Balance," Jenny answered in a voice that could make millions with a 1-900 number.

"Hey, Jenny, it's me. How's it going?"

"Great. I just stocked the smoothie bar and hung all the glassware. It looks so pretty. I can't wait for you to see it. The grand opening is going to be amazing."

"People are talking about it all over town, and I've been dropping hints about it on all my farm visits. I'm so excited for you." Brooke's relocation had been a necessary step to keep her sanity through the divorce from Keith. Yet Jenny's move was working out just as well, or maybe better, for her. "Speaking of talk all over town, I've got Adams Grove gossip from my farm visits today."

"Oh, goody. I love the juicy gossip in this little town. You coming by?"

"On my way." Brooke paused as she caught a blur of blue in her rearview mirror. A car had appeared out of nowhere right behind her. *I hope I didn't cut him off on that last turn.* "I'm going to stop by the house and pick up some library books that are due back, and then I'll be there."

"Awesome. I'll test out the blender and new recipes on you."

"Lucky me," Brooke said with dread. Jenny was always trying to trick her into healthy stuf

"That's what friends are for."

Brooke ended the call and glanced

earview mirror again. The car wasn't on her bumper anymore; that was good. She turned into her neighborhood and motored down the curved road. Her house was on the last street near the lake. It was comforting that there was no way Keith could cruise by without her seeing him coming or going. One way in. One way out.

She pulled into her driveway and dashed inside to grab the library books. Just as she closed the front door, she opened it again and turned on the porch light. No telling what time she might get back home with Jenny so excited about the grand opening, and she'd promised herself she would be extra-cautious after all the goings-on with Keith. That was easier to say than to remember, because things seemed so safe and easy in this town.

When she and Keith had split, she had been hurt, but at least things were polite; when he'd decided that he wanted to be back together, it had gotten creepy and uncomfortable. His infidelity and lies were unforgivable in her book, and the way he continued to insert himself into her business was unsettling. More than once she was pretty sure he'd caused the trouble that he'd tried to rescue her from. Then there was the whole thing with him telling his lawyer that she was the one who had abandoned the marriage, and fighting for possessions she'd brought into it. Proving all of that was becoming a real pain.

Moving had been the best choice, and being

the glass and set it down. "This one is a definite yes."

"Good."

"What is it?"

"I'm not telling you."

"That means you're feeding me weird stuff again. Why do you always sneak healthy in on me? You know I'm not into that new age lifestyle."

"It's good for you." Jenny handed her another glass. "Besides, if I tell you what's in it you won't give it a fair taste."

"You think that's going to make me feel any better about it?" Brooke took the glass full of a thick yellow concoction. She took a sip, thinking it was banana, only to get a tart lemon taste instead. Her face puckered up like a kissing gourami.

"Not good?"

"No. It's good. I was just expecting banana and got sour." Her lashes fluttered, but she took another sip. "Wow. But good. Yes, it's good."

A skinny, dark-haired man walked through the front door.

Jenny smiled and waved, but the guy, carrying a small satchel, barely broke stride as he headed toward the back of the space.

Brooke leaned forward and whispered. "Who's that?"

"He's painting the murals in the locker rooms."

Brooke glanced over her shoulder. "Good, because he doesn't look like your type or the social, smoothie-makin' type."

"No, he's not, but he's one hell of an artist." Jenny came from around the bar. "Come follow me. He's done with the guys' locker room already. You've got to see this."

She pushed the door labeled WARRIORS open and motioned Brooke inside.

"My goodness! This guy *is* talented." A serene countryside mural spread from one end of the room to the other. Deer drank from a small pond, and the flowers in the meadow looked so real Brooke thought she could smell them, and the sky . . . the sky extended to the tall ceiling and was so clear she half-expected to see a bird fly by. It was like The Venetian in Vegas, where you really had to keep reminding yourself that you were not outside. "How long did it take him to do this? And how did you keep it a secret for so long?"

"He's been working on it for about two weeks. He gave me a deal on it if I let him stay in the space while he worked."

"You're becoming the bartering queen."

Jenny nodded. "I know. Wish I'd been this good of a negotiator during my divorce. Maybe I would have come out a little better in that deal. I still can't believe I just let him have the beach house."

"True, but he'd been sleeping with his little

22

mistress in that beach house at the time and I'm still glad you didn't do something crazy like burn the place down."

Jenny smirked. "Don't think I didn't think about it. Thank goodness for the don't-do-anything-you-can't-undo rule. Keeps us out of trouble every time."

"Probably the best gift my dad ever gave us. He was good for something after all." Brooke walked closer to the painting. "The only problem I see with this artwork is that the guys that live around here might try to shoot those deer out of season, they look so real," Brooke teased.

The sound of someone clearing their throat made both women spin around.

"You scared me to death." Jenny lowered the hand she held to her chest and let out a breath. "I didn't hear you come in. I was just showing my best friend your work. This is Brooke. Meet Dan."

"Nice to meet you, Dan." Brooke stepped forward to shake his hand. "Your work is amazing."

"Thanks." He shook her hand, holding it a little too long. A slow smile softened the hard lines of his face.

Brooke felt an uneasy pull as the man just stared at them. "Are you from around here?"

"For now."

Brooke waited for more, but he didn't continue. "Have you checked in with Jill Malloy down at the artisan center? I bet she'd love to showcase your work."

"No. Haven't. One thing at a time," he said.

Alrighty then.

He turned to Jenny. "I just wanted to pick up a couple things and I'll be out of your way."

"No worries." Jenny turned and started heading to the door. "We were just leaving."

He turned sideways as they passed.

"He's a little odd," Brooke whispered as they walked back out front. "And quiet. I never heard him come up."

"Yeah, quirky, but I can't believe I got an artist like that for just the cost of crashing in an old building and a few hundred bucks. So what were you going to tell me?"

Brooke ran down the details of her visit over at Kasey Phillips's farm.

"I can't believe you didn't tell me you were going over there. What if Cody Tuggle had been there?"

"Then I'd have probably fainted, and you'd have found out when they took me to the hospital because you're my emergency contact!" Brooke laughed. "No, I'd probably have just stood there mumbling and drooling."

"That's attractive."

"No, it wouldn't be, but that's okay. The guy that I'll be working with isn't a troll either."

Jenny gave Dan a quick wave as he walked past

them and left the building. "So what's this about the guy at the farm? Is he single?"

"His name is Mike. He's tall, probably like six-three, dark hair, muscles to die for, ex-Marine, polite—"

"Sounds like someone's interested."

"Me?" Brooke shook her head. "Oh, heck, no. If I ever get out of this marriage, I'll never date again." She crossed her heart. "He is hot, though."

The bells on the door tinkled and a young woman in black yoga pants and a pink tank top came in.

"There's my girl. Hi, Ashleigh." Jenny called out to the girl. "Come meet my best friend in the whole world, Brooke Justice."

"Nice to meet you, Ashleigh." Brooke gathered her things. "I'm going to let y'all get down to the yogurt, grass, and fruit-shake making."

Jenny turned to Ashleigh. "First order of business. Never ever, under any circumstances, tell Brooke what is in our smoothies."

"Secret ingredients?"

Jenny shook her head. "Nothing that savvy. My best friend here has a serious aversion to healthy food . . . and men."

Brooke picked up her purse and turned to leave. "On that note, I'm outta here, but for the record I don't think avoiding health food or men has ever killed anyone."

❖ Chapter Three ❖

Mike Hartman knew his dad had ulterior motives for inviting him over for dinner. He always did. Ever since Mike had gotten back from Iraq, his dad kept in constant contact. There was something unsettling about someone, especially your dad, thinking you might snap at any minute.

He wasn't fragile, but war changes a person. Mike knew that, and he was sure that's what his dad was worried about. Suddenly the clear rules and strong camaraderie of being abroad in uniform were gone and civilian life seemed like one big free-for-all. It had been a little overwhelming at first, but he was making his peace with it. Translating military skills into civilian experience was a stretch for some, but Mike had gone to college before he decided to join the Marines, and he'd been able to land a civilian job with ease. Problem was, he just wasn't fit for a desk job. Sitting on his ass for eight hours a day was pure torture.

Of course, Dad didn't understand that. When he heard the salary that government contractor was willing to pay for sitting behind a desk answering questions and advising servicemen on the software package they'd just installed, Dad couldn't understand why in the world he'd chuck all that to work for himself. Especially in this economy.

After his time in the Marines, Mike had considered training service dogs as a career alternative, as kind of a way to give back to the program, but his experience working for four years side-by-side with First Sgt. Gunner, a highly skilled and decorated German shepherd, hadn't prepared him for all that was involved. So he took a small step and signed on to foster a German shepherd pup through its first year in preparation for service work. It wouldn't be easy to give him up at the end of the twelve-month period, but knowing that he'd helped prepare a pup for a lifetime of service felt like a good step in the right direction. Of course, that didn't solve his desire for satisfying work.

That desk job was driving Mike about half-batty when he reconnected with Perry Von, and when Von suggested Mike start his own private-investigation outfit in Holland County . . . it had felt like the right move. Von said he had more work than he could handle and he'd pass those cases along to Mike until he was up on his feet with his own clientele. Being his own boss had much more appeal, and the work was varied and interesting. He could also work in time for training the service dog, while keeping tabs on Kasey's place. Being in business for himself was a better fit for sure.

So he'd quit the desk job and changed course.

Mike pulled into the driveway of the house he'd grown up in. It looked just like it had for as long as he could remember. Even the flower-beds looked the same—squared-off hedges and rows of yellow and orange marigolds nestled between wide-leaf hostas. Dad was a creature of habit. One trait he was glad he hadn't picked up.

"Hey, Dad," Mike called when he walked inside. He could only guess what Dad might need fixed this time. His needs were turning into a honey-do list, and he thought he'd avoided that trap by never remarrying.

He wandered into the kitchen and dropped off a box of pastries from Mac's Bakery. The aroma of Italian food made his stomach growl. A big tossed salad in a decorative bowl brightened the kitchen table, and a huge pan of the cheesiest lasagna he'd ever seen sat on a cast-iron trivet on the counter. *What have you gone and done now, Dad?*

He grabbed a beer from the refrigerator. From the looks of the number of settings at the table, four, he was going to need it.

Mike opened the slider to join his dad and the obvious mother-daughter duo on the deck. He smiled, although he'd rather have turned and left.

"Son!" Dad popped up from a deck chair and seemed to dance as he jockeyed through the intro-ductions. "Meet Beth and her daughter, Katie." He leaned in close and whispered into Mike's ear, "She's a beauty, isn't she?"

Mike smiled and nodded to Katie, who looked as stuck as he felt. That somehow made it less awkward.

"Beth here goes to my church, and she makes the best lasagna you've ever had," his dad bragged.

Beth blushed. "Thank you. Your daddy is such a charmer."

"He is that," Mike agreed.

"Katie lives in Raleigh," Beth continued. "Not too far. Easy drive. She just got an amazing promotion at her firm. I'm so proud of her. She came up to help me work on the big church bazaar. Now if she could just quit working long enough to find a nice man."

Katie looked like she wished she had a bread stick to throw at her mom.

"You hungry?" Mike's dad asked.

"I wasn't until I walked through your kitchen and smelled that lasagna."

"It's my specialty." Beth got up from her chair, and motioned to his dad. "Come on. Help me in the kitchen."

The two of them scurried away like they were pulling off a big coup.

Mike and Katie let out a sigh at the same time, causing them both to laugh.

"You didn't know I was going to be here, did you?" Katie asked.

"No. I didn't know anyone was going to be here.

I thought I was coming to fix something for Dad. They think they're tricky, don't they?"

Katie nodded. "Don't blame your dad. I'm sure it was all Mom. She fancies herself quite the little matchmaker. I'm not sure why. She's been trying to hook me up for at least the last seven years and I've never been attracted to even one of the men she's picked for me. That woman has a weird definition of handsome."

"Well, I do clean up nice," Mike said.

She clasped her hand across her mouth. "I didn't mean it like that. You're very good-looking . . . oh, gosh . . ."

"I'm just kidding."

"Sorry," she said. "The truth is I'm kind of seeing someone, but I just don't want the hassle of dealing with Mom and the scrutiny of the family on every holiday until it's a for-sure thing. It's simpler to pretend I'm alone and have to work."

"I see you have a few of your own tricks up your sleeve. Must run in the family."

"I guess I do. It'll work until I'm forced to come back and take care of her. She'll never leave this town, but she's getting a little forgetful and I do worry. Maybe I'll get lucky and your dad will take care of my mom and vice versa."

"Maybe. Never really pictured my dad remarried again, but you never know. He's a good man."

"Have you always lived in a small town?"

"No, not always. But mostly. It appeals to me."

Technically it was true. Although all his civilian time had really been right here in this small county, he'd been all over the world as a Marine. Longer story than he planned to share with this gal, though.

"Divorced?"

Mike took a swig of his beer. "Nope." It wasn't a lie, but he knew her real question was had he ever been married, and that was a whole other story. But then again she was already rambling along about herself, so maybe she didn't really care what his status was.

"I was married for less than two years right out of high school. Big mistake. I ended up getting a divorce, then I went back to college and started fresh. I've had a couple serious relationships, but nothing that felt like forever. I'd like to have a couple kids, but my career does keep me busy."

They ate dinner and Beth carried most of the conversation with chitchat about the church and her ladies club. It seemed like the longest dinner on earth to Mike and he was glad when his phone rang and gave him the chance to pretend he had a business call to go on.

"Sorry, folks. I'm going to have to run." He tapped his phone. "Duty calls." He turned toward Beth. She seemed nice enough and Dad seemed to really enjoy her company. "Thanks for the lovely dinner, Beth."

The woman blushed and grinned like she'd just

won the blue ribbon at the fair. "It was my pleasure."

Mike's dad rose from the table and followed Mike to the door.

"You're not mad, are you?" his dad asked.

"No, Dad. I'm not mad, but I'm okay. I don't need you setting me up on dates."

Dad's eyebrows pulled together like they did right before he went into speechifying mode. "Son, you've been alone too long. You need to move on. You're missing out on precious time in your life that you don't get back. Trust me. You'll wake up one morning and you're too old to do all the stuff you put on that list for someday. Make today that someday."

Mike cuffed his dad's shoulder. "Don't worry about me. I'm not pining away. That Beth seems real nice, though."

"She is. Her daughter seems nice too."

She was pretty, even seemed nice, but that was a complication he would not be adding to his life. Not now. Not ever again.

❖ Chapter Four ❖

Ever since she'd made the visit to the farm on Nickel Creek Road, Brooke seemed to be right in Mike's path. It seemed funny that she'd never laid eyes on him until that farm visit and now it was like every time she turned around—there he was.

The next day she'd bumped into him at the post office when she picked up her mail, then he showed up at the grand opening of HAPPY BALANCE. Yesterday he was picking up bear claws at Mac's Bakery when she arrived to get the order for the office, and this afternoon on her way home he was in the Piggly Wiggly.

All three times he'd stopped and chatted her up. He hadn't mentioned dinner again, and she finally had let her guard down deciding he'd just been being polite that day they'd met. Which was a relief.

They'd talked so long in the parking lot that her frozen goods had all but thawed. Maybe her heart had too since, when he brought up his dinner offer out of the blue, she'd let him pin her down to go together to the local Ruritan Club steak dinner Friday after next.

At least they wouldn't be alone. Everyone in town would be there.

For someone who was almost divorced and sworn off men, she'd had zero willpower when it came to saying no to Mike.

She left in a hurry, worried about what else she'd agree to if she stuck around. As she pulled into her driveway she was relieved to just be home and be able to put him out of her mind for a while. At least until Friday after next at that dinner.

As soon as Brooke stepped out of her car, the

summer heat sucked the air-conditioned chill from her skin, but that didn't keep goose bumps from crawling up her arms. She shifted her purse and the grocery bag up on her hip.

The dense line of red-tip Photinia had been a selling point when she'd bought this house, but now the long row of hedges just looked like a convenient place for someone to lurk.

Moving here was supposed to have eliminated these feelings, and Keith was nearly a two-hour drive away. Even if he had figured out where she'd moved, it wasn't likely he'd be riding by her house all the time like he'd been doing when they lived just miles from each other. That had just become unsettling. Out of sight would be out of mind . . . she could only hope.

I'm safe here in Adams Grove. When the thought didn't do anything to relax her, she tried to convince herself by humming the song that had been playing on the radio.

Her heels clicked against the pavers. Just feet from the front porch, she stopped midstride.

"I know I left that light on this morning." *Great. Now I'm talking to myself.* She distinctly remembered going through the motions to leave the porch light on this morning because she thought she wouldn't be home until late tonight. Thank goodness the summer days were long and she'd left the office early for a change, so it wasn't dark out, but . . .

Maybe the bulb burned out—or not.

Recent incidents clicked off in her mind—missing items that magically reappeared days later, gas siphoned from her car, and the phone line pulled from its clip on the house. *How often does that ever happen?* Both times the police had come, they'd written it off as harmless pranks by kids with too much time on their hands.

Brooke positioned a key between each finger like spikes. She'd seen that in an action adventure film once, and that girl had kicked ass. Armed and ready as she'd ever be, Brooke headed for the front porch. *Why am I acting all ninja girl? It's broad daylight.*

She pulled out her cell to dial the police, then stopped.

What am I going to say? Hello, 911, my porch light is off?

That wouldn't fly. Sheriff Calvin had been really nice about it, but with no evidence there wasn't much he could do. Still, she hadn't liked the way that deputy with the Northern accent talked to her in that tone they use on crazies.

The hairs on her arms tingled as the adrenaline built. A sense of prying eyes, someone watching, forced her to run up the steps where at least she could lock the door behind her.

Brooke lunged toward the front door, twisted the key in the lock, and rushed inside to safety. She slid her purse and grocery bag off her shoulder to the sideboard table, kicked the door closed, and twisted the newly installed dead bolt.

She exhaled the breath she hadn't realized she was holding, then flipped the light switch and peeked out the side-light window next to the front door. The front porch light worked fine.

A chill crept the length of her limbs. Was it possible that Keith was picking up right where he left off? Maybe ninety miles wasn't far enough after all.

She threw her phone in the top of her purse and pulled out a small spiral notebook to jot down the disturbance. Collecting data was like breathing. Of course, it had to align with her gut and those lucky signs that she lived by too. She tossed the notes back into her purse.

"Stitches? Where's Mama's girl?" The little dog's hearing was going, but she'd usually have wandered out to greet her by now. Brooke clapped and called for the fourteen-year-old dog again.

Brooke took in a deep cleansing breath, the kind Jenny always swore by, even before they started doing yoga. She let out the breath to the count of five as she stepped out of her shoes. Silently, she recited the self-affirmations she'd been practicing.

I am fine.
I am fearless.
I am in control.
I am independent.
I am strong.

Then, like every other time she'd tried that self-affirmation thing, her mind wandered into a chorus of "I Am Woman" by Helen Reddy. The memory of her mom singing that song so off-key that dogs whimpered and whales fled for deeper waters made her laugh. So it wasn't exactly how the whole affirmation thing was supposed to work—it was still empowering.

Her hand froze, hovering in midair over the sideboard. The one blemish on the otherwise perfect surface was in clear view. Alarm slid through her. The wooden bowl she'd positioned to hide the scratch was about two inches out of place.

Even though she'd spent hours in a dingy warehouse auction to buy the old piece of furniture, it had been a liberating first step in putting her broken marriage behind her and starting fresh. It was a style Keith hated. That in itself was worth the price she'd paid.

Unclenching her fingers, she dropped her keys into the bowl, and nudged it back into place over the scratch with her index finger. That's when she noticed the familiar spicy scent. Dad had worn it. Keith wore it. Half the men in America had splashed it on at one time or another, and their commercials were making a comeback, but why was it in her house now? *Keith, you know where I am, don't you?*

A noise came from the kitchen. She drew her

fists to her chest as if she were ready to take on the intruder, but realization struck just as quickly. *The icemaker.* Brooke dropped her hands. Doing battle with the icemaker would be overkill, but it was still clear that someone had been in the house and that was unsettling.

She'd rather look overcautious than stupid, so she called the police. The dispatcher told her to wait on the front porch. She prayed the same deputy wouldn't show up. It was getting embarrassing. This would be the third time in as many weeks, but even changing the locks hadn't made a difference.

"Where's my sweet girl dog?" Brooke wasn't about to leave Stitches inside while she waited out front.

When Stitches still didn't appear, Brooke propped the front door open and went down the hall to her bedroom to look for the dog. But after searching every room, there was no sign of Stitches, and that just didn't make sense.

She ran out the French doors, searching the backyard, hoping for a spot of white amid the colorful landscaping.

"Stitches, are you out here, girl?" She clapped her hands and called out again. It was highly unlikely she would have left Stitches out all day in this kind of heat. Helplessness consumed her.

Where was that cardinal that usually darted through the trees and tangled shrubs? Not seeing the lucky bird only heightened her apprehension.

A high-pitched yelp came from the far side of the deck.

Brooke took off in that direction. She cleared the three steps to the gazebo in one long leap toward the hot tub. Sickness rolled in her stomach when she spotted the hot tub cover folded back.

Stitches's tiny eyes bulged and her black nose stretched just above the water in a desperate doggy paddle in the center of the hot tub. Brooke plunged across the side into the bubbling water to scoop Stitches to safety.

"It's okay. I'm here." Brooke climbed out of the water and grabbed a towel from the trunk next to the hot tub.

Stitches continued paddling the air, still in a panic for survival.

She wrapped Stitches in a terry-cloth cocoon and pulled her close. They both trembled. The tiny dog's heart pounded like a hummingbird on a caffeine overload.

"Thank god, you're all right." Brooke rocked Stitches as water dripped from her soaked jacket to the deck. She grabbed another towel and headed inside. She raced through the French doors to the kitchen, then dropped the towel and stood on it, still dripping, as she grabbed the magnet from the side of the refrigerator. She dialed the veterinarian's office. Even though she and Stitches had only been there once, they agreed to wait for her when they heard what had happened.

Soaking wet, Brooke stripped down to her panties right there in the kitchen before she remembered the front door was propped open. She picked Stitches back up and sprinted across the living room down the hall to quickly change into dry clothes.

Stitches lay trembling on the bed where Brooke had set her down. She dressed as fast as she could, then swept the scared dog back into her arms.

As she stepped out on the front porch, the sheriff's car pulled into the driveway. That same deputy, the one who talked to her like she was a nut job and said that until she came along this had been a quiet neighborhood, stepped out of the car.

She didn't break stride as she headed to her car.

The deputy walked toward her like he was in no hurry at all. "Are you okay, ma'am?"

She swept past him. "I told you my ex-husband was up to no good. He almost drowned Stitches."

He followed her to the car. "Slow down. What happened?"

"I can't. I just rescued my dog from the hot tub. Maybe I can't prove it was Keith, but I know. I told you something was going to happen." She stabbed a finger in the air in his direction. "This is *your* fault for not listening to me." She opened the passenger door and set the dog inside. "I've got to get her to the vet. I can't deal with this or you right now."

He handed her a card. "That's fine. Give me a call when you get back. I'll come back out and see what we can do. Doesn't matter what time it is."

Oh, yeah. Like you've been so much help before? She snatched the card, her voice still shaking but quieter. "Thank you. I'm upset."

"I can see that. Go on. Doc Brady'll take care of her. He's a good guy."

She nodded and jumped in the car, trying not to speed out of the neighborhood right in front of the very guy who could give her a ticket. That would just really top things off.

❖ Chapter Five ❖

After eight long years, Frank "Goto" Gotorow knew to the hour how long he'd been a free man. He made parole seventy-one days and seven hours ago.

How the hell did they expect him to lead a normal life on the outside? He could barely afford to take care of himself. In seventy-one days and seven hours the best job he could land was at that damn pizza shop with a bunch of college-aged kids.

He'd been a hell of a mechanic at one time. He'd never realized how the oil and grime had married with his skin until the oil began leaching out for months on the white prison sheets. It had taken a long time for his nails and skin to get clean and now that they were, when he said he had years of mechanic experience, one glance at his hands and folks thought he was a liar. No mechanic had hands that clean.

He'd pounded the pavement looking for decent work. The dealerships wouldn't hire him because of his record, and even the small garages wouldn't hire him when they found out he didn't have his own tools. His old lady had sold all of his tools at a garage sale, and split with the cash when she realized what he'd done to that woman. Just imagine how mad she'd have been if she knew about the others.

"Bitch," he seethed. "It's not like I ever did anything to her," he muttered to the Jesus air freshener swinging from the rearview mirror. His buddy, Rabbit, had turned him on to Wheelie. Wheelie was already on the outside and he was the guy who'd hooked him up with the car. It had taken nearly all the money he had to his name, but he had to have wheels. Wheelie had thrown in the Jesus air freshener and a "Support Your Local Police" bumper sticker, swearing it would keep the cops off his ass.

It had been a pretty sweet deal, but it didn't leave him much to live on. He'd given up his weekly rental hotel room, and bought a ten-dollar blanket and a five-dollar pillow so he could save some money by sleeping in his car. He spent the rest of a twenty-dollar bill on canned Vienna sausages and Beanie Weenies at Kmart. His car had served double duty, bedroom and dining room, until he'd worked out the barter with the yoga chick to do those murals. He'd worked out a crash-and-cash deal with her and he'd liked staying in the big old building by himself, but now that she'd opened, that luxury was a thing of the past.

Probably a good thing too, because he'd been worried when he met her friend that she'd recognize him as the guy who delivered pizza to her. That wouldn't have been good. Especially since he'd used a fake name with her friend. He knew her name though. Brooke Justice. She was hard to forget.

The money he'd earned had helped him stay on track with his internal deadline though. He still hadn't figured out exactly what that plan was going to be, but getting justice was going to be sweet and Mike Hartman would never see it coming. Goto scrunched down in the seat as the front door of the house opened.

❖ Chapter Six ❖

Mike had settled into a productive routine between his new business, spending time on Kasey Phillips's property, and starting to renew friendships and family ties. Mornings on the farm had given him a reason to look forward to waking up. First of all it was quiet. No one asking a million questions, and no crowds. And there was a lot to do. Staying busy appealed to him and taking care of the goats had turned out to be a fun chore. Even though the local 4-H'ers showed up to do it on most days, he'd taken a liking to coming over to check on the property as part of his morning routine. Riding the Polaris along the fence line to check things out while he drank a tall mug of coffee from Mac's Bakery was a nice way to start each day.

He'd even kept up the small garden in the backyard, something he couldn't do in his place on Main Street. It was still early in the season, but he'd already harvested some broccoli from Kasey's well-established plants. At least her attention to the plants was yielding him the luxury of fresh veggies even if she wasn't around to enjoy them. If nothing else grew, he was enjoying having his hands in the dirt. Being busy had been good medicine as he continued to transition back to civilian life. There was no doubt in his mind that he was spending more time here than Kasey had ever expected him to, but the extra workload had brought a balance to his life that he hadn't realized was missing. For the first time in a very long time he was feeling more like his old self.

After securing the barn and locking up the place, he headed back to town. He pulled around to the back of the old bank building that housed the Buckham and Baxter law offices, where he'd rented out the second apartment on the second floor. Carolanne Baxter had lived there until her house was built in the new neighborhood over by the artisan center, the same place where he was having his house built.

Mike punched the code into the back door and collected his mail from the partitioned mail slots just inside the huge doors. He flipped through the stack of envelopes as he headed upstairs. As Mike opened the door, Hunter pranced from foot to foot in his kennel. One ear still tended to flop when he got excited, but he was a pretty dog. Mike dropped the mail on the desk and opened the kennel. Hunter raced out and circled the office, then sat in front of Mike waiting for attention. Mike nuzzled the dog and grabbed the leash.

It had taken a few weeks for Hunter to get the hang of the steps, but now he trotted down them at a safe and steady pace, not breaking into a jog until Mike gave him the signal when they hit the jogging path in the park.

Training Hunter healed Mike a little every day. He could feel it, and he couldn't wait until they could move into the house and Hunter could run the yard on his own free will.

Garrett Malloy had broken ground on the house of Mike's dreams months ago but it would still be a while before he and his German shepherd puppy could move in. Until the house was finished, the apartment in town was perfectly suited as his office and living space.

Mike had been at the right place at the right time that day he'd run into Connor. Carolanne had just moved out and Connor Buckham hadn't even decided what he was going to do with her apart-ment, or his now that they were living in her house together. When Mike told him he was looking for an office space that could double as an apartment until the house was done, Connor had liked the idea of renting to him.

It had turned out to be a good fit, since the two lawyers had already thrown some work his way. He'd remodeled the space to include an office in the front portion and then a separate door to the living quarters that he could later turn into storage or a second office.

After a good run in the park, and time for Hunter to explore, they headed back to the apartment. Mike fed Hunter and poured a glass of tea for himself.

He walked to the window. The view from up here gave him a clear panorama of Main Street. A shiny black Corvette pulled in front of the veterinarian's office. Like the rest of the businesses here in Adams Grove, the vet was normally closed by now. He watched a woman get out of the car.

Her shoulders hiked as she raced to the passenger side.

He pulled the curtain to the side and leaned forward to get a better look. When the woman turned to open the door, he could clearly see her face.

The extension agent. Brooke. *Nice gal. Nice ride too.* She hadn't seemed the sports car type, but then he'd only seen her in the county truck. He'd surprised himself when he'd asked her out right there on the spot. Something about her had outwitted his good sense, but what was done was done.

He watched as she messed with something in the passenger seat. Finally, she stood with a bundle in her arms. As she pushed the car door closed with her hip, a white scruffy head popped out above her shoulder. She carried the dog into the vet's office like she was rescuing a baby from a fire.

There was a time when he didn't understand how people treated their animals like family, but that was before he had been partnered with Gunner overseas. After being paired with the German shepherd, an enlisted bomb sniffer, he had a whole new appreciation for that relationship. They'd formed a bond that was closer than he'd ever had with another human being . . . with the exception of Jackie. But then if Jackie had still been around, there'd have never been a military career or Gunner.

He tugged the curtain closed. Hunter had joined him while he watched and looked up at him with that one lazy ear flopping. He reached down and straightened it, then knelt beside Hunter and stroked his side. "You're a good one, Hunter."

Thoughts of Jackie still sent his heart on a nosedive. He wasn't sure why Brooke had made those thoughts come back, but he wished they'd stayed where he'd tucked them safely away.

❖ Chapter Seven ❖

Brooke muttered all the way into the veterinarian's office. Thank goodness it was only a couple blocks away. If it had been a longer ride, she'd have probably been a danger to the drivers in her path. Her no-fault divorce had turned into a series of twists that made her stomach turn and Stitches didn't deserve to be caught in the middle. On top of the crazy lawyer fees, she'd had the expense of moving, and now that seemed to be a big fat waste of money. This had Keith's name written all over it.

She rushed into Dr. Brady's office and just as she began to speak, she broke down in tears.

His assistant took Stitches from her and told her to take a seat.

I must look like one crazy woman right now. And the truth was she felt at her wit's end. Just this morning she'd read an article on the Internet about divorce. Some staff reporter, *a single one no doubt,* had reported that divorce rates were up and his hypothesis was that it was because it's easy to get out of a marriage. Easy? The only sure thing in the divorce process that was easy, as far as she could see, was the guarantee of emotional highs and lows.

That article made it sound like divorce was a kiddy slide to take with your hands in the air grabbing divorce papers and your maiden name on the way down. Hers had been anything but fun or easy. It had made her want to lose her lunch a few times, but instead she'd lost more important things like pride and self-esteem, not to mention the material possessions Keith was trying to take from her. *Easy? I don't think so.*

She should've known her marriage to Keith Farrell would end in disaster. On the day he proposed, there hadn't been a single lucky sign. Not a rainbow. Not a ladybug. Not even a cardinal showed up, and that's the Virginia state bird! The morning of the wedding, she'd had her doubts too, but dismissed them as jitters.

When I don't follow my gut, I make mistakes. Keith was a real doozy.

She pulled herself together while the veterinarian and his assistant took care of Stitches, but when Dr. Brady walked out to the lobby, she leaped from her seat like she'd been shot out of a cannon.

"She's fine," he said, then placed the dog on the floor.

Stitches ran across the tiled floor to her.

"Thank you so much for checking her over."

"I'm going to give you a prescription for her just to calm her down." His assistant rounded the corner with a blue bottle of pills. "Think of it as the doggy equivalent to Valium," he said, handing it to her.

She held the bottle in her hand. *I wonder if I can google the safety for human consumption. Lord knows I could use one of these myself right now.* Actually, she'd prefer a cold beer, but she had a hard and fast rule against drinking and driving and she had someplace to go.

She settled with the girl at the desk, and must have thanked Dr. Brady and his staff a hundred times before she finally got out the door.

Thank goodness Stitches was okay, but now that worry had turned to anger and she was madder than an old wet hen. If she'd been gone any longer . . .

She couldn't even face that horrible thought. She eased onto the street from the parking spot in front of the vet's office with her grip on the steering wheel so tight it made her hands ache. "Keith will *not* get away with this."

Stitches walked a circle in the passenger seat, then climbed onto the center console and settled her chin on Brooke's lap.

On a Friday night she knew exactly where Keith would be. At Walker's Pub hanging out with other folks obsessed with hot rods and muscle cars. She knew because there was a time when they'd done that together. Her worry continued to build to anger at twice the rate, and the speedometer was registering it too.

She glanced at the clock. She had time to make it there. Heck, at this speed she might catch up to Keith, or even pass him. He couldn't have been gone long.

Her ringing cell phone broke her trance as she sped down Route 58. She checked the caller ID, then answered.

Jenny's voice came across the line. "Where are you? I've been at your house for like ten minutes. Are you okay? The neighbor said the sheriff was here again."

"I'm fine, but you're not going to believe what's happened."

"What?"

Brooke felt her adrenaline pick up speed. "I know it was him. I swear I could kill him."

"Slow down. Brooke, you know our rule. Don't

do anything you can't undo. I suppose this has to do with Keith. What's he done now?"

"Fine. I won't kill him, but he's going to at least get a piece of my mind." Brooke spilled the rest of the details to Jenny as she weaved in and out of traffic.

"Thank goodness you're both okay. Hey, are you driving? Where are you headed?"

"I'm headed to Walker's."

"Oh, lord. Girl, you better pull over and get yourself together. You're going to get another ticket. Or worse, have an accident."

Brooke lifted her foot off the accelerator. "You're right, as usual."

"That's why we're best friends. We keep each other out of trouble."

"There *is* that." Brooke had to admit that every embarrassing moment she could remember had been with Jenny. "Hang on. I'm stopping." She pulled into the next parking lot and shut down the engine.

"Look, I'm not saying you don't have every right to go postal on Keith, but you can't do it. You don't want to be the one who looks like the maniac here."

Brooke knew she was right. Just talking to Jenny was already calming her down a bit.

"Call the police and have them meet you at Walker's. It's their job. If you report it, they have to investigate it."

"I need a better plan."

"I don't like the thought of you going to confront Keith, not that it's going to stop you. You're still going, aren't you?"

It was a statement, not a question. Jenny knew her so well. "Yes, I have to."

"Tell you what," Jenny said. "Swing by here and pick me up. We'll approach Keith together."

Brooke's throat tightened. "You don't have to do that." She ran a hand under her nose to stall the tickle. "It's over an hour to get there. It'll be late as heck when I get back."

"Seriously, do you think I'd miss you telling Keith off? Not a chance."

Tears of gratitude wet Brooke's lashes. Jenny had always been there for her.

"Where are you right now? I'll meet you somewhere so you don't have to backtrack."

Brooke started the car and headed back in the direction she came. "Sit tight, I'm coming back to get you."

A few minutes later Brooke pulled up to the curb in front of her house and Jenny climbed into the passenger seat.

"Took a swim, did you, girl?" Jenny patted the dog's head, then pulled back. "Whew, she smells like chlorine, but she sure is chilled out for a dog that just went through all of that."

Brooke sniffed Stitches' fur and wrinkled her nose. "I think her puppy Valium is already kicking in."

• • •

Jenny and Brooke pulled into the front lot at Walker's Pub right at eight o'clock. Brooke cruised the lot once on the lookout for Keith, then parked at the end of a long line of cleaned-up vintage cars. Brooke got out of the car with Stitches against her hip.

"That didn't take long." Jenny slid out of the passenger seat and came around to the driver's side of the car. She tugged on Brooke's sleeve and nodded across the parking lot. "You won't have to go hunting down Mr. Evil after all. Look who's heading our way."

Brooke handed Stitches off to Jenny, turned in Keith's direction, and straightened to her full five-foot-four. Every muscle in her body tightened.

Keith gave Jenny a nod, but focused on Brooke. "Thought you said you'd never step foot on this lot again. Having second thoughts? Miss me?"

Jenny took a step back, and Brooke closed in on Keith. "I don't miss you one bit. In fact, I can't wait until the minute I'm finally free of you completely."

"Aw, come on. Not even just a little?" He reached for her cheek. "All you ever do anymore is work and send out for pizza. Pining away for me, aren't you?"

She smacked his arm, twisting out of his reach. "You've *got* to be kidding me." She prayed the remark was a lucky guess, but her instincts told her he was still stalking her. There was no way she'd give him the satisfaction of letting him see he was scaring her right now.

"Then why are you here?"

She glanced over at Stitches. "You've gone too far this time. I know it was you." She pointed her finger at him the way she knew drove him crazy. He didn't flinch.

"What are you talking about?" Keith looked innocent, but she wasn't buying the act. She'd fallen for that look one too many times.

"Thank god, Stitches survived. You could have killed her tonight."

He snickered. "Little mutt looks fine to me." Then he leaned in and whispered in Brooke's ear. "You're looking pretty fine too. You're hot when you're mad."

She shoved him. "Shut up. I know you did it!" Her hands balled into fists.

"Did what?"

Her stomach wrenched. "You smug bastard." She wanted to scratch the smirk right off his face. "You stay away from me, and everything I own. You hear me?"

"You sure are stressed out. Maybe you should go take a soak in that hot tub of yours."

Her eyes went wide.

"I could play lifeguard and make sure nothing happens to you," Keith said.

Her stomach turned at the thought. "How did I

ever think you were charming?" She raised her hand to hit him, but he caught her arm.

A good foot taller than her, he outweighed her by an easy hundred pounds. "Stop it. You're making a scene. I don't know what you think I did this time, but I haven't done anything to piss you off. And if we're talking about tonight . . . I've been here for hours."

"I don't believe you. I'm warning you—you'd better leave us alone."

"Technically we *are* still married. We could be a little family again. You, me, and Stitches."

She used to love his perfect smile. Now it just made her gag.

"That will never happen." She glared his way while trying to steady her voice. "Sign the divorce papers. Or don't sign them. I don't even care at this point, but I promise you this. We will never be together again. So deal with it."

"That's not what I want." He leaned in closer, whispering, "I always get what I want."

"Aaaaagh." She swung her purse with all her might, but at the last moment he jumped out of the way and the full weight of her purse slammed against the side of her car, cracking the fiberglass.

The collective sucking of air hung around them.

"Oh. My. God." Jenny scrambled closer.

"Daggone it!" Brooke dropped her handbag to the pavement and ran her fingers across the splintered damage. She spun in Keith's direction

56

and shook her finger in his face. "I wish I'd never met you. You ruin everything. Every single thing you touch."

Keith laughed. "You're nuts."

"If I am it's because you made me that way. Stay away from me. I mean it." Brooke stepped closer to Keith. "Leave me *alone*. Leave Stitches *alone*. Leave my house *alone*. It's over."

Brooke turned and ran her fingers across the splintered fiberglass. She loved this car. She'd rolled the odometer past the nines long ago, but it still looked new. She bent down next to the car, as Keith backed away.

Jenny moved in and squatted next to Brooke. "He's gone, honey."

"I was such a fool to ever get involved with that man." Brooke pushed her bangs back and shook her head. She took Stitches from Jenny and hugged the dog close. A tear of frustration slid down her cheek.

"Don't feel bad. He had us all fooled. For a while anyway." Jenny put a hand on her friend's back. "Please get a restraining order against him. I'll go with you. He has to be stalking you. That pizza comment just proves it. How else would he know that?"

"Because I just about live on pizza?"

"True, but he threatened you, didn't he?"

"I can't believe I ever loved that man. I'm an idiot."

"Stop it. You are not. He was a perfect charmer when you met him. We all thought so. Those good looks were deceiving," Jenny continued. "Up until now the incidents haven't been a big deal, but this thing with Stitches is a whole new level, and creepy to boot. I think Keith is really losing it, and that could make him dangerous."

She'd made excuses for him long enough. Jenny was right. It was creepy. She stroked the little life in her arms that was hers to protect. "Tomorrow. I'll take care of it tomorrow. Right now, I just want to go home." Suddenly worn out from the events, Brooke opened the car door.

"Have Keith arrested. I'll tell the cops I heard him threaten you. Whatever you want. Please? If it won't make you feel better, do it for me. It'll make *me* feel great."

Brooke slid behind the wheel and twisted the key in the ignition as Jenny climbed into the passenger seat. The car didn't turn over. "What else could possibly go wrong?" She knocked twice on the burlwood console to ward off any more bad luck. If the divorce had taught her anything, it was not to tempt fate.

Jenny said, "Is it in park?"

Brooke slapped the shifter. She must've been so distracted she'd shut it down in gear. She grabbed the leather-wrapped knob and pushed it back up to the letter *P*.

"Now try it."

The car started right up. Brooke pressed her lips together, and rolled her eyes. "How stupid."

"Not really. All those years hanging out in the garage with Granddaddy paid off. People do that all the time. Now, take a breath."

Brooke plopped back against the seat.

"Are you sure you can drive? You're so upset. I don't mind driving back."

"No. I'm fine," Brooke said.

"Okay. So what are you going to do?" Jenny pulled Stitches into her lap.

"I'm going to drive us home, then I'm taking a long, hot bath so I can pull myself together and then I'll figure that out. If I don't decide to drown myself and put myself out of this misery."

"Not even funny. But I'm not surprised to hear you're headed to the bathtub. When things aren't working, *ker-splash*. I swear you're part mermaid." Jenny closed her eyes, and put her fingers on her temples. "Then I predict you'll fire up that computer and type up a plan."

"Fine. Fine. I get it. I'm a little predictable," Brooke conceded. She eased onto the interstate and set the cruise control. No sense letting her mood earn her a speeding ticket tonight on top of everything. "I can't believe Keith still hasn't signed the divorce papers." Brooke toyed with the buttons on the console. "This should have been over a long time ago. I think it's time to call an investigator like my lawyer suggested and prove he's up to no good once and for all."

"Sorry, sweetie. I know he's getting under your skin." Jenny placed her hand on Brooke's arm. "Hey, I can make my famous Kamikaze on the rocks when we get home. If that doesn't make you forget him for a while, nothing will."

"No. I just need to slow down and figure out what to do next. Sorry I messed up our dinner plans tonight." Brooke stroked Stitches, who could just barely keep her eyes open.

"That's fine. It's not about the dinner anyway. This is the most unusual girls' night we've had in a while though."

"True." Brooke nervously scratched the shape of a question mark in the center of her steering wheel.

"I'll call Connor Buckham in the morning and get that investigator guy's number."

"Good. If Keith did put Stitches in the hot tub, he could do something to hurt you next." Jenny raised her hand. "I know. Don't say it. I'm just saying, it's a possibility and there's no sense putting yourself in that position."

"He just wants me to think he's in control. I don't think he'd ever hurt me."

"How can you say that? He could've killed Stitches."

Brooke's words came out just above a whisper. "He was my husband."

"Tell that to Laci Peterson, or OJ's wife or . . ."

Something that felt akin to a glop of cold oatmeal sat in her belly. "Fine. I get the point. When you're right, you're right." Brooke looked at the horseshoe-shaped crystal and beads that hung from her rearview mirror.

Brooke's good luck philosophy on life had rarely let her down. Yeah, her friends could tease her all they wanted to about making decisions based on the presence or absence of lucky signs, but they worked. She had the charts to prove it.

"You're a walking contradiction, my friend." Jenny inhaled, clearly preparing to continue the lecture.

But Brooke wasn't up for an argument or a lecture. "I'll call Connor. I'll get that investigator's help and take back control of this situation."

"And I'll help."

A short while later they pulled into the driveway at Brooke's house. "Thanks for coming with me. I don't think it did any good. Just a waste of time and gas, but I had to do something."

They both got out of the car. "You going to be okay?" Jenny asked. "I can stay the night."

"I will. I'll let you know what I'm going to do, and I promise I'll be smart about it."

"Good. I'll call you in the morning."

Brooke walked Jenny to her car and gave her a hug. Jenny waited until Brooke got to the door and opened it before she pulled away from the curb. She lived around the block in an apartment over the new yoga studio. Brooke might have really been crazy by now if Jenny hadn't made the move to Adams Grove too.

Brooke looked out the window into the night sky, and said a quick prayer for a shooting star to get her through another day.

❖ Chapter Eight ❖

Mike looked up from his desk. Footsteps echoed from the hall. His first after-hours customer? Hunter sat up from under the desk and let out a soft woof.

"It's okay, boy," Mike said. "Down."

Hunter lay back down under the desk.

The doorknob twisted and Rick Joyner walked inside. "What? I have to hear from your dad that you set up shop in Adams Grove?"

"Rick. Good to see you, buddy." Mike came around the desk and shook his hand. "It's been too long. I was going to call you."

"Sure you were. Your dad said you've been back for a while." Rick looked around. "From the looks of things you're pretty settled in too. You avoiding me?"

"No. Just busy." But maybe he had avoided facing Rick. They'd been friends since their school days, and even though Rick swore he'd never blamed Mike for his sister's death, Mike had still carried that guilt. "Trying to figure out what the hell life is going to be from here on out."

Hunter let out a soft woof from under the desk.

"Come here, Hunter. We have company."

The dog bounded out into the middle of the room. All legs and ears, the seven-month-old puppy greeted Rick like they'd been friends forever.

"Pretty dog. Never knew you to have a dog though."

Mike nodded. It was true. Jackie had always wanted one but he'd never given in. *Another regret.* "I had one assigned to me when I was overseas. Good dog. Good partner. Guess the Marines changed that in me too."

"I'm sure the Marines will miss you." Rick shrugged. "After seeing your dad, when I drove by and the light was on I had to stop. Hope you don't mind." He scanned the office and gave the dog a pat on the head. "Looks like you've got yourself set up right nice here."

"It's working." Mike shifted his hip up on the desk. "It's actually been a pretty big adjustment back to civilian life."

"I'm glad you made it back. Everyone will be glad you're back, as soon as I spread the word. You shouldn't have kept it such a secret."

That was just like Rick—always the one to get the gang together. Large and in charge. Mike said, "I'm just taking things a little slow. It's an adjustment. You get it."

"Sure. I get it. Your dad mentioned something about giving up the job of the century to play *Magnum P.I.*"

"He doesn't get it. I'm just not the white-collar type."

"But are you the investigator type? That's the question." Rick's face grew serious. "Don't think it'll bring back too many memories, do you?"

"I'm taking it a day at a time."

"Well, don't be a stranger." Rick plopped down into one of the chairs in front of the desk. "Your dad had a rather attractive old gal fawning over him when I ran into him in town. He's getting more action than I am. How sad is that?"

"Must have been his new lady friend, Beth. He tricked me into dinner with her and her daughter the other night. I think all the ladies in town are spoiling him. I think he spends more time driving them around to different things than he does at home anymore."

"I should be so lucky," Rick said.

"He's probably the only single senior who still has a car. I never pictured him with anyone but Mom, but he sure seemed to be enjoying the attention."

"I guess a guy with a car is just as big of a deal at seventy as it is at seventeen, but you Hartman men always did have a charming way with the ladies."

"Guess I'll have to work a nice ride into my retirement budget to hedge my bets."

"You and me both." Rick laughed and looked around. "Wouldn't have pictured you as a private investigator. So, you spying on cheating wives? Shit like that?"

Mike laughed. "Guess it could come up, but mostly it's been cases Perry Von has been too busy to handle. The lawyers downstairs have also had me on a few things. I've been locating missing relatives, looking up a few bond skips. Nothing too sinister."

"Your dad is really glad that you're back. He worried about you when you were in Iraq. We all did. I think he was afraid you wouldn't be careful."

"I didn't take any unnecessary risks. No one needed to worry."

"I don't know, man. When you left . . . none of us were in a real good place."

Mike shook his head. "Let's not go there."

"Fair enough. So, you're back for good?"

"I better be. I'm building a house here."

"You rebuilding over at the old place?" Rick looked surprised.

"No." The old place. He couldn't build there. He hadn't even been able to bring himself to drive by the property. Under the circumstances he wasn't sure why he'd hung on to it, but selling it just seemed wrong. "No, man. I'm having one built over in the new neighborhood."

"That log cabin you always wanted?"

"Exactly. I think it's time to settle down in one place. This ought to tie me down a little."

"Shackles couldn't tie you down, but I'm sure that'll set you back a pretty penny."

"You got that right, but you only live once." Mike stood up.

"Your dad said you aren't seeing anyone."

"I'm not. I'm busy. He's way more worried about it than I am."

"You're afraid," Rick said. "You were in the Marines, not a monastery, man. You need to get back in the game. Life's too short to live it alone."

Rick was the last person he wanted to discuss this with.

"Jackie wouldn't like you to be alone. She wouldn't like it at all," Rick added.

She would have said that. Rick was right, but if it had been the other way around, she'd have understood. It's one thing to say it. Another to live it. "I'm working on it."

"If you say so." Rick didn't look convinced. "Eight years is a long time to be alone."

"I'm not pining away. I even asked someone to the Ruritan Club steak dinner Friday." Mike didn't know why he'd offered up the information. It was no one's business, and he hadn't even meant to ask her, but somehow he felt like he needed to prove that he was okay.

"Really? Guess the old man didn't know about that. Someone serious?"

"No. Just met her. Nothing serious. First date."

"Mike, it's okay if it is. It's been a long time since Jackie died. You can move on." Rick started laughing. "But it is kind of funny. Showing up at a Ruritan dinner is like ringing the bell on the gossip line. Everyone will be talking about y'all whether it's serious or not. Hell, I'd have at least done coffee or something easy to get out of."

"Kind of didn't think about that part. Too late now."

"I'm just giving you a hard time. It'll be fine." Rick's face grew serious. "It's really good to see you, man."

"Yeah. It is." The old friendship hadn't changed despite the years since they'd last spoken. "Can I get you a beer or something?"

Rick raised a hand. "No. I'm not going to stay long. I'm just glad you're back. Wish I'd known. I'd have thrown you a big welcome-back barbecue on the farm. It would have been better than the high school reunion, which you missed, by the way."

Mike cast him a sideways glance. "Maybe that's why I didn't tell you."

"Seriously, don't be a stranger. It's been too long."

"I'll stop by one day next week," Mike said. They'd been like brothers at one time. In a way, they'd always be family.

"That would be good. You won't even recognize the farm. I've done a lot while you've been away."

"I'm thinking a farm looks like a farm."

"Oh, no. I gave up the hog farming, thought my luck with the ladies might change after that, but it hasn't. Tore down all the hog barns and replaced them with a state-of-the-art horse barn."

"I hadn't heard you'd gotten out of hogs." Mike had done a stellar job removing himself from everything he left behind when he'd joined the Marines, and that had felt good at the time, but now it was making it hard to ease back in.

"I'm just doing the horses and running a few cattle now."

"Small world. I'm farm-sitting over at Kasey Phillips's ranch. They are getting ready to stable some racehorses on that property."

"Racehorses? You're not talking about Denise Hill's new location, are you?"

"Yeah, exactly. She's Cody Tuggle's mother. He and Kasey are building a new place down the street, and his mom is going to use that acreage. I'm working with the extension agent to ready the pastures and stuff while they get everything figured out."

Rick's face lit up. "I've been talking to Denise Hill about buying an interest in one of the Hillcrest racehorses. Put in a good word for me."

"I don't think I have any pull, but I'll mention you if it comes up. Least I could do."

"Call me if you need any help over there. It'd be good to work on a project together again."

"I will. Thanks, man." Mike knew Rick would be as good as his word. He always had been. "So, when are you going to quit being so picky and settle down?"

"I haven't found a woman who can keep up with me, who wants kids too. I might be forty by the time I find her. I just hope I haven't already found her and was too stupid to realize it. Maybe now that you're back you can be my wingman and I'll find Mrs. Joyner."

"Like the old days." Mike grinned at the memory. They'd been a hell of a team back in their Virginia Tech days. "Don't you worry. When you find the right woman, you'll know it." Mike felt that familiar pang deep in his chest . . . in his heart.

He walked Rick out and then locked up.

"Load up, Hunter," Mike said. The shepherd pup ran into his kennel and lay down. Mike gave him a pat on the head. "Good boy."

Back in his bedroom he got undressed and pulled back the comforter. He sat down on the edge of the bed and lifted the picture of Jackie that sat on the nightstand. "Maybe it's time. But damn, it's hard to say good-bye to you." He slipped the picture in the top drawer of his night-stand, then got up and walked over to the kennel.

He unlatched the kennel door. "Come on,

buddy," he called to Hunter as he walked back into the bedroom with the pup at his heels. He got into bed and patted the edge. "It's okay." Hunter leaped up and curled up next to Mike. "Just for tonight."

❖ Chapter Nine ❖

Sinking down into the lavender-scented water until her chin just barely cleared the frothy softness, Brooke wished she could float in a warm tub until this divorce was behind her. She extended her leg out of the bubbles and used her toes to twist off the oil-rubbed bronze faucet.

Pools and the ocean scared her to death, but bathtubs and hot tubs were just her speed. Jenny had a good point. With the amount of time Brooke had spent trying to soak away the stress, it was a wonder she hadn't sprouted mermaid fins.

"*Mer*maid. If I ever get through this damn divorce, I'll welcome becoming an *old* maid." Either way there'd be no more wedding bells in her future. The twinkle in Keith's eye when he saw her anger rise played on her mind. She'd never be his victim again. No way. But the police around here were not on her side, and she had no proof anyway. Not really. Just her gut instinct, which was enough for her, but no one else.

Brooke soaked until her fingers and toes turned

pruney, then gave up and pulled the plug to let the water swirl out of the tub. She dried off and put on her favorite pair of pajamas.

Stitches snoozed on the living room couch, staying as far away from the sound of running water as possible. Who could blame her? Brooke settled down on the couch with Stitches in her lap. Flipping through the channels, she hunted for a distraction. The Travel Channel was touring Cape Cod. She'd always wanted to visit Woods Hole on the way to Martha's Vineyard. Maybe a couple weeks away somewhere would give Keith time to find something new to focus on. No, that was too much like letting him win.

He'd already run her out of her hometown—she darn well wasn't going to flee Adams Grove too.

She switched over to the Food Network. A little food porn always did the trick to chase away her troubles, but tonight the shows were all reruns.

Nothing worth watching again, or was it just her mood?

She turned off the television and carried Stitches to the back door to let her out. A cool front had pushed through, reducing the humidity to something bearable and making the air feel fresh for a spring night. The crickets and clean night air made her yearn to sleep with the windows open. That wasn't going to happen tonight, though. She'd already checked windows and doors twice.

An open window would be her undoing for sure. She'd be on the alert all night.

Stitches toured the yard, disappearing for a moment in the shadowy darkness. Brooke rushed outside in a panic, only to have Stitches greet her halfway across the deck.

Brooke forced herself to let the dog walk into the house on her own four paws.

Tears of frustration hit Brooke's cheeks as she realized there really wasn't any other way to handle this. She grabbed the phone and dialed Connor.

It was after hours, but at least calling now would keep her from changing her mind in the morning.

"Hi, Connor, this is Brooke Justice. Last time we talked you mentioned a private investigator who might be able to help me with my ex. Can you touch base with me in the morning? Thanks so much."

She grabbed a pad and pencil and jotted down some more notes about what had happened, then resigned herself to dealing with it in the morning.

The night sky gave way to the morning sun, and she was ready for coffee. She headed to the kitchen and poured a piping-hot mug to take out on the deck. She sipped and listened to the birds waking up. They chirped and twittered, and she was thankful to see the familiar cardinals darting in and out of the tangle of vines along the fence. Cardinals, good luck. What a relief.

A garbage truck clanged through the neighborhood as the sun broke the horizon. Being on the Saturday route ruined any chance of sleeping in. Relieved to have made it through the night, Brooke went back into the kitchen and punched the second speed-dial number on her phone. Her brother, Dean, answered on the first ring.

"What time is it?" he grumbled.

"After seven. You never were a morning person."

"Sis?" he grumbled. "Did we have plans this morning? Please don't tell me you're calling to see if I want to grab coffee or some happy shit like that." Sheets rustled, followed by the sound of something crashing to the floor. She winced, as he cussed under his breath.

"I'm not calling about coffee. I'm calling because you're right."

"I must be dreaming. Did Brooke Justice just say I was right?"

"Aren't you just a funny guy? Fine. Yes, I admit it. You were right. Are right. Whatever. I left a message for the lawyer here in town. He said he knew an investigator." Brooke felt some of the frustration lift just talking about getting help. "Keith's been in the house." It sent a shiver through her. "I never thought he would do anything dangerous. But frankly, I'm a little freaked out. I should have listened to you before."

"Damn right you should've listened to me. You told me to stay out of it, but it's been killing me.

Get the restraining order like I told you to weeks ago."

"I knew that's what you'd say, and don't you worry. I am going to do just that. But you have to admit. It's . . . weird. How can someone who once loved me enough to marry me suddenly do something so horrible? I don't get it. Now he's saying he wants to get back together after all he's done. Not that that'll ever happen."

"Hey, that's a question for Dr. Phil, not your brother. And definitely not for me at this hour. What do you need me to do?"

"Nothing. I just wanted you to know." Brooke caught her reflection on the side of the toaster. This divorce was making her look old. Pulling a hand through her bangs, she noticed a gray hair. Thirty-three was way too young for gray hair. She plucked it, frowning at her reflection.

"'Bout time you started listening to your big brother."

"I always listen to you." Her childhood had been such a hodgepodge of unplanned events. Between her OCD daddy and manic mama, before she hit junior high, she knew the one thing she'd do different in life was always know what was ahead. The one sure thing she could count on was Dean. He was the best brother she could have ever asked for.

"Yeah, right. As long as I'm telling you what you want to hear."

"Thank you, sweetest, dearest, most wonderful big brother." Brooke wasn't sure what a private investigator could even really do, but the constant looking over her shoulder and worry was beginning to wear on her. She had to do something.

❖ Chapter Ten ❖

It only took Brooke a few minutes to drive from her house to her office on Main Street. It never took long, but Saturday-morning traffic was nonexistent. She only had to work a half day today, and that was always a treat. Just as Brooke sat down at her desk, her phone rang.

"Glad I caught you. It's Connor Buckham."

She closed the folder in front of her and turned her attention to the call. "Hey there. Thank you for calling me back so quickly. Thought I might not hear back from you until Monday."

"If this is about that almost-ex-husband of yours again, better to not let it wait. Sometimes these things get nasty. I do have the name of an excellent private investigator. He's got some military background, great guy, and really fair prices too. Got a crayon?"

Brooke grabbed a pen and a sticky pad. "Sounds perfect. I've got a pen handy."

Connor rattled off the number. Brooke jotted each digit as he gave them. "Got it."

"His name is Mike Hartman."

She underlined the number twice.

"His office is right upstairs from mine," Connor said. "He's good people. He's usually in the office in the late afternoons if you'd rather just stop in."

"I'll give him a call. Thanks again." But rather than make the call, she stared at the number. Was it possible this was the same Mike Hartman that she just met over at Kasey Phillips's farm? It was a common name, but it was also a very small town. He'd said he was just helping out, but how awkward would it be to hire him to help with her disaster of a divorce, after she'd agreed to go to dinner with him. Damn him for being so good-looking. She never should have said she'd have dinner with him.

She got up and snagged the slim phone book from her credenza and flipped to the *H*'s. She swept her finger through the short list of Hartmans. Only one Michael.

"It had to be you, didn't it?" She closed the directory and tossed it aside. After an hour of pushing work from one side of her desk to the other and feeling anxious about another connection with Mike, rather than make the call, she got up from her desk and walked down the block to see Jenny at the yoga studio.

"Knock-knock," Brooke called out as she pushed through the tall doors on the old building. What a stroke of luck that the building had been for sale when Jenny was with her on the house-hunting trip, else Jenny may not have gotten the wild idea to relocate with her.

She could still see the look on Jenny's face when she'd spotted the bright-orange building. Brooke had laughed because it was about the tackiest pumpkin-orange building she'd ever seen, but the yoga chakras or good karma must have reached inside the car and tapped Jenny right on the shoulder, because Jenny had nearly jumped out of the car before they stopped to go look in the window.

She'd bought and closed on the building before Brooke even closed on her own house. As crazy as it had seemed, Brooke wasn't about to talk her out of it. Besides . . . she'd have missed Jenny like crazy if she hadn't made the move.

Jenny came skipping out from the back carrying an armful of colorful yoga mats. "Hey!" She dropped them off on a counter next to the door and gave Brooke a hug. "I didn't know you were stopping by this morning."

"I had a few minutes." Brooke stepped into the middle of the room and twirled in the wide-open space. "It's great. It feels so peaceful compared to the bustle of the grand opening party."

"That was fun, but I like this better."

Brooke sniffed the air. "What's that smell?"

"A new candle. Lavender and vanilla. Isn't

it divine?" Jenny inhaled deeply and closed her eyes. "I swear I'm tempted to wear it as perfume."

"Nice. You nervous about your first set of classes?"

Jenny's face lit up. "Not at all. I'm so excited. I have twelve people all signed up for the one this afternoon. The Monday-morning class is completely sold out. I thought I'd have to do a lot of free stuff to talk people into trying it, but that hasn't been the case."

"Maybe that other lady had already whetted their appetite for a yoga class."

"Well, then I should find out who she was and thank her."

Brooke started laughing. "Yeah, about that . . ."

"What's so funny?"

She winced, hoping Jenny wouldn't take the news as bad karma. "I heard the story about what happened with the yoga center that was supposed to have opened up here before."

"What?" Jenny looked worried. "Tell me."

"Turns out that lady is in prison now."

"No way. Stop. You're lying." Jenny took a step back. "You're serious?"

Brooke nodded. "Dead serious."

"Bad joke, Brooke."

"It was a little funny, admit it."

"Okay, no thank-you notes to jailbirds. I'll just take the good karma and roll with it," Jenny said.

"Good idea."

"Are you coming to the class this afternoon?" Jenny asked.

Brooke hiked herself up onto one of the stools in front of the smoothie bar. "I wouldn't miss it. I need the balance, that's for sure." But Brooke's nerves were on edge and Jenny was giving her the look. She could always tell when something was on her mind.

"What's up?"

Brooke let out a sigh. "I talked to Connor. I got the name of the investigator."

"Thank goodness. What did he say?"

"I haven't contacted him yet."

"Why not?"

"Maybe I'll call Monday once we get past your first weekend of classes and all."

Jenny picked up the cordless phone on her counter. "Don't you dare use me as an excuse to delay this any longer, Brooke Justice. Lord, girl, call him now."

"I think it might be the same guy I told you about over at the farm."

"The 'not Cody Tuggle, but not a troll' guy?" Jenny's face lit up. "The one you are interested in whether you care to admit it or not?"

Brooke hid her face with her hands to keep Jenny from seeing her smile. Jenny knew her too well. She dropped her hands and tried to look serious. "Stop. It's not like that, but seriously, wouldn't it be weird if it's him?"

"Why?"

"Because I said I'd go to dinner with him, and now I'd be airing my dirty laundry."

"There's nothing dirty in your laundry. It's Keith that's the dirty scoundrel. Call him," Jenny said, nudging the phone toward her.

"I can call him when I get back to the office. What if he can see me today, and that makes me late for the class? I just didn't want to—"

"Let me down? Don't be stupid. If we don't take care of this mess with Keith, you might not be around to let me down. And I have gotten used to you being around."

Brooke rolled her eyes. "You're being dramatic."

"I'm being practical. Dial!"

"Fine," Brooke said. She took the piece of paper from her purse and dialed the number before she chickened out. He answered the phone on the first ring. He could see her as soon as she could get to his office.

"So? You're on your way?" Jenny asked.

"Yeah. Apparently. Just how good can this guy be if he can see me like right now? What's he doing? Just sitting around waiting for business? Doesn't sound like the best to me."

Jenny snagged the phone from Brooke's hand and sat it back on the charger. "Is it him?"

"I don't know. I didn't ask. But yes . . . it sounds just like him." Brooke let out a sigh. "It's going to be so weird."

"Quit stalling."

"Fine." She got up and gave Jenny a hug, waving as she walked out the door.

"Call me and let me know how it goes," Jenny called after her.

"I will," Brooke said, only her gut told her that was just Jenny's way of making sure she really went.

Brooke's stomach swirled. Talking to someone she didn't even know about this mess with Keith was embarrassing. Plus, it somehow just seemed more real when you said it aloud. Out of habit, she swished her hand through the top of her hair, then raked the bangs back into submission across the front.

Brooke had walked as slow as she could but it still hadn't taken long to reach his office. She stood in front of the law offices of Buckham and Baxter on Main Street. The numbers above the door of the old bank building were 11515. Ones and fives. Her favorite numbers. To some a mere coincidence. To Brooke, a lucky sign.

HARTMAN SECURITY AND INVESTIGATION, LLC in red letters scrolled professionally across a metal sign. It swung from two lightweight chains at the second-story level. Flower boxes hung from the windows, filled with happy splashes of color from the marigolds that overflowed from them. She wondered if they were his doing or part of the Main Street beautification guidelines. It didn't matter. She loved marigolds.

"Marigolds. Good luck." *The ones and fives in the address may have been a stretch, but marigolds were a sure thing.* They'd been her favorite flower since she and Granddaddy started planting them each year from ten-cent seed packets. Whenever she happened to see them, she felt happy for the memory and very, very lucky.

❖ Chapter Eleven ❖

If the car had a thermometer, Goto would've bet his life that it would read in the triple digits. If not, it had to be close, because it sure felt that way after sitting in the sweltering heat for over an hour.

Suddenly, he straightened behind the wheel of the beat-up Grand Am, and wiped the back of his hand across his sweat-beaded lip. A whole six weeks of tracking the do-gooder, and all had seemed pretty much a waste so far.

He cursed himself for letting pride win over practicality when he bought this piece of shit Grand Am. No air and the bucket seats made sleeping in it no picnic. He could've been chillin' with some cool air-conditioning in that minivan. It wasn't like he was out trying to pick up women, so why had he allowed himself to get sucked in by the sportier car when Wheelie gave him the choice?

One mistake. He always allowed himself one. Didn't do you any good to try to be perfect. That would just drive you insane. So he'd made his one mistake already and got it out of the way. Just as well. He wouldn't want to make one when it really mattered.

He leaned forward. "Well, well, well. How do you like that? It's about time." He hadn't seen anyone interesting come or go from that office except Mike Hartman in the weeks he'd been watching—until now.

He watched intently as a short brunette made her way up the stairs. His legs tugged against the seat as he leaned over to pull a small pair of binoculars out of the glove box. As he shifted his weight to his right butt cheek trying to unglue himself from the vinyl seat, his sweating legs resisted the movement. It was like pulling himself off a big-ass Band-Aid every time he tried to move.

He raised the binoculars to take a closer look, but she was already out of sight.

Coming back here after eight years of being in the slammer was like landing on a new planet. You used to be able to get a courtesy cup of ice water anywhere; now it cost you a buck just to quench your thirst. And nothing looked the way he remembered.

He leaned back in the seat, fixing a stare on the front of the building. Maybe she wasn't a customer. Maybe he was getting him a piece of that hot ass right this instant. He closed his eyes. He could almost hear the sounds of it, smell the sweat, and hear the screams. He did love a good scream. Not that kind, but a scream was a scream in his book.

Goto slapped the steering wheel. Then slapped his face to make himself quit thinking about that girl and sex.

When he was in prison they'd called him Goto.

Not Franklin or Frank. Not Daniel or Dan like his mom always had.

Not Gotorow. Goto.

At first it made him mad that they didn't get his name right, but then he'd fallen in love with it because the nickname had come from all the media coverage he'd gotten all those years ago.

The "Goto Hell Murderer" had splashed national headlines.

Those news guys—they loved a good story. And he'd loved the attention. He wouldn't mind giving them another.

He pulled a spiral notebook out from under the seat and flipped to a back page. Putting pen to paper he started drawing small circles and waves. *Three circles and a row of waves. Three more circles and a row of waves.* The exercise was supposed to help him get past *that feeling* whenever it came over him.

His teeth ground. *Three more circles and a row of waves.*

He'd faked it a million times when he was in prison, but now he needed it to work.

Focus. That's what he needed. He only had a few weeks to finalize and execute a plan. Not just any plan either. The perfect plan. He hadn't waited this long to screw it up, but if he didn't get it done and get the hell out of Dodge, he'd probably end up back in prison and he had no plans to do that.

There was no room for error, and a woman would be a distraction. He bore down so hard on the next row of circles that he ripped the paper.

❖ Chapter Twelve ❖

Brooke stood outside the door of Hartman Security and Investigation, LLC trying to push back the swell of nausea. She let out a long, slow breath.

Was she letting Keith win by letting him get under her skin? Was she overreacting? Sometimes it felt that way, but standing here made the situation last night feel more real, more threatening. More importantly, was the nervousness she was feeling right now an overreaction to Mike Hartman?

She'd earned the reputation of being in control

no matter what, yet these things were leaving her frazzled and feeling a bit helpless, and *helpless* was not a word she wanted to describe her.

She patted her sweating palms against her pants. Asking for help wasn't one of her strong points. With one last deep breath, she knocked and pushed the door open.

The man behind the large wooden desk looked up and smiled.

"Hello, again." His confident smile reached his eyes.

She extended her hand, almost speechless. She'd hoped she was wrong, but here he was . . . again.

"You knew it was me when I called?" She shook his hand. Her skin looked so pale against his. Those fine lines that danced like exclamation marks around his bright-blue eyes made her breath hitch. His muscular frame pulled the shoulders of the white dress shirt tapering into worn blue jeans, his slim waist accenting the width of his shoulders. He cleaned up nice. "Why didn't you say something on the phone?"

"Didn't think it mattered."

"I guess it doesn't." She hadn't mentioned it either. Guess that evened the score. She set her purse next to the chair, but remained standing, hoping her nerves would settle and he wouldn't notice the shake in her voice. "Thank you so much for seeing me on such short notice."

"No problem."

"Connor recommended you. He says you're good people."

"I put that on top of my résumé." He smiled and those little lines danced around those blue eyes like skipping rocks sending out ripples. "That's why I get paid the big bucks."

Their eyes held for one of those extra-long moments, and she fought an unexplainable urge to bolt from the building.

A bark from somewhere across the room sent Brooke into a spin. "What?"

"Hunter. It's okay," Mike said. "Sorry about that. We're still working on his manners."

Brooke laughed off the nervous energy, and stooped down as the German shepherd moved to Mike's side and sat right next to him with just a hand signal. "He's beautiful," she said. She reached out her hand and Hunter not only gave it a sniff, but gently licked the top of it and then looked up at Mike.

"I think he likes you," he said.

"Good thing. He's going to be a big dog. Look at the size of those feet."

"He's a good boy. Hunter, load up." The dog ran across the room and went into his kennel and lay down.

"He's smart too." She stood up, feeling a little less apprehensive. "I wasn't sure if I should have called someone in Virginia Beach. I mean, we are kind of out in the boonies."

"I have all the same high-tech solutions as they do in any city. Trust me. I can take care of you just fine."

"I didn't mean it like that. I mean, Keith, my hopefully soon-to-be-ex, he's in Virginia Beach. I'm here. I just wasn't sure if it mattered." Great. Now she was rambling. "I hope I'm not wasting your time. My brother thought I should've called someone a couple weeks ago. I've been having some problems and I think my soon-to-be-ex might be behind them."

Mike seemed to be sizing her up. "Have you called the police?"

"Of course." Did he think she was stupid? "They've been out to my house a few times. They think I'm a fruit loop. Well, not Sheriff Calvin. He's nice, but that deputy of his definitely thinks I'm crazy."

"Well, you're here now, so let me be the judge of that."

She wasn't sure if him judging her was exactly where she wanted to start. "What do we do?" She followed his lead, taking a seat in a nailhead-trimmed leather chair in his office. She stroked the soft, worn leather, tracing it slowly with her fingertips.

He grabbed a pen and wrote something on the pad in front of him. Even his hands looked strong. Butterflies, extra big ones, knocked around her stomach. Was it the situation, or was it Mike?

Being around him should not have this effect on her. Her focus was on getting rid of a guy, not getting one.

"Tell me what's going on," he said without looking up.

"I don't even know where to begin. I . . ." Still avoiding his gaze, she leaned forward in the chair.

"Relax." He leaned back in his chair. "Just start from the beginning. Take your time."

She let out a slow breath. *Here goes nothing.* "I'm in the middle of an ugly divorce," she explained. "It's been a huge mess. At this point, he can have the material stuff. I just want out, but now he's decided he won't sign the papers."

He tilted his head. "Why won't he sign the papers?"

"He's the one who originally filed the separation, but now he's saying he wants to get back together."

"You said he lives in Virginia Beach. Right?"

"Yes.

Mike took notes. "What's his name?"

"Keith Farrell." She paused to spell it for him. "He was originally from Pennsylvania. We met at a charity car show event a few years back. He was so different back then." Or maybe she'd really just *wanted* him to be different back then.

In hindsight, someone else had dragged Keith to that event. He really didn't have a charitable bone in his body. He'd even been too selfish to support the kids who'd come knocking on the door to raise money for school athletics, and every time they'd gone to a fund-raiser he'd belly-ached about the cost of the tickets versus what was in it for him. She'd learned to tread lightly around those discussions to avoid his rants.

"Keith can be a little . . . unpredictable. You never really know which mood or attitude you're going to get from him."

"What's he do for a living?"

"He's a computer guy. He works for a government contractor out West, but he works from home. He can do his job from anywhere."

Mike nodded, encouraging her to continue.

"The trouble all started when I was still living and working in Virginia Beach. I figured he had kept a house key or something. Plus I was so close, it was easy for him to come over and mess with my mind. Snip a phone wire, siphon my gas, and put goldfish in the hot tub we had . . . stupid stuff. Not dangerous. Just a hassle more than anything. I thought maybe it was sour grapes because I was living in our house. When the job opened up in Adams Grove, I put in for a transfer."

"But it's still happening? The mischief, I mean. Even after you relocated?"

Brooke ran a hand through her hair, dipping loose strands behind her ear. She looked up at him and their eyes caught for a moment too long. "Yes." She swallowed. What color crayon would those blue eyes be? "At first it seemed so crazy I didn't tell anyone. But then stuff kept happening and I called the police. Keith's been in my house in Adams Grove. I can't prove it, but I know it. Things have been moved or shuffled around. Potted plants toppled. I smell his aftershave. That kind of thing."

"Things moved? Do you lock your doors and windows?"

"Yes. I've even had the locks changed and upgraded, but it hasn't helped. I'm no domestic goddess, but everything has a place. I started getting freaked out, so I started a list to be sure it wasn't in my head and to see if there was a pattern."

"Did you?"

Her brow wrinkled. "Did I what?"

"See a pattern?" Mike asked.

"Oh, no. It's just a really long list."

"And that's why you're here. Can I see the list?"

"Sure." She dug the notebook out of her purse. "It was all little stuff . . . until yesterday. Yesterday he went too far. If I hadn't gotten home when I did . . . my dog would . . ." Her gestures showed her frustration, and her hands slapped her thighs as she let them drop to her lap.

Mike leaned back, elbows on the arm of the chair. "Your dog?"

"She's fine, thank god. You have a dog. You know. They're like family."

He nodded.

"If anything had happened to Stitches . . ."

"Stitches is the dog?"

"Yes. She was a stray. She had stitches across one of her legs when I found her, so I named her Stitches. I notified all the local vet clinics, but no one ever claimed her. Who loses a dog that just had surgery?" she rambled. "Anyway, that isn't important, is it? When I got home from work yesterday, Stitches was outside in my hot tub treading water." She pushed back the tears that threatened to spill.

"Could it have been an accident?"

"No. She was in the house when I left that morning. I've gone over it in my head a hundred times. I have no idea how long she'd been out there. She could've drowned. That's when I called Connor and got your name."

"And this happened in the house here in Adams Grove?"

She nodded, biting back tears. Still the thought of something happening to Stitches scared her. "Yes. Just last night. I haven't lived here that long, but I've called the police practically every week over things. Adams Grove is not turning to be the safe place I'd hoped it would be."

"Well, let's fix that." He raised a brow. "How do you think he got into your house?"

"I haven't the foggiest idea. No sign of forced entry. Again." She shrugged. "I confronted Keith last night about this. He swore it wasn't him, but I don't believe him. He's recently become obsessed with us getting back together."

Mike jotted a couple of notes on the pad in front of him.

"You're frowning. What? You think I'm crazy, too, don't you?" Great. It would be a little hard to be able to do her job advising on the pasture and grazing plan if he thought she was a nut job. This was a huge mistake. She should've found someone else.

"No. That's not it at all."

Brooke peered across the desk, trying to see his notes. "You look all serious over there. Do you think it's *not* . . . not so serious?"

"Maybe." It was a statement, not a question. "No children?"

"No." She answered without hesitation.

"Okay." Mike took note.

"That didn't sound right. I love other people's kids. I just don't think I'd be a good mom. I never ramble like this, or maybe I do, but not this badly. Even *I* think I sound like a crazy idiot today. I'm sorry."

Mike didn't even look up. "Any chance of reconciliation?"

"What?" She nearly shouted it.

"I had to ask." He tapped his pen against the pad on his desk and shrugged.

"Not a chance," she answered firmly, crossing her legs.

Mike set down his pen and focused on her. "People can pull some crazy stunts when they feel they're running out of options. Keith Farrell might fall into that category. Give me a week. If nothing else, we might figure out how he's getting into your house. Better safe than sorry."

"I don't know, listening to what I just told you, I feel like a neurotic worrywart. I'm probably wasting my time, not to mention yours." Her mouth pulled into a tight line and she felt the color rise in her cheeks.

"One week and if there's nothing there, it's on me."

"I can hardly pass that up, can I?" She shifted in the chair. "I sure hope I'm not blowing this out of proportion."

"Brooke, if more people followed their gut feelings there'd be a whole lot fewer problems in this world. Besides that, estrangement homicide is on the rise. It isn't something to play off lightly."

"Homicide, like murder?" She grasped the arms of the chair.

"Basically. It's a homicide that is driven by the feeling of a loss of control. You see it in couples, sometimes parent-child relationships too. This could fit that escalation profile."

"Are you trying to scare me?" Brooke folded her arms across her chest. She didn't like being in the damsel-in-distress role. She could take care of herself . . . usually.

"It may be nothing at all. I just don't want you to take this lightly." He came around the heavy wooden desk and balanced a hip on the edge, crossing one long leg over the other. "One week. We can decide after that. At the very least, you should get some peace of mind." He leaned back against the desk. "It's your call."

She stared out the window like she was expecting to see an answer pop up on a cue card. "Cardinal, good luck," she said just above a whisper as she spotted the lucky bird dancing in the flower box just out the window.

Mike swung his attention toward the window in response.

Guess I said that in my outdoor voice. "I guess there isn't much harm in one week," Brooke said, trying to act nonchalant. "Figuring out how he keeps getting into my house would be a good start. So what do we do?"

"Aside from a few additional details today, you don't do a thing. Be yourself, go about your business. I do all the work in this relationship."

"That'll be a switch. I might just enjoy that."

He walked to the corner of the office, patted the chair in front of the computer, and gestured for Brooke to take the seat there.

Mike reached across her and, with a tap, the screen came to life.

He was giving her instructions and she'd already missed half of them while she was focused on that wedding ring on his finger. It hadn't been there the other day on the farm visit; she was sure of it.

"The software will walk you through a series of questions. If you don't know it, just skip it. It ensures I don't waste our time finding out what you already know." He clicked through a couple preliminary screens, assigning a case number and startup questions, and then patted her shoulder. "I'm going to grab a cup of coffee. Can I get you anything?"

"No, I'm fine, but thank you."

He walked out of the office and she got down to the business of filling in the screen with information. She was able to fill in most of the blanks, which she wasn't sure was good or bad.

When he came back in the room, she was pushing back from the desk. "One last thing and we're done. I need your itinerary for the week."

"I have it electronically. Let me grab it." Brooke walked across the room to her handbag and retrieved her smartphone. "I live by this thing." She grimaced. "Isn't that awful? I can't remember a thing without it."

"I know what you mean. Even the kids have them these days. How did our parents ever get along without technology?"

"Beats me." She walked back over to the desk and updated the details on the calendar. "Done. Thank you so much."

Mike shook her hand. "Great. We'll sync up when we get together for that steak dinner on Friday anyway. I guess I won't have to call for your address now."

"Do you think dinner is really a good idea under the circumstances? I mean with the case and everything, and . . ." How do you just blurt out that you aren't that kind of girl? If he was married there was no way in hell she was going to give people in this town something to gossip about.

"I don't think it breaks any rules. Besides, it's a community event."

"I was thinking you and your wife should just make it a night out. I mean, she'll probably appreciate the alone time if you're working on this case for me."

He looked a little dumbfounded at first, then held up his hand. "The ring? I don't have a wife waiting at home if that's what you're asking."

"You're not married?"

"No."

"Then why let people think you are by wearing a wedding ring?"

"It's a long story."

Maybe it was part of his undercover work. "But you're not going to tell me right now, are you?"

"Right. So dinner as planned? I'll pick you up at seven on Friday."

"Yes. I guess so, and thanks for working me in so quickly." She turned to leave but then turned back and smiled. "You know, I was really uncomfortable about this. Thanks for making it so easy. Thank you. I mean it. Did I just say 'thank you' like a hundred times?"

"Just three, but who's counting?" he teased, and Hunter let out a high-pitched whine as if he wanted to be a part of the conversation, making them both laugh. "You're welcome. It was nice to see you again too." He let his hand fall under her elbow as he guided her to the door and downstairs.

He opened and held the door for her, then scribbled his home and cell phone on the back of his business card and handed it to her. "Call me if anything else comes up. Anytime, day or night. Got it?"

"Got it." She flipped the card against the thumb of her other hand, and then pointed the card his way. "That's why you get the big bucks, right?"

"Yep, that would be it," he winked, then led her down the stairs and out to the sidewalk.

"By the way," she said as she turned around. She pointed toward the window boxes. "Those flowers. Did you plant them?"

He looked up and grinned. "Marigolds. A housewarming from my dad."

"They're my favorite. My granddaddy and I used to plant them from those ten-cent seed packets." She smiled and glanced back up at them. "Good memories."

She turned to leave. "Thanks again," she called out.

"Later, bye," he said as she walked away. He watched as she headed up Main Street and disappeared around the next corner. Still standing there, staring at the empty sidewalk, he heard his cell phone ring, bringing him back to reality. "This is Mike."

"Just testing it out," she said. "You're hired."

❖ Chapter Thirteen ❖

Goto ripped the circle-and-wave-covered page from his notebook and crumbled it in his palm when the girl walked out. Mike was right at her heels. Goto's tongue flicked across his dry lips as he watched her flip her long hair over her shoulder as she moved gracefully down the block.

His eyes narrowed as he watched her walk away. Mike was watching her too.

Goto pulled his binoculars to eye level and twisted them into focus. Mike wore a goofy-ass smirk.

"Stupid bastard." Goto lifted his hand in a gun-like motion and pulled the fake trigger with his forefinger.

He could picture the six-foot-something bastard

gasping and grabbing for a pool of red in the center of his chest, then falling to the sidewalk. He could do it right now and be done. Too easy, though. No sport to that. "Soon, my friend. Soon."

Maybe that girl would factor into the final plan. Could he be that lucky? He dropped the binoculars into his lap and grabbed the notebook. Balancing it on the steering wheel, he started sketching. He pushed the pen, first lightly brushing it against the paper, then pressing hard to refine the image.

Pretty damn good, if he said so himself. The girl stared back at him from the page. Okay, so she had some extra cleavage now, but it looked good that way. And then it dawned on him. This was the girl that he'd met at the yoga studio the other night. Brooke Justice. *I knew I'd seen her before.*

He shoved the notebook back under his seat, finally feeling satisfied with the surveillance mission and himself. According to the digital clock on the dash, he had just enough time to stop and get a lottery ticket and get to work at the pizza shop on time—if he hurried.

Holding down the job was a pain, but he needed to be close to his prey to make the plan, and he sure didn't want to send up any red flags with his parole officer. As long as he was on time for his check-ins there shouldn't be any problem.

❖ Chapter Fourteen ❖

The moment Brooke clicked Accept on the computer at Hartman Security and Investigation earlier that morning, state-of-the-art software was at work unraveling the recent events of Keith Farrell's life and hers.

On Monday morning, armed with the information on Brooke's case, Mike headed out early to Virginia Beach to begin following the leads. He couldn't go to Virginia Beach without stopping to see Perry, so he picked up a box of bear claws from Mac's Bakery on the way out of town.

Almost two hours later he pulled up in front of Perry Von's office. It was just a little shotgun house-turned-office building, but it served the purpose. Mike walked inside to the smell of fresh-brewed coffee and an adorable little blonde working Perry's phone.

"He in?" Mike asked.

"Yes, sir."

Mike's ego deflated a little. *Sir? Really?* He eased on past the girl, went into Perry's office, and dropped the bakery box on the desk. "Better than doughnuts. This *is* what guys in your line of work eat, right?"

"I think you mean *our* line of work. I see all

those years in the Marines couldn't grind the smart-ass out of you."

"Never at risk." Mike opened the box and stuffed half a bear claw into his mouth. "You're one to talk."

"I'm sure Riley would agree with you on that one."

"Where is that beautiful wife of yours? Didn't you tell her I was coming to town this morning? Or are you keeping us apart so she doesn't fall for a real man?"

"She's in Nashville with Kasey. Again. You know those two are inseparable. I'm on my own this week."

"Not totally alone." Mike lowered his voice. "When'd you get the cute secretary? And does Riley know about her?"

"That's Riley's handiwork. When she heard Mrs. Reynolds was going to Nebraska to help her daughter for a few weeks, she offered up the position to one of the local college kids."

"Tell Riley she can hire workers for me anytime, and since the little woman is out of town, you can buy me dinner tonight."

Von arched his brow. "That's eight hours from now. You don't think I'll be sick of your sorry ass by then?"

"I can almost guarantee it." Mike plopped down in the chair in Von's office.

"What are you doing in this part of town anyway?"

"I've got a client with an ex who won't leave her alone. He lives here in Virginia Beach so I'm going to check on some things. I knew I couldn't come to your town and not stop by. I'd never hear the end of that."

"Got that right. You're settling in okay? How's business?"

"Good. The lawyers in the office below have already pushed a couple things my way. Got this case on Saturday. I uploaded all the data into the system on the new case. I figured it wouldn't hurt for you to have it since it was kind of in your neck of the woods."

"Sounds good." Perry walked around to his desk and flipped the remote to activate the big screen. His logo of a bloodhound projected on the wall. Perry grabbed the mouse and repositioned the windows of data on the screen side by side so they could see the whole case on the wall. Perry and Mike had designed the investigation and tracking software all those years ago and it had been a critical part of cracking the case to put Jackie's murderer away. The two of them still received a nice income from the licensing of the Hound software, although they'd quit updating the product for the public not long after Mike joined the Marines. Now, they reserved any enhancements to Hound for their own use.

"She's got a louse of a husband bugging her."

"You know I hate a guy who treats women poorly."

"I know." Mike knew it all too well. After Jackie's death, Mike had been frustrated with the pace of the investigation to find her killer. When talk turned to the case being tied to others in Virginia, he'd tracked down some of the other families. It's how he and Von had met. They shared the worst nightmare imaginable, and they'd been friends ever since. Tragedy did that— brought people together in ways you could never force. The two of them had spent over a year tracking down the guy responsible. Long after the police had moved onto new cases they'd stayed laser-focused and they'd tracked that loser down and turned him over to the authorities themselves.

And as good as they thought putting that man behind bars was going to feel, Mike still remembered the loss the two of them felt after the sentencing. Even the death sentence wouldn't have been enough. It was true that the evidence didn't prove he'd killed all of those women, but Mike and Von both knew from the profile that he'd been behind them. Sadly, nothing would bring any of those women back, and nothing would ever erase that scene from his mind.

Still to this day, Mike hadn't been able to forgive himself for not being on time the night Jackie died. Had he been there at the time he'd promised . . . Jackie would still be here. He'd have

104

protected her. Nothing and no one in the world would ever change his mind about that.

The sleepless nights, the to-the-bone sorrow was more than he could take and, rather than crack beneath it all, Mike had joined the Marines and tried to escape the memories.

It had been his only option. He couldn't bear to see one more person look at him with that "I'm so sorry" expression, or hear that it wasn't his fault. It was slowly killing him every day. But that had been a long time ago and now he was back. The pain was there, but it wasn't so raw like it had been back then.

And now, all these years later, he and Perry would be working together again on occasion.

Mike sat. "Let me bring you up to date on this one. Her name is Brooke Justice. She used to live here in Virginia Beach, but she took a transfer up to Adams Grove to put some distance between her and the ex."

"Probably a smart move, and that's how she found you, I take it."

"Connor Buckham, the lawyer downstairs, gave her my name. Her husband is still living down here. Or at least that's what she said. She believes he's been getting into her house in Adams Grove and that makes me wonder if he's really still in Virginia Beach or not. So between here and Adams Grove . . . we should have this pretty well covered."

"What kind of trouble are we talking about?"

"Nasty divorce."

"Cheater?"

"According to the information she gave me, that was part of it, but not our problem. He's been stalking her. Bothering her. Making a nuisance of himself. I guess he doesn't want out, although he sure wasn't all in the marriage when they had one, from what she says."

"There's always two sides."

"I know."

"You have a pretty good starting point," Von said, clicking through a screen of data and then expanding one of the boxes for more detail.

"Right," Mike said. "She didn't think her ex had had any prior run-ins with the law. Public records from his hometown showed otherwise. Keith Farrell has a history of trouble there, including a domestic dispute."

"That's not good."

"He also made a recent real estate transfer. Not sure what that means. Maybe he's moving on." Mike turned his attention from the screen back to Von. "I actually met this girl the other day, before she came to me about the case. On Kasey's farm. She's an ag extension agent out there in Holland County. She's the one I'm working with on the pasture upgrades."

"Small world."

"Got that right." He thrummed his fingers

against the arm of the chair as they discussed the details of the case. "Tell you what," he said in closing. "I'm going to get to work on this."

Von headed for the door. "I have to head down to the courthouse to pick up some things. Let's touch base midday. How about we meet at The Brew in Town Center?"

"Sounds good." Mike got up and walked out with Von right behind him.

"Always loved that car," Von said.

Mike nodded. He knew Kasey's late husband, Nick, and Von had been best friends. Mike had promised Kasey he'd drive Nick's car on occasion. Nothing undercover about a classic baby-blue Thunderbird, but then sometimes overstated was even less obvious and it wasn't like he was planning to tail the guy.

After just a couple hours of cruising around Virginia Beach, Mike had found out that Keith had quit his job, broken his lease on the apartment that he'd gotten after the separation, and his cell phone was no longer in service.

Could be good news, but his gut told him otherwise. The little things that Keith Farrell was doing to his wife were not the actions of a guy who was going to give up. Not enough to get him in big trouble, but a definite sign she was always on the top of his mind. If Mike had to guess, the guy was obsessed with getting her back just because he couldn't.

At least the guy at the apartment complex had told him about a new vehicle Keith had purchased. Brooke only knew about the red Cadillac, but Farrell's former neighbors had complained that he also had a big green four-wheel-drive pickup now. That information, along with the names of a couple of Farrell's old haunts from the guys he used to work with, gave Mike high hopes that if Farrell were still in town, he'd run across him today.

Mike headed over to The Brew to grab some coffee and update the information he'd gathered so far. The Hound app on his iPad fed the data real-time to the database and would keep both him and Von up-to-the-minute with any new information.

❖ Chapter Fifteen ❖

Mike took the list of Keith Farrell's hangouts and punched in the addresses on the tablet. Not only did the information get logged into the Hound application, but the software also charted the most succinct map like a GPS on steroids.

Technology sure made the job a breeze.

He tapped the red dot closest to his current location. Pappy's Pool Hall. One more click and the GPS picked up from there.

It didn't take but about twenty minutes to get to

the dive. In front of the small brick building there were a couple motorcycles and half-dozen cars. He was getting ready to leave when he spotted the big Dodge pickup parked around back.

Mike pulled the T-bird across the street and settled in. No telling how long Keith would be in there. He'd known guys like Farrell. He could be downing a liquid lunch and shooting pool for hours.

About thirty minutes later Keith Farrell walked out of the building and got into his truck. Mike eased onto the road behind him. It was a hassle trying to follow him in the downtown traffic, but once Keith got on the interstate it was smooth sailing, and it didn't take Mike long to figure out exactly where Keith was headed. Back to Adams Grove.

He dialed Von to let him know he was on Keith's tail and cancelled their dinner plans.

Once they got onto Route 58, Keith pulled into a gas station. Mike rode on by. No sense blowing his cover. He went up the road about a mile and stopped to top off his own tank, then waited for the green truck to catch up.

Mike watched Keith drive by and then waited to let a big rig pass and pulled the vintage car behind it.

Forty-five minutes later they were tooling down Main Street in Adams Grove. Keith pulled into the parking lot at the post office. He rolled the window down, his elbow dangling out, as he sat in his truck right across the street from the County Agriculture and Extension office where Brooke worked.

Mike parked around the corner where he could see them both but Keith wouldn't have a clear line of sight on him. When Brooke walked out of her office building, Mike saw Keith straighten and crank up the truck.

Brooke walked up the block and met up with a blonde-haired girl, then both entered the diner.

Keith gunned the engine on the big truck and took off.

Mike followed him at a distance. He had a pretty good idea where Keith was headed.

Mike passed and went down to the end of the street as Keith pulled into Brooke's driveway. He turned around at the culvert near the lake then pulled to a stop down the street where he had a straight-shot view of the side of Brooke's house. He watched Keith saunter up the front steps, and from where he sat, it looked like Keith used a key to get inside.

"One mystery solved." Mike hadn't had time to set up any type of internal surveillance yet, so he watched to see what would happen next.

A few minutes later, Keith walked out of Brooke's house, busy working his thumbs across a small device in his hands. Mike would put his money on it that Keith was synchronizing his own smartphone to Brooke's. It was easy enough to do if she was keeping her home computer calendar synced to her phone.

Mike followed Keith back to Brooke's office.

Keith parked up the street and sat watching until she walked out of the diner and headed back to her office. He moved up the street and parked right across from her office. He was being bold. New wheels or not, that was a smug move.

He was on her every move, and so absorbed in watching Brooke that he hadn't noticed there were eyes on him too.

❖ Chapter Sixteen ❖

Goto slowed as Mike turned into one of the nicer neighborhoods. He knew this area well. He'd delivered plenty of pizzas out here over the past month.

He considered his options before turning in behind Mike. There was only one way in and out of this neighborhood. At least there was one advantage to working that pizza gig. He knew this area like the back of his hand already. The cul-de-sac at the very back of the neighborhood opened up to a large park. He'd slept there a few times. That was before he'd manipulated that kid at the pizza shop to let him crash at his place. Nice kid. Too bad he didn't have a clue that he had a criminal in his midst. Pizza Boy would probably freak when the plan was done and he saw his own roommate on the front page of the paper.

Goto could picture Pizza Boy saying, "He was such a nice guy. I can't believe he'd ever do something like that."

A belly laugh flooded the car at the thought. He waited another minute before turning down the street behind Hartman to look less conspicuous.

Goto tugged on the neck of his T-shirt. Between the humidity and nerves, his shirt was soaked. The neckline hung. He swept the back of his hand across his forehead and began to slowly drive down the street.

Steady.

Don't speed up or slow down.

Head forward, only look with the eyes.

Don't want to get his attention.

He crept down the street at the posted 15 mph.

This neighborhood was known by the guys down at the pizza shop as the best tipping area. In fact, the guys had fought over the new lady who had moved in. They'd even given her the nickname Tipper. But he knew she was the one he'd met at the yoga studio that day.

He drove past her house, but there was a green truck there he hadn't seen before. Two doors down, parked on the street, Goto passed Mike parked along the curb.

It nearly killed Goto not to look the man in the

eye; his insides were screaming to react. This was the closest he'd been to him so far. His jaw ached, reminding him not to clench his teeth, but every muscle was taut being this close to his mark.

Mike was watching someone.

He was watching Mike watching someone.

Not just anyone, though. He was watching the house he was familiar with. A good tipper. Brooke Justice.

What were the odds?

"It's like she was tossed down on a silver platter just for me," Goto cried out to the Jesus air freshener. In the yoga studio, the same one from Hartman's office yesterday, the one whose tips were keeping him afloat to execute his plan. Destiny. She was meant to be part of the plan.

Hot chick. Hot car. The guys in the pizza shop said she hadn't lived there long. The tips were nice, but what he liked was how she answered the door with a warm smile, like he was doing her a favor.

She smelled good too. Like honeysuckle, or something fresh like that. His mind connected to the scent, but then he breathed in a little too quick, swallowing his gum, choking on it.

He still hadn't figured out exactly what that plan was going to be, but now he was sure that Brooke Justice was going to have a pivotal role in it. Small world.

❖ Chapter Seventeen ❖

When Brooke got out of yoga class Monday night, she'd just opened her locker to go shower when her phone rang.

She picked it up and glanced at the display—Mike Hartman's number. "Hello?"

"Hi Brooke. It's Mike. We need to talk."

"Okay, I could stop by in the morning if you like."

"Actually, I was thinking more like now. I made some progress today, and I'd like to go over it with you and take care of a couple of things. Could you meet me over at your house?"

"My house? Sure." She pulled her clothes out of the locker and draped them over her arm. "I'm on my way."

Brooke threw her lock in the top of her handbag and headed out of the locker room. She spotted Jenny over by the smoothie bar with a group of new clients. She'd never miss her.

Sweaty from the class, she yanked the ponytail holder from her hair and headed for home. Mike was sitting on the front porch when she got there.

"I look a mess. Sorry. You caught me just after yoga."

"I think you look pretty."

Pretty? She ran her hand through her hair, feeling very conscious of her appearance.

Mike stood. "Didn't realize that stuff was so exerting though."

"Oh, you'd be surprised." She walked up the steps. "Come on in."

He followed her inside. She let the dog outside, then went to the kitchen and came back out with two glasses of ice water. "So, what's going on?"

"I tracked down your ex today. He's been busy."

She took a long sip of her drink. "What's he done now?"

"Quit his job, moved out of his apartment, switched to a burner phone. Even stopped by here."

"He was here?" Her heart dropped. "Today?"

"In your house. I saw him."

She looked around. Feeling vulnerable. "How?"

"It looked like he had a key to me. We'll file a complaint against him, but I'd like to get my guys over here to change the locks and install a security system. It's good technology. I think it's important that you do that, especially under the circumstances."

He looked at home in her house, but heck, it seemed like anyone could make themselves at home in her house these days. How had Keith managed to get a key to the new locks? "Okay. When can they do it?"

"I called them this afternoon and let them

know we might need them tonight. If you're okay with it, I'll get them right over."

"What's it going to cost?"

Mike pulled a sheet of paper out of his pocket and spread it out on the coffee table between them. He reviewed the system and its cost.

"That seems like a fair price. That's installed?" She leaned forward and sighed.

He placed his hand on her arm, then moved it away. She wondered if he'd felt that tingle between them.

"I know it's a lot to take in. It's a good deal, and yes, that's the price. Completely installed. It also includes two external surveillance cameras. Nothing on the inside of the house. I think you need that privacy, and you can have any of it disconnected if you decide you don't need them later."

"Great. Let's do it."

Mike pulled his phone from his hip and made the call. "They'll be here in about thirty minutes."

"That's fast."

"I'm a little concerned about this guy. With him cutting all ties, it seems like something is up. There's more too. He's got a sketchy past with the law. I don't think we want to take any chances."

"Thanks." She chased the chills that ran the length of her arms.

"Let me walk you through how the system will be installed while they're headed over." He'd just finished walking her around the house and discussing the placement of the external cameras when his guys showed up to do the installation. He introduced them to Brooke and unloaded ladders and supplies.

"How long will all this take?" she asked.

Mike jumped in before the guys could answer. "I thought I'd take you for a ride so they could get to work. They'll be done before we get back."

"I'm a mess. Maybe I should shower and change."

"Come on. I've got my truck. We'll bring Stitches too."

"Seems like you're not going to take no for an answer."

He shrugged. "No reason to primp. It's not like it's a date. Come on."

It's not a date. He's just a nice guy. She picked up her purse and lifted Stitches to her hip. "Deal."

Mike and Brooke rode in silence for twenty minutes until he honked the horn twice as they crossed the North Carolina state line.

"My daddy used to do that," Brooke said.

"Mine too." He seemed to enjoy the memory as much as she did. "In fact, he probably still does."

"It's good luck."

"You have a lot of lucky beliefs. I like that about you," Mike said. "Are you hungry?"

"A little."

"Good. I'll take you to one of my favorite places. It's just up the road here."

"Unless it's a drive-through, I don't think I'm dressed for it."

"You're dressed just fine. It's an old train depot that's now an antiques shop and they make a great sandwich. I think you'll like it. The owners are a couple of old ladies—sisters, I think. Trust me. We'll be the only ones in the place."

"You're not going to let me have a say anyway. You're borderline bossy, you know."

"Look who's talking."

She knew he was right. "Just get there already, would you? Before I regain my fashion sense and refuse."

"We're here." Mike turned into the lot, crunching through the deep gravel, and pulled the truck near the front door. He rolled down the windows for Stitches, then got out of the truck and moved quickly ahead of her to open the front door.

Brooke dipped under his arm, entering first, and getting a whiff of his cologne. The old wood floor creaked. The smell of home cooking filled the air. They took their time poking around the cluttered collection of items. Each room had its own theme, filled with glorious old pieces of furniture, trinkets, linens slightly yellowed with age, and hand-crocheted doilies. She headed for a big mahogany dresser and pulled the top drawer open. The workmanship was beautiful, and the knobs were all original. "This is wonderful," she said to Mike, realizing that he was just barely within earshot.

"Sorry, I didn't hear you."

"I was just saying I love this place. What do you have there? Some kind of animal trap?"

"No." He dangled a pair of antique spurs he'd just picked up from a huge tabletop of goods. "They're spurs. I collect them."

"I love this kind of stuff. You can feel the memories." She looked around and took a deep breath as if the air would share the details of the decorative items among the old furnishings.

"Let's go place our order and we can look around while they're cooking. I'm starved."

Brooke let Mike lead her to the lunch counter, where he ordered BLTs and limeades for the two of them. They circled back and returned to browsing through the old treasures.

"Mostly I love the stories behind these things," admitted Brooke. She lifted a teacup, admiring the beautiful intricate design on the inside. She turned it over to examine the mark on the bottom.

Mike picked up an old cast-iron skillet. "Okay, what's the story? Lay it on me."

"Well," she said with a playful glint in her eye, but an oh-so-serious tone. "Grandma Vivian used to use that pan every Sunday morning."

"Really?"

"Oh, yes, every single Sunday. She would fry up

bacon, from the hog she'd slaughtered right out back of her house. A local 4-H project, no doubt. The hog's name was Ham Bone. His sister was Riba."

"Reba, as in the great country singer?"

"Uh, no, Riba, as in barbecued ribs."

"Of course. How could I have not known?"

Brooke continued in full animation. "Then she, Grandma Vivian that is, would fry up eggs in the bacon grease until they were crispy on the edges. She made the best darn fried eggs for miles. That pan is quite a steal, you see, because it has made memories for so many people over the years. In fact," she said, lowering her voice, and looking around as if to make sure no one was listening, "it's really quite hush-hush, but rumor has it that Grandma Vivian once made fried corn bread in that very pan for," she cleared her throat and looked around before leaning in and lowering her voice again, "the King himself."

"The king? As in the King of England, I presume?" he asked.

"Oh, don't be silly. The real king." She flashed a mischievous smile. "Elvis, hello!"

"Grandma Vivian and Elvis? Scandalous," he teased.

"You know Elvis wasn't really crazy about jelly doughnuts. The truth is, he was really all about Grandma Vivian's corn bread. And yes, he did put jelly on that too."

"Interesting." Mike twirled the heavy pan in his hand.

"Oh, yes, the memories of Grandma Vivian's corn bread . . ." Her voice drifted off.

"I see. Making memories. That's what it's all about, isn't it?"

"Of course," she said. "Even if you have to make them up."

"Better than my story, I guess." Mike held the pan. "Some woman beat the crap out of an intruder with this. Guy had a big knot on his head that was covered in bacon grease and fried egg pieces. End of story."

"Stick to your day job," she teased.

"Here's something with a real story." He motioned for her to come over to a long oak glass-front counter. "It's an old postcard. Pretty cool." He flipped it from front to back reading the message and looking at the picture, then passed it to her. "They look like myotonic goats."

"Goats pulling a cart. I love it. Hope they aren't myotonics. Those are the fainting goats. That could be a problem if they're supposed to be pulling a cart."

"True. Probably just Spanish goats," he said.

"You do know a little about livestock. I'm impressed."

"I've got friends."

"That man in the cart looks like a giant compared to them. We grow goats a lot bigger these days."

"Learn something new every day, huh?" Spending this time getting to know her layered the feelings that had been sprouting inside him lately, feelings he thought had been tucked permanently away after that tragic event over eight years ago.

When she turned around he was standing right there, practically toe-to-toe with her.

He tipped her chin up with his knuckles. "I love rustic stuff. There's lots about me you don't know."

"I think I'm going to like learning about you." She hadn't felt this carefree in a long time. It felt good to be silly with no strings attached, and he was good company. "You know, that postcard would be really neat in a shadow box. You should get it for your friend." Brooke edged along the counter. "Hey look, a lucky horseshoe." Then her mouth dropped wide as she moved to a velvet-tray display of jewelry and trinkets. "Now *that* is exquisite."

"Which one?" He was so close his shoulder brushed hers. A comfortable energy ignited between them.

"That one. Right there. She pointed to a white-and yellow-gold-filigree hair comb studded with tiny pearls and gemstones, maybe even a few rubies. "Isn't it beautiful? I wonder how it ended up here."

"That *is* pretty." He signaled to the blue-haired shopkeeper to open the case.

Brooke balanced the beautiful piece in her hands. "This is the kind of thing you pass on for generations. Maybe the woman had no family to leave it to, or she became desperate for money and had to give it up to save the farm. I bet there's a beautiful story behind this comb."

"Do you know anything about this piece?" Mike asked the shopkeeper.

"It came from an estate sale. Sorry. No details."

"She may have worn it in her hair on her wedding day." Brooke imagined a young woman with perfect skin, hair swept up, nervous about the nuptials.

Mike placed a hand on Brooke's shoulder. "I bet you were a beautiful bride."

"Order up." The ding of a bell followed.

Brooke felt literally saved by the bell from the awkward moment just then.

She avoided the comment as she and Mike meandered back to the counter and hopped up on the barstools. Brooke caught a glimpse of herself in the old warped mirror behind the counter. "I can't believe I'm out in public looking like this."

He pushed a wisp of hair back from her right cheek, quietly leaning into her. "Actually, I wasn't going to say anything, but I did hear those two ladies over there talking about how they couldn't believe a frumpy chick like you ever landed a good-looking guy like me." He gave her a convincing look, but she knew he was teasing her.

"You'd better quit picking on me. You're on my payroll, you know."

"I'm not billing you for this. Besides, you look beautiful to me. And you're fun to pick on."

"Hey, quit with all the flirting and just eat, would ya?" she said, then bit into her sandwich.

"Can't you even just take a compliment?" He rolled his eyes.

They munched on their BLTs without much conversation and then headed back home.

"This was great," she said, looking out the window. "Do you think they'll really be done with the security system by the time we get back?"

"Should be." He looked at his watch. "Or close to finished. We'll have to do this again."

"I don't want to mislead you. I'm not looking for a relationship," she said. "I don't mean to sound harsh, but I'm just not cut out for it. But dinner. With a friend. I could totally do that."

"Friends is good," he said. "Maybe even better."

They drove back over the Carolina line to her place. Mike pulled into the driveway alongside the security guys' truck. They were already packing up.

"Looks like you were right," she said.

"I'm right a lot. Get used to it."

"We'll see about that, but thanks for the distraction while they got this done. I appreciate it." She got out of the truck and headed for the door with Stitches right behind her. A second slam made her spin around. Mike was falling in step right behind her. "What are you doing?"

"I thought I would take a quick peek and be sure everything looked safe and sound."

"Thanks."

Mike walked in behind her and sent the installers on their way. Then he gave the place the once-over, and when they were both convinced everything was safe, he gave her the two-minute alarm tour and they did a couple of practice runs.

"I can handle it," she said. "Thanks." Brooke walked Mike to the door.

After an awkward moment, Mike placed one hand on the door, and pulled her to him with the other. "I had a great time tonight. Thanks for humoring me."

She looked up at him, and smiled. "It was nice. Thanks for being so bossy and forcing me to have some fun. It felt good. It's exactly what I needed."

He tipped her chin, and for a second she thought he might kiss her, and yet she didn't move. Instead he moved away.

"Bye," he said with a nod, then he pulled the door open, stepped out onto the porch, and headed to his truck.

As she watched him leave, she considered what it might have felt like if he'd covered her mouth with his. Kissed her slow and soft. But then why would he? She'd just given him the I-don't-do-relationships speech.

She set the alarm and stood there at the door, watching him leave. She wondered what might have happened if she'd kept her daggone mouth shut for a change.

Glancing at the caller ID, she grinned and answered sweetly, "Hey, Mike."

"You know my ring?"

"I'm psychic." Her whole insides danced at the sound of his voice. It had been nearly a week since he'd had the alarm system installed. He must have taken the *friends* speech to heart.

There was a trace of laughter in his voice. "Caller ID?"

"Did you ever consider the private investigator business?"

"Think I'd be good, huh?"

"Oh, yeah. Glad you weren't my dad. A girl can't sneak anything by you."

"Well, quit trying, would ya?" he said. "I know we made plans for dinner, but what are your plans on Sunday instead?"

Brooke tried to recall her schedule from memory. "I've got plans with Jenny on Saturday afternoon, but aside from that, nothing important. What'd you have in mind?"

"I want to take you somewhere on Sunday," Mike said.

Instead of the steak dinner, and he hadn't called it a date. That was a plus. "Where?"

"Can't tell you where. It's a surprise."

"Oh, come on. I hate secrets," she pleaded. "Maybe I'd rather do the dinner."

"You'll have to just trust me that you'll like this better."

"You think you know so much about me already, do you?"

"Oh, no. I wouldn't dare go there, but I'm pretty sure I'm right about this."

"Now I'm really curious. How will I know what to wear, if I don't know where we're going?"

"Dress casual. We'll be outside," he said.

"I'm not athletic at all. I run like a girl, throw like a girl . . ."

"I didn't say anything about sports. Jeans and tennis shoes—something comfortable."

"Fine. Keep your darn secret. No one else could get away with this."

"I'm honored."

"You should be. Can you hang on a sec? I just got home, let me put my stuff down and get inside."

"Okay."

Brooke unlocked the front door, then dropped her keys in the bowl on the sideboard and hung her purse on the coat closet door. "Feels good to be home." She kicked out of her shoes, then something in the backyard caught her attention through the French doors. "Hang on."

"What's the matter? I can hear it in your voice."

"I'm not sure. I thought I saw someone." She ran to the back door and peered out the window.

"What's wrong?"

She held the phone close as she scanned the yard. "It's okay," she said to Mike. "Must have been a bird or something. Sorry." She walked back into the living room with the phone against her ear. "All right, so where were we? Oh, yeah, you being all honored, or was it ornery?"

Mike snickered. "How about I pick you up at eight Sunday morning, and plan to be gone most of the day."

"All day? This better be good." She feigned annoyance.

"It's only a couple days away. I think you can make it. See you Sunday."

"I'll be ready. See you then." Sunday couldn't get here quick enough.

❖ Chapter Eighteen ❖

On Sunday morning, Mike pulled into the driveway at Brooke's house at eight o'clock on the dot. Brooke stepped outside looking cute in her jeans, red hiking boots, and blue-and-white-striped top. She balanced two travel mugs looped through the fingers of her left hand as she turned the deadbolt.

He lowered his window as she walked up, and

Hunter sprang across him and pushed his nose out the window.

"I thought the least I could do was supply the morning caffeine fix." She handed him a mug. "Goodness. I didn't think to bring one for you, Hunter."

"He's not a coffee drinker." He pointed to the red mug she'd just handed him and then to her blue one. "But blue is my favorite color."

She trotted around to the passenger side of the vehicle to climb in. "The blue one will cost you some four-one-one on where we're going."

He raised a brow. It was way more fun to make her wonder.

"Yeah, I didn't think so; besides, the blue one is mine and has girly flavored cream in it. I pegged you as more of a simple cream-and-sugar kind of guy."

"You're right. I'll stick with the red one." He took a sip and dropped the truck into gear.

"Uh-huh, thought so," she said, looking pleased with the early win. She stroked Hunter's ears as the truck eased out of her driveway.

As they pulled onto the street, movement in the backseat startled Brooke. She swung around to see what it was. "What do we have here?"

A soft thump, thump, thump sounded from the backseat. A black-and-white rough-coated border collie anxiously shifted from paw to paw.

"What? Are you going to make me have a

guard dog now too? Have to tell you that Hunter looks a lot more menacing, even as a puppy, than this little border collie in the back." Brooke leaned back and stroked the dog's head. "What is it about Mike and damsels in distress?" she asked the dog. "Or is this little gal your date?" she asked Hunter. She regretted using the word *date* as soon as it slipped from her lips. She didn't want Mike to think she was thinking of today as one.

Mike turned his attention to the backseat. "Brooke, meet Jubilee. Jubilee, Brooke."

Jubilee lifted her paw to shake as if she understood the introduction process.

"Well, I'm glad to see that he only rescues brilliant, well-mannered damsels." She shook Jubilee's paw.

"Jubilee belongs to my friend, Rick Joyner. We're giving her a ride."

"And to where would that be?" she asked, looking hopefully back and forth between Mike and Jubilee for an answer.

"You'll see. I told you it's a surprise."

Brooke turned to Jubilee in the backseat. "He's been driving me crazy all week with this secret."

"It wasn't a whole week."

Brooke ignored his comment. "Does he torture all the girls like this, or do you know where we're going?"

Jubilee barked a response, and that sent Hunter

into a spin. "Down, Hunter," Mike said, and the dog calmed right down.

"Even you know where we're going?" Brooke gave Mike the stinkeye.

"Jubilee has to work today. She's a career girl, like you."

"Oh, so you do have a type."

"Yep." Mike kept his eye on the road. It was fun watching Brooke squirm about where they'd be going, but he was surprised she hadn't guessed yet now that they were almost there.

"Ah-ha, I know where we're going!" She pointed at the yellow-and-red banner announcing the Southampton County Fair.

Mike steered the vehicle into the grassy lot to park. "I thought you'd enjoy it, plus it gives me a good chance to put Hunter through some socialization practice in a crowd. He's working on his Canine Good Citizen manners."

"Like Scout badges for a dog?"

"Sort of. I'll introduce you to Rick too."

"This will be great."

She looked genuinely pleased and that made his day. "So I was right. You like the idea of spending the day here."

"Absolutely, especially when I don't have to work it. The only thing I don't like is having to admit you're right."

"It's not a bad gig." He got out of the truck and Jubilee leaped out to the ground, then sat and waited for Mike to put on her lead. Hunter held his position until Mike called for him. Mike handed Brooke Jubilee's lead, and then he turned his attention back to Hunter.

"Good boy." Mike leaned down and gave him another command as he put a Gentle Leader on Hunter. "Forward."

Mike moved and Hunter didn't pull or stray from the path. Brooke held on to Jubilee's leash and they both walked through the gates with a stream of other folks. The colorful tents and banners made the usually bare fairgrounds look festive.

"Let's take Jubilee to Rick first. Then we can walk around," Mike said.

A tall red-and-white-striped tent housed the livestock arena. Metal gates formed a maze of pens that opened inward and outward, creating paddocks to move the animals through. Jubilee seemed unaffected by the livestock.

"She's so calm," Brooke said. "I love border collies."

"This is familiar to her. Jubilee here is a champion. You'll be able to see her work this afternoon. If this impresses you, I'll have to take you with Hunter and me to one of his classes. Those service dogs will blow you away."

"I've been around the agility dogs more than the herding dogs. Some of those breeds are rambunctious. Jubilee seems to have her company manners on. Is she competing?"

"No. Jubilee is way above the caliber of the other dogs. Rick's doing a demo with Jubilee before the pups compete." He leaned on one of the red pole gates, propping one foot on the bottom rail.

She looked out across the arena, and then bumped her shoulder against his. "Thanks for bringing me here."

"I'm glad you're having fun."

A man in sharply creased Wrangler jeans and a straw cowboy hat threw a hand up in their direction. "Hey, man. How ya doin'?" He slapped Mike on the opposite shoulder while shaking his hand with the other.

"Great. Got your girl here," Mike said.

Rick gave an approving look at Brooke. "Well, thanks. You *are* a good friend," he said, dipping his hat in approval, his eyes never leaving her.

Jubilee barked to get his attention, saving Brooke from having to respond.

"Aw, you mean this girl here?" Rick tapped his chest once and Jubilee leaped into his arms at chest level, with hardly an effort. She licked him on the cheek. Rick nuzzled her muzzle affectionately. "That's my girl. You didn't think I was talking about this other pretty gal, now did ya?"

"Rick, this is Brooke."

"Nice to meet you," Brooke said.

"Same here. I've heard a lot about you from Mike," Rick said.

"Really now?" Brooke glanced in Mike's direction.

Mike knocked the dirt from his boot against one of the stall rails. "Not *that* much."

Rick stepped toward the gate. "We have a lot to do. Trimming, shining. I hear you're an extension agent, Brooke. Can I put you to work?"

"No. We're here for a day of fun," Mike said. He grabbed her hand and tugged her out of Rick's reach. "She's all mine today."

Brooke gave Rick a sheepish grin. "Yeah. What he said."

Rick tipped his hat back and put one foot up on the gate. "Y'all are staying for the show and auction later, right?"

"That's the plan," Mike said, moving Hunter's lead from one hand to the other.

Brooke nodded. "Looking forward to it."

"Good. Nice to meet you, Brooke. When y'all come back, come around the north side of the arena." He pointed to one of about five sections marked in green streamers. "The 4-H kids decorated our spot."

"Great, we'll check ya later," Mike said.

Brooke waved as she pivoted to follow Mike out of the livestock area. "Nice meeting you, Rick."

Jubilee lifted her muzzle and gave a single bark.

". . . and you too, Jubilee," Brooke called back over her shoulder. "He is so nice."

"He's a good guy."

"Good people," Brooke said. "That's how Connor described you. Guess good people gravitate toward one another."

He opened his mouth and caught himself before he uttered the words on his mind. That he hoped she was gravitating toward him. He liked her company. She was easy to be with, but maybe being with her was so easy because he knew she didn't want anything more than a friendship.

Brooke and Mike made their way through tents of local arts and crafts, award-winning vegetables, and desserts. Children tried to catch slippery oiled pigs, and tractors raced to pull heavy boxes across a finish line. Then they sat along the tree line in the shade to listen to a band out of northern Virginia called Blackstrap Manassas. They had a rock sound with a cool country vibe and sang mostly original songs with a few standard Southern rock songs that everyone sang along with.

"I'm having the best time," Brooke said as she swayed to the music.

He enjoyed watching her move, even if her singing was totally off-key. "I'm going to get us something to eat. I'll be right back."

"Okay. I'll watch Hunter." She tucked the edge of Hunter's lead under her shoe and gave the dog an encouraging pat on the head as he watched his master walk away.

Mike turned back and just that quick look put a smile on his face. Mike went to get them some lunch and came back with corn dogs and Orange Crush in bottles, and a cup of water for Hunter.

He stepped up behind her and lifted a cardboard tray over her head in front of her. "For you," he said with her trapped in the circumference of his arms and the tray. A CD was tucked between the two sodas.

"You got me their CD?"

"Yep, and nutrition."

"Thanks. That was so nice." She took a soda and then held the corn dog up in the air by the stick and twisted it in the air. "So I wonder why someone thought it was a good idea to put these on a stick. I mean they are already perfectly suited to fit in your hand."

"Don't tell me you've never had a corn dog."

"Never."

"It's fair food. You have to have a corn dog. I think there's an unwritten law on that."

She took a hesitant bite, then nodded. "It's actually pretty good." She chewed and swallowed. "Good food. Good company. Good music."

"Can't beat that. They are pretty good, aren't they?"

"They're great," she said. "You meant the band, right?"

"I sure wasn't talking about the corn dog." At the end of the set everyone cheered and Mike and Brooke headed back to the arena to watch the livestock show.

In the crowded arena Brooke jerked to the right at the sound of someone calling her name. "Did you hear that?" she asked Mike.

He pointed toward a blonde in faded skinny jeans and a bright-yellow top. "I think it came from over there. You know her?"

The girl had climbed over a gate and was heading their way with a camera in one hand.

"I do. What is she doing here?" Brooke stepped down the bleachers, pushing her hair behind one ear as she balanced her way down to the bottom rail.

"You're the last person I would've expected to see here on your day off," Jenny said.

"Ditto. What are you doing here?"

"One of the girls in my yoga class has a kid showing today. She invited me to tag along." She kicked the dirt against the gate with a dusty three-inch-heeled designer boot. "She's been introducing me around. I met a really nice guy."

"Uh-oh, should I be worried? Nice, or nice-looking?"

"Both." Jenny nodded her head toward the auction ring. "Not only is he nice, he loves kids, and he's good-looking as all get out."

Brooke rolled her eyes. "Aren't they all?"

"So I take it that's Mike. You're right. He's no troll. Cute." Jenny waved to Mike, who had stopped to watch the kids walk the ring. Brooke gave her friend a warning look. "He's just a friend. So where's this guy *you* met?"

"The one in the straw cowboy hat." Jenny leaned over and pointed toward the holding pens.

"Rick?" asked Brooke, surprised.

"You know him?"

"I just met him a little while ago. He's a friend of Mike's. He's one of the reasons we're here."

"Well, this must be one of those synchronicity things you're always talking about. I was just breezing along daydreaming about a gorgeous guy who loved kids, and asking God just how long he was going to make me wait to find the perfect mate. Then, *wham-o*. I looked up and there he was."

"Well, I'm not sure that's exactly synchronicity, Jenny. You dream about that twenty-four hours a day, seven days a week. It *is* a coincidence that we both ended up here today, because I didn't even know we were coming here until we got here. Mike wanted to surprise me."

"No one told Mike that you hate surprises?"

Mike walked up behind Brooke. "Did I hear my name?"

"You did. This is my friend, Jenny. She just got introduced to your buddy, Rick."

"Small world," Mike said.

Jenny looked back over her shoulder toward Rick. "Seriously now, is he hot enough to melt a snow cone or what?"

Brooke blushed. "You have to excuse Jenny. I swear she only says that stuff to watch me blush."

"It's working," Mike said.

"Isn't she adorable when she blushes?" Jenny shook a finger in Mike's direction. "Don't you go telling him what I said."

"You have my word," he said.

"Excellent." Jenny excused herself to help corral children and their animals into the ring for the first showmanship class.

"Nice to meet you, Jenny," Mike called after her.

"You too." She threw a hand up in the air over her shoulder.

It had been a long day and it was starting to get dark by the time they headed back home. Mike and Brooke rode in quiet, not even turning on the radio.

"What are you all deep in thought about over there?" Brooke asked.

"You."

"Me?"

"Yes, you." It had been a great day and the last thing he wanted was for it to end. He wanted her, but she didn't seem to be picking up on his signals. Either that or she wasn't interested. If she wasn't interested, he'd be better off knowing now. Time to figure it out. He slowed and pulled off the road at the next red light, and put the truck in park.

Brooke turned to him. "Everything okay?"

He leaned across the truck and kissed her before she could ask another question. Her lips were as soft as he'd expected them to be. He moved his mouth over hers. He gazed into her eyes in the red shadows cast from the stoplight. Her lips parted. They still looked moist from his kiss, but she didn't say a word.

The light turned green. He put the truck in drive and pulled back on the road, neither of them saying a word about it until they stopped at the next light.

"Mike?"

"Yep."

"What do we have going on here?"

"What do you want it to be?" The car behind him tooted its horn when the light turned green. He cursed and gunned the engine.

"I had a great time today."

". . . but?" He braced himself for what he didn't want to hear.

"But we barely know each other, and . . ." Oh, god, she didn't even know what she wanted. Her heart and her head were like those angel and devil cartoons on her shoulder. *Do it. Don't do it.* "I'm just not ready. Are you okay with that?"

"Sure," he lied. Jackie's memories were getting easier. The bad ones finally fading, the good ones a treasure to hold. He could thank Brooke for that. Whether they got together or not, something about this little lady had given him back what he thought he'd long lost.

"Mike. I'm sorry. I can tell this isn't the conversation you wanted to have." She turned and looked out the window. "I just need time. I don't want to make another mistake like I did with Keith. I just don't trust myself yet."

"Take all the time you need." Mike didn't want to wait, but after spending time with her he also knew he would wait as long as it took to be with Brooke. Like when he fell in love with Jackie. It had been an immediate flip of a switch. Unexpected. Hell, he hadn't wanted it. But here it was.

They rode in silence for so long it became awkward.

Brooke blurted out, "I'm going to the Tides game later this week. I was wondering if you'd go with me."

"As friends? Or as your hired gun?" He sucked in a breath.

"I don't need a hired gun, do I?" She shook her head. "Never mind. Does it matter?"

"I love baseball." He turned and looked at her. "Yeah. I should go. You know, to check things out. Just in case. I can be sure Keith doesn't show up and try anything. Keep you safe."

"It should be fun too. Some friends I used to work with have the skybox for the doubleheader Tuesday."

"And fun. Definitely." Mike patted the steering wheel. "I'll pick you up at the office." *And if I still feel like I do right now, I'll find a way to make sure you own up to how you feel too. That kiss was no friendly kiss.*

"You're always the perfect gentleman, aren't you, Mike Hartman?"

Yeah, and look what that got me. Not the kind of home run I had my hopes on. Don't count on that again.

Thank goodness, they were almost to her house now. He pulled in the drive and left the truck running while he walked her to the door.

"I had a great time," she said, looking up at him under the cast of golden light from the front porch lamp.

And as she stood there looking into his eyes, he'd have sworn she was hoping he'd kiss her again. But he didn't risk it. Instead, he gathered his wits and stepped down from the porch.

"Me too." He walked back to the truck as she let herself in the house. He got in the driver's seat and waited until he saw the living room lights come on, and then pulled off wishing it could have ended in a different way. With her in his arms.

He knew about not being ready, not trusting your heart. Hell, he'd been protecting his own for eight years.

❖ Chapter Nineteen ❖

Brooke and Mike had a great time at the Tides game. It was a very lopsided win to the Tides' favor, so they slipped out in the middle of the ninth inning to beat traffic. There'd been no sign of Keith at the game and he hadn't made any visits back to Brooke's house since they'd installed the new alarm system.

On the drive back, Mike turned down the radio. "I'm going to be hauling some stuff up to Rick's brother's ranch as a favor. It's just a couple hours away. I thought you might want to ride along. They have plenty of room for us to stay overnight." Then he quickly added. "Separate rooms of course."

"Of course." Still caught up in the casual and easy afternoon at the ballpark, she didn't even hesitate. "Sure. Sounds great."

"I'll have someone cover the surveillance while we're gone. We'll move your car and see if Keith tries anything. We might catch something on the tape if he's still up to no good. Him going silent has me a little worried."

"Do you think he might show up?"

"Guys like him don't give up that easy," Mike said.

That was Tuesday. Now that it was Friday

she was wondering what the heck she'd been thinking at the time. What happened to not getting involved? A sly inner voice reminded her she was already involved. The time she spent away from him was spent mostly daydreaming about the next time she might run into him. If she was honest with herself, didn't she wish they could spend even more time together? Every time he left, didn't she wish he'd stay? Didn't she wish she could see more of him? Preferably shirtless. She was doomed.

Her stomach swirled, and she could feel a headache threatening. She popped a couple Tylenol and chugged a bottle of water hoping it would go away. It was too late to cancel, and she really didn't want to, but she was afraid what disaster another relationship might bring with it. Her only choice now was to go with the flow for a change. Jenny lived her whole life that way. It worked fine for her. Maybe she did need to loosen up a little. Was it possible to find her inner Jenny?

She caught a glimpse of her hands clenched into fists in her lap. She lifted them and shook them out. This was no way to start. She shimmied her shoulders, shook her hair back, closed her eyes, and did the "slow breath in, slow breath out" thing. And again one more time, just for good measure. Then she shut down her computer and pulled it from its docking station. She slid open the bottom-right drawer of her desk, tucked the laptop inside, then kicked the drawer closed with her foot. It would be the first time she'd left her laptop behind over a weekend in as long as she could remember.

She stood back and brushed her hands together, proud of herself for the first step to a wild, carefree weekend. Hoisting her overnight bag on her shoulder, along with her purse, she gave her office one last look to make sure she hadn't forgotten anything, and headed out to wait on Mike.

When she stepped outside, she saw a gold pickup with a horse trailer behind it stretched across the front curb, taking up no less than twenty-five feet end to end. This was not what she'd pictured when he said he was hauling stuff. *What the heck are you up to now, Mike Hartman?*

She pushed through the heavy wood doors of the old building. Mike was already in front of the passenger door by the time she got there. He tossed her bag behind the front seat of the extended-cab truck, and gave her a boost into the passenger seat.

"There are horses back there," she said, gesturing to the big eyes peeking through the side vents of the trailer.

"You *are* good at your job." He feigned surprise.

"Smart-ass. Why do we have horses with us?"

"I told you we're doing a favor for Rick." Mike closed her door, crossed to the front of the truck, and hopped behind the wheel of the rumbling diesel engine.

"You didn't bring Hunter along?" she asked.

"No. He's better kept on his schedule. The vet tech at Doc's loves him. She was happy to come in and puppy-sit."

"Whose truck is this?"

"Rick's."

She gnawed on her bottom lip. "Do you know how to drive this thing? It's way bigger than yours."

"Of course. I'm a man, aren't I?" The truck jerked a little at the weight of the trailer, clanging as they bounced over the cobblestones back onto the paved road toward the interstate.

Brooke grabbed for the door handle, and pushed her foot to the floorboard.

"The brake over there doesn't work."

"Real funny."

Mike clicked the CD player volume up a notch and began humming along to the latest Toby Keith cuts. Brooke tried to relax in spite of herself. By the time they got on I-95 northbound she was getting the hang of the "go with the flow" state of mind.

"How far away is it?" She was just making conversation, because she'd already googled and figured out where they were going, and mapped the route out of curiosity. The lister and planner in her couldn't resist, and it never hurt to be prepared anyway.

"Not too far past Tappahannock. We should be there in less than two hours," Mike replied.

"We've been friends for years. Rick's brother has a pretty cool place." He tapped the steering wheel for emphasis. "They have hills, not just the gentle roll like we have around here. Like Rick, Jack is an excellent horseman." He shifted in the seat. "The main house was built in the seventeen hundreds."

"Neat. You said Rick will be there too, right?

"Yep. He rode up with the big trailer of horses yesterday."

"You mean this isn't the big one?" They rode along without a lot of conversation in a comfortable quiet until they took the exit and slowed down to navigate the winding hillside path. Brooke enjoyed the simple scenery.

By her watch, they should be there anytime now. Brooke's palms started sweating, and her throat tightened when the truck moved from the pavement to a dirt road. Dirt kicked up under the tires in a billow of smoking dust that trailed behind them. The occasional drooping limb scraped across the top of the thoroughbred-height trailer, snapping the bough under the pressure of its own weight. The lane became wider and then suddenly everything opened up in front of them. It was like the trees all stepped aside and gave a celebratory "ta-da."

"Oh, Mike, this is lovely."

"I know."

"Beautiful." She scanned the lush green of the rolling pastures and outbuildings. "Where's the house?"

Mike pointed by way of nodding his hat toward the northeast. "Just up the hill over there. That cluster of trees kind of hides it."

"Oh, yeah, I see it. How do we get all the way over there? There's no road."

"We open the gate. Jack left the lock off for us."

"I'll get it." She jumped out of the truck and swung the shiny red pole gate open as Mike pulled the wide load through.

"Watch the hot wire on the fence there," he called out.

She swung it shut and shook it to be sure it was secured, then ran around to get back in. "I got this. I work with these things all the time."

Finally, they pulled up to the main house. A paved road ran only a couple hundred feet from the front door. She flashed an accusing look Mike's way as they got out of the truck. "Hey, why did you take me through the fields to get here when we could have just pulled in the driveway?"

"For your information, little Miss Know-It-All, it's tough to make the turn into that driveway with this long trailer."

"I guess I should just keep my mouth shut."

"I think that's going to be easier said than done for you."

"Oh, you think you know me so well?"

"Don't I?" He walked toward the house, leaving her in his boot-heeled dust.

He had a point, but she wasn't about to admit it. "Hey, wait for me." She ran to catch up. He grabbed her around the waist, took her hand, and walked toward the house with her as if they'd been a couple for years.

Rick stepped out on the porch.

Mike let go of Brooke's hand and took the beer Rick had extended his way. "Thanks, man." He pulled a long sip.

"What can I get you, Brooke? You the beer type or would you prefer a glass of wine or something else?"

"A beer would be fine. Thank you."

Rick spun around to an old-style cooler box and took out another long-neck bottle. "Need a glass?"

"I can manage the bottle. Thanks."

He tapped his bottle to hers. "My kind of girl." Then he turned back toward Mike. "Jack asked me to have you go to the barn as soon as you got here. He has a stall ready for the horses, and he wants to show you his new pride and joy." He turned to Brooke. "You can ride along with him, or if you'd rather stretch your legs after the ride I'll give you the five-cent tour."

"I'll take the tour," she said.

Mike jumped in the truck and started down the

path toward the barn, disappearing down a steep slope.

Rick led Brooke through the backyard to an oasis he called "the garden." Whitewashed fencing partitioned off a large space. The gate was nestled under a beautiful carved archway adorned by deep-purple clematis in full bloom climbing the intricate design. Next to the gate a cluster of three rural-size mailboxes sat atop an old tree stump. Each one was painted a different color.

"Tree-mail?" Brooke chuckled as Rick reached to open the big mailbox.

"Yeah. We recycled the mailboxes that the big farm equipment are famous around here for knocking over. My brother, Jack, is so thrifty he never wants to throw anything away. These store garden tools to keep them from getting rusty."

"That's a fun idea."

"I'm glad you came with Mike. He's a super guy."

He didn't have to tell her that. "I know. He's great."

"I mean I guess I'm a little biased being his brother-in-law, but it's good to see him with someone in his life again."

"His brother-in-law? I thought y'all were just friends."

Rick's eyes snapped up to meet Brooke's. "My sister was Mike's wife. He hasn't told you?"

"No. Well, I know he wears that wedding ring

sometimes. I assumed he's divorced. Why? Is there something else I should know?"

"I guess I shouldn't be surprised. He still doesn't talk about her much, even after all these years. It's still too painful. Don't take this the wrong way, but I was shocked when Mike called and said he was bringing someone up here. He hasn't dated or talked about anyone since . . . well . . ."

"What?"

Rick shook his head. "The way we lost Jackie was horrific."

"An accident?"

Rick motioned Brooke to follow him to a table and chairs near the fence. He leaned against the table. "Mike hasn't told you any of this?"

"No."

"Jackie. That was my sister's name. She was murdered. He was the one who found her. It was awful. She was bound to the pillar on the front porch of their house. He didn't even know she was dead at first."

"Oh, my goodness." She suddenly felt like she could barely breathe. "What happened?"

"She was raped. Strangled." His voice was distant. "There was a lot of press about the whole thing."

Brooke's body seemed to drop ten degrees from the sorrow in his eyes.

"It was awful. There'd been a couple of sexual assaults in the area. Everyone was aware and extra-careful because of it." Rick looked a million miles away.

Brooke watched the black cloud of emotion cross his face.

"We all wondered how he had gotten to her, and why he'd targeted her. She was an angel. She didn't deserve that kind of death. Not that anyone does, but you know what I mean. That happens to faceless people in the news. Not your friends. For damn sure, not your own family."

"How awful. I'm so sorry that happened."

"They hadn't been married long. He's carried the guilt for years; hell, he still carries it. He thought if he'd been home it wouldn't have happened. He worked late that night. He half made himself crazy over it. He tried to work through it, but that's why he left town and joined the service. We all did some serious priority shuffling after that."

Rick's pain was easy to see. She could only imagine what Mike carried around. "I'm sorry."

"It was awful. It hit us all very hard."

"Did they find the guy?"

"That's just it. The police weren't doing much. The case remained open and unsolved for the longest time. Without a lead, for months, Mike finally started gathering every detail he could find from Jackie's case and from other unsolved cases with a similar M.O. That's how he met Perry Von. Perry's wife was murdered in a similar way. He and Von became close friends. Allies. They tracked every lead and eventually they hunted down the guy. They solved what the police hadn't been able to. Of course, Mike and Perry had more invested in it. If he hadn't found Frank Gotorow in a public place, I know Mike would have killed him. I wouldn't have blamed him either."

Brooke rubbed her hands up and down her arms. Her heart ached with pain for their loss. How awful for anyone to go through.

"If you're from Virginia Beach, you probably remember the case. The headlines were 'Goto Hell'; the bastard's last name was Gotorow."

Brooke's jaw dropped. "I do remember that. I remember not going anywhere in smaller than a group of four."

"It was an eerie time."

"I'd forgotten all about that," she whispered. It was easy to forget horrible events when they didn't touch your own life. She couldn't imagine having been wrapped up in that nightmare.

"He should've gotten the death penalty as far as I'm concerned, but that's justice for ya." Rick knocked back the rest of his beer. "Sorry. I didn't mean to be such a downer."

"No. Don't apologize. I'm glad you told me. It explains a lot, actually."

"Mike was so distraught after losing Jackie. We all needed something to concentrate on. That's when we started working on this place. We all needed a distraction. Mike spent the better part of a year out here working on it with us."

"Thanks for sharing this with me." No wonder Mike never talked about his late wife. His past was way worse than hers with Keith. Two wounded lovers. They were both a mess in their own way. Their own supersized baggage.

Trying to lighten the mood by changing the subject, Brooke asked, "How did y'all come up with the name 'Painted Prairies' for the farm?"

"It was a combination of the paint horses they breed here, and the fact that there are three cottages over on the top of the other hill. Each has a different-color tin roof."

She peered in the direction he was pointing. "You can't see the cottages from here?"

"Only from upstairs. You can see the whole property from the second-story balcony. I'll show you later if you like. It's the perfect spot for stargazing. If you like that sort of thing."

"I do. I love watching for shooting stars." *Because I can use all the good luck I can get.*

"Mike never stays up here at the house. He always stays in the blue cottage. You'll love it. It isn't decorated like the house. It's more 'rustic lodge.' Mike decorated the blue cottage. It was the last thing he did before he joined the Marines. Just wait until you see it."

"He doesn't seem the decorator type. This should be interesting." She spun around at the clang of the empty trailer against the dirt road that let them know Mike was headed back to the house.

An hour later dinner was served family-style on colorfully painted farm-style tabletops that lined the long dining room for a few neighbors, Jack, Rick, and them. Local pottery heaped with veggies, mashed potatoes, and breads made the rounds, while Jack carved beef tenderloin with white country gravy. To top it all off, blackberry cobbler was served over homemade ice cream.

"I'm stuffed," Mike declared as he pushed back from the table without touching his dessert.

"Do you mind if we skip dessert and head down to the cottage?"

"Not at all." He held her chair as she placed her cloth napkin on the table.

"We're going to call it a night, guys." Mike led Brooke by the elbow around the long table toward the side door.

"Everything was wonderful. Thank you so much," Brooke said. "Can I help clear the dishes before we leave or anything?"

"Thanks for the offer, but I've got this," Rick said. "Y'all sleep well. We'll see you in the morning."

"Night," Jack said.

Mike slapped Rick on the back as they walked by on the way out. It was pitch-black outside. Brooke blinked, hoping her eyes would adjust quickly. He'd promised separate rooms. She hoped she wasn't getting ready to be surprised.

❖ Chapter Twenty ❖

Brooke followed Mike down the porch and was pulling the passenger door of the truck open before she realized Mike wasn't right behind her. "I thought you said we were going to the cottage."

"I wondered where you were headed. We can just follow the lighted trail. It's just down the hill a little ways."

"What about our stuff?"

"I dropped it off earlier and opened the place up."

"Oh." She felt nervous about walking down the dark path. Not because of Mike, she trusted him, but her insides were churning with the memories of being in college when the police were looking for the Goto killer. To think that Rick's sister, Mike's wife, had been one of the victims . . . even just the thought made it hard to breathe. Trying to act nonchalant, she said, "You're not going to whip out your Boy Scout sash of badges next, are you?"

"Would it impress you?"

He'd already impressed her. Fear stacked on top of all the stuff from Mike's past that Rick had shared with her were throwing her emotions into turmoil. "You don't have to impress me."

"Come on."

She hesitated.

"Are you okay?" he asked.

She pressed her lips together and looked toward the path and then back at Mike. "I'm feeling some anxiety about walking through the woods. I didn't used to be such a fraidy cat. I know it's silly, but—"

"Come on. You're safe with me." He held a hand out toward her. "I promise."

She stepped forward and took his hand.

His thumb rubbed the smooth skin on top. "You okay?"

His touch subdued the fear, but amped the sadness she felt for what he'd been through. She couldn't even begin to imagine how that scarred someone. "Yeah. I'm good." She pulled her hands up around his bicep and let him lead her down the path.

The night air was cooler compared to the hot day, and the darkness was alive with chirping crickets and frogs.

Mike stopped as they cleared the tree line. "Listen," he whispered, stopping her in her tracks.

"What?" Her heart started to beat a little quicker. She was thinking bears, or scary critters. "I don't hear anything," she whispered.

"Exactly." He pulled her in front of him and rested his chin on top of her head. She leaned back into his embrace. "Isn't it great?" He wrapped both arms around her.

"Oh?"

"Look." Mike pointed out ahead of them.

"At what?" she whispered back.

"Lightning bugs. Everywhere."

"I love fireflies!" Brooke's eyes were still adjusting to the darkness, but he was right. Now that she looked closer, there was a light show going on and it was all natural. "There must be millions of them."

"A million you almost walked right by," he teased.

She sputtered and laughed. "You're right. I really didn't notice a thing." Her mind was miles away . . . or years away in the past.

"Sometimes you just have to slow down and enjoy what's right in front of you."

She knew he was talking about the frogs and the lightning bugs, but how many other things was she missing, like this great guy standing right behind her?

"It's a free laser light show," he said.

"You're right. It looks choreographed." Brooke leaned into Mike's arm, her chin skyward. "The stars seem so close. It looks like they fell from the sky and landed in the yard."

"Your senses really come alive out here, don't they? Seeing, smelling, feeling, hearing . . . touching." He brushed her cheek with the back of his hand.

She nuzzled against his hand.

He turned her around to face him. Pushing her hair back from her face, his thumb skimmed her lip.

She pulled away, changing the subject back to the safe topic of lightning bugs. "I almost hate to admit this, but when I was a little girl we would collect lightning bugs off the big hedges around our house and put them in a jar. At night, we would pluck the little lights right off their butts and make jewelry. You know, diamond rings and earrings." She pushed her hair behind one ear.

Mike stared down at her with a lopsided grin. "I just can't picture you pinching lights off lightnin' bugs."

"Don't try to tell me you never did anything like that?"

"Never."

"Liar."

"We never made jewelry. We made war paint."

"War paint?"

"Yeah, we'd smear the fluorescence on our cheeks like war paint." He ran his finger down her cheek.

"Stop it," she said with a laugh, only there wasn't anything funny about the tingling that he'd just set off on her from head to toe.

Mike let his arm rest easily across her shoulders. "Want to make some new memories?"

"Maybe," she whispered. Her mind was reeling. She knew what she wanted, but she knew she'd promised herself she wouldn't go there again. She swallowed and looked to the stars. What the heck was she supposed to do with this mixed-up heart of hers? Just as she looked to the sky for an answer, she got one. She broke the silence with a squeal. "A shooting star, good luck! Did you see it?"

"I saw it. Did you wish on it?"

"Of course." She was relieved by the lucky sign. She must be in the right place after all. "Thank you, Mike."

He tilted his head down toward hers. "For what?"

"This. I feel so relaxed. This place." She held her arms out. "This wonderful place. Thanks for sharing all of this with me. I feel very lucky."

"I'm glad you like it. C'mon, I want you to see the cottage."

She stood her ground.

"What's the matter?"

She took his hand in both of hers. "Mike. I'm really sorry about your wife."

His smile disappeared. "Rick told you?"

She nodded. "You must miss her."

"She was my wife. Of course I miss her." He stepped forward. "You've been married. You know you can't just make the past disappear."

"Mine's different," she said. "I'd like mine to disappear. I'll settle for the divorce, though."

"But my marriage was a long time ago."

"He said you've carried a lot of unnecessary guilt."

He let out a choked sound. "He never blamed me, but I know if I'd have been there, it wouldn't have happened. No shrink, no one, will ever convince me otherwise." He sucked in an audible breath. "But it was a long time ago. Being with you has made me feel something I haven't felt in a long time." He placed his hands against her face, stroking her jawline. "This is now and tomorrow." He kissed her. "And the day after that." He kissed her again. "And as soon as we get that crazy ex out of the way."

She laughed at that.

"Now are you ready to see the cottage and drop all this downer talk?"

"Yes." She let out a breath. "I just didn't want to have a secret."

"Thanks. I appreciate that."

She stepped up next to him and hugged his arm. "So, rumor has it that not only did you design this place, but you decorated it too."

"Rick doesn't know when to keep his mouth shut," Mike said.

Mike led Brooke up the steps, then stopped.

"What's wrong?" she asked.

"Nothing. Everything's fine. Come here and close your eyes." He placed cupped hands over her eyes.

"Why?" Her hands flew to his.

"Because I asked you to," he whispered into her ear. His warm breath tickled.

She relaxed under his hands, letting him guide her. "I suppose you always get what you want, don't you?"

"Most of the time."

"Figures."

"Like you don't?" Mike stepped up right behind her, his body lined up right behind hers, holding her tight against him again. "Walk with me. Keep your eyes closed. Left foot." They started to walk, one step at a time, and Brooke giggled, but followed along. She felt completely safe in his grip. She'd never felt that way with anyone, not even in the good days with Keith.

One of Mike's hands left her face, but even peeking it was so dark she couldn't see anything, so she closed her eyes and went along with it. He leaned forward, and she heard the door knob turn and the front door of the cottage swing in with a creak. Air-conditioning rushed against her skin as they stepped through the threshold. "I'm going to move my hands. Keep your eyes shut, and stay right there."

"What are you doing?"

"Just a second."

She heard him moving around the room. She stood still in the darkness, excited by the mystery of it all. A moment later, his hands were back on her face, cupping her cheeks, one thumb playing over her lips.

Her breath caught and her heart raced. "Can I . . ."

she started to ask, but before she could finish the sentence his mouth was on hers, and the warmest, most passionate kiss was taking hold of her. Her knees wobbled, and she wondered if she might fall.

Mike pulled away. "Now you can look."

She blinked, taking a moment for her eyes to adjust and her knees to regain control of her stance. Candles glowed along a rough-cut wood mantel, and an arch of candles flickered in the floor-to-ceiling fireplace.

She scanned the room, surprised at the size of it. The furniture was heavy and leather. A bearskin rug sprawled in front of the flagstone fireplace. In the far corner more candles were lit behind a glass block wall. "What's back there?"

"The bathroom. Claw-foot tub and all."

"Ooooh, I love those." She walked in a small circle, trying to take it all in. "This is amazing. I'm not sure what I expected, but this is wonderful." *Like a dream. One I've had often.*

"I know." In one quick sweep Mike had her off her feet and in his arms.

Brooke squealed with surprise, "Put me down!" She slapped his shoulders playfully. "Why did you do that?"

"Because you're tiny," he said. "Because I can, and it makes me feel manly." There was no arguing that, so she let Mike carry her to the back of the cottage to the glass-blocked bathroom. He lowered her onto an antique trunk, then stepped back and lit two lanterns that hung gracefully from the corners of the room. They brought a lot of light to the bathroom. He flipped the old-style porcelain hot and cold knobs on and the water started rushing into the old tub. Mike lifted the lid on a large glass cookie jar. The smell of rose petals and fresh lavender permeated the air. He scooped a handful of the dark and scented leaves and tossed them into the running water.

"For me?"

"Enjoy. There's a robe behind the door. I'll be in the living room. Take your time."

"Perfect." She stood on tippy-toes and put her arms around his neck. "This is very nice. I'm glad I came with you."

"I'm glad you came too." His eyes locked with hers for a long moment. "I need to get out of here. Enjoy your bath, and don't worry about saving hot water for me."

She giggled as he walked out of the room. "Aren't you too sweet?" She could see his silhouette through the glass block as he went back to the living room.

Mike answered as he continued to move through the living room, "Not really. I have a feeling I'm going to need a cold shower. You're making me crazy."

She caught her reflection in a full-length free-standing oval wooden-framed mirror. She almost didn't recognize the smiling face in the reflection. She knew she was giving him mixed signals. As much as she didn't want to be interested, to feel what she was feeling, those butterflies in her stomach weren't going to let her off the hook so easy. She wondered if he could see her stepping into the tub through the distorted glass, but pushed the worry aside and sank into the deep tub. Brooke soaked until she was pruney and then forced herself to get out of the cooling water. She eased into the plush robe and quietly padded across the candlelit room. "Whew, that was great." The ends of her hair were damp and curling.

"Good." Mike toyed with the rolled hem of the heavy robe from his position stretched out on the couch.

"Where's my stuff? I want to brush my teeth."

"I put your stuff in the downstairs bedroom on the bed."

"There's more than one bedroom?"

A smile spread across Mike's face. "There's a loft. See the stairs off the kitchen? Had you worried, huh?"

"Well, I don't know that I would say worried, but I wondered. Okay, yes. I was worried."

"Afraid I was going to take advantage of you?" he asked, patting her hand.

She pressed her lips together. "Who says I was afraid?"

Mike looked pleasantly surprised. "I like the

sound of that." Mike stood. "I'm going to go jump in the shower."

"Can I brush my teeth before you get in there?" she asked.

"There's another bath off the bedroom. You can unload your stuff in there."

"This place didn't look that big from the clearing."

"It's full of surprises, like me."

So I see. Brooke got as far as the doorway to the bedroom, but the pitch-black room made it hard for her to maneuver. "Hey, Mike?" She yelled from the doorway.

"Yeah."

"Where's the light switch? I can't see a thing."

"Just clap twice, the lights will come on."

The clapper? *I hope he's kidding. Oh, my god. Okay, so now the tacky maleness is showing in the decorating.* She clapped twice. Sure enough, a soft flood of light filled the cozy room. A canopy-style lodgepole bed filled one end of the room. The pristine white duvet, clean and crisp, was in sharp contrast to the burgundy-and-black Western blanket that was casually folded at the footboard.

She unzipped her bag that, like Mike had promised, was on the bed. She retrieved her toiletries and headed for the bathroom, brushing teeth and hair and then trading the robe for her own pajamas. She now regretted bringing the conservative cotton pajamas. When Brooke got back to the living room, she saw the cup of tea Mike had left for her on the wagon-wheel coffee table.

She sipped it slowly, letting it relax her. She noticed his silhouette through the glass block. Even through the distorted glass she could see the wide span of his shoulders and athletic taper. She felt naughty spying on him. She wondered if he had done the same from this very seat when she was in the tub. She grabbed a soft pillow from the end of the couch and snuggled it under her head and chin.

An owl woke her from a dead sleep. She must have drifted off before Mike ever finished showering because she woke up all alone on the couch to the sound of that hoot owl. A matelassé coverlet was tucked around her hips. Thoughtful.

She lay there relaxed and comfortable. The thought of Mike excited her. She squeezed her knees together, trying to ignore the feeling by pressing her hips back into the leather.

But her mind was filled with thoughts of him. She swept the cover back and headed for the bedroom. It was empty.

She contemplated crawling into the master bedroom bed, but hated to mess up the crisp coverlet for just a couple of hours of sleep, and knowing that he'd been the gentleman after all and taken the loft just made him more appealing.

She headed back to the couch, but instead she took the stairs to the loft. She took each step carefully, hoping they wouldn't creak and alert him before she made it to the top. At midpoint up the stairs, she got a little dizzy, and realized she was holding her breath. She took in a deep breath and steadied herself, then made it up the stairs to the edge of the rail.

Mike was sprawled across the queen-size timber-framed bed, similar to the one in the master bedroom. Rather than a canopy, this one had an intricately carved scene of running horses in the headboard. He looked tan against the light-colored linens, and she wondered if he had anything on under the sheet that was covering the lower half of his body.

She watched him sleep, then walked over, slipped into the bed, and spooned up against him. He didn't budge. She relaxed into his warmth. Her breathing fell in sync with his slow, deep breaths, and before she knew it, she was dreaming again of shooting stars and lightning bugs.

In the last couple of hours since she'd snuck into Mike's bed, they had switched positions. She remembered crawling in behind him, but now he was spooning her. He had one arm across her body, his hand cupping her breast, and as nice as it felt, it made her regret the bold move.

"Good morning, Brooke," a half-asleep muffled voice whispered into her ear, then dropped a kiss in her hair.

Embarrassed for having been so forward to sneak into his bed, she squeaked out a "Hi."

He embraced her, giving her a gentle squeeze. "Mmmmm, this was the nicest surprise . . . to wake up with you in my bed."

"Glad you didn't mind. You're not the only one full of surprises," she said brazenly.

"I see that."

"Good morning." She rolled over to face him, thinking about the recurring dream, more of a fantasy really, with the log cabin and wondering if this was the man who went with it.

He shifted up on an elbow to look into her eyes, then kissed her softly on each of her eyelids. "You're not like anyone I've ever known."

She smiled, eyes still closed from the kisses. "Thank you," she paused, then opened one eye. What did that even mean? "I think."

He leaned into her neck, making her gasp as his face made contact with the soft skin between her shoulder and ear. "It was a compliment." He swept her hair back from her face.

She shifted toward him. "It must be the country air."

He rolled over quickly on top of her, but on his knees, not letting his body touch hers.

She felt a rush of desire, and at this moment she

didn't care what won—her head or her heart—as long as it didn't make her stop.

The heel of his hand made a path between her breasts and then slowly but firmly down to her belly button over her cotton pajamas. She closed her eyes, but she was anything but relaxed. The weight of his palm slowly made the leap to the place that made her wish for more.

She gulped in a breath of air.

"Like that?"

Brooke felt cheated when he laid one short kiss on her, and then stood up out of bed. She heard him clomping down the stairs two by two, before she even opened her eyes.

"Better get up and get a move on if we want to have breakfast before we hit the trails," he called to her.

She lay there for a moment, trying to pull herself together. The shower started downstairs, so she hightailed it down to the master bedroom to get dressed before he could notice how he was knocking her off-kilter, if he hadn't already.

In jeans and white T-shirt she started to join Mike in the other room, and then decided to grab a different shirt from her bag. An oversize yellow blouse would combat the morning nip and the afternoon sun. She grabbed her hiking boots and headed to the living room, where Mike was already on the couch sipping a cup of coffee.

"You about ready?" he asked.

"Yes." She tied the laces on her boots, then sprang to her feet and led the way to the door. "Let's go, I'm starved."

After breakfast, they headed down to the barn and saddled up for a trail ride. Marsha Mellow, a beautiful tan horse with a soft white mane and tail, was Brooke's ride for the day. She laid her hands on the ribs of the large animal, then moved toward Marsha Mellow's front. The horse snorted softly. Brooke placed her hands on the animal's huge head. Speaking quietly to the beast, she struck a bargain that she hoped would get her through the day in one piece. "My, what big eyes you have. If you're nice to me and don't go real fast, I promise you a nice brush-down at the end of the day. Don't embarrass me or make me squeal like a girl. We understand each other?"

The horse tossed her beautiful mane.

"Good," Brooke said just as Mike walked up behind her to help her onto the saddle. Marsha Mellow took it from there, falling in step behind Mike's horse.

She reached forward and patted Marsha Mellow's neck, almost losing her balance as she tried to sit back upright. "Thank you, pretty girl."

It was late afternoon by the time they headed back home. They'd left the trailer there, so the return was much more comfortable, and after all the fresh air, Brooke slept most of the ride home. She sat up when the truck stopped moving. "You didn't have to bring me home. I could have driven from the office."

"You were asleep. Kind of. I saw your head jerk up three or four times."

"Mmmmm, guilty as charged. I am pooped. Thanks for the door-to-door service," she said sleepily, trying to stifle a yawn.

"I'll come by in the morning and give you a ride to your office."

"Or you could stay," she said, grabbing her bag and heading for the door. "I could fix you something to eat. It's nearly dinnertime."

Mike walked her to the door. Brooke unlocked and pushed it open with a hip, dropping the overnight bag just inside.

Stitches came running across the yard, with the neighbor's daughter chasing behind her. "For a dog that can't half hear, she sure is intuitive. She knew as soon as y'all drove up," she said.

Stitches ran up the steps to greet Mike.

He petted the dog, then lifted her in his arms and stepped in front of Brooke. She was a step higher than him so they were eye to eye for once. He casually reached his free arm around her, his hand crossing over behind her resting on her butt.

Brooke tried to hide the pleasure of his touch as she thanked the girl for watching Stitches.

When the neighbor finally turned and walked away, Brooke swatted at Mike playfully. "You were tickling my butt. That's not funny."

"It was kind of funny. Admit it."

"I'll do no such thing." She couldn't help but grin at his silly charm. "Are you going to stay for a little while?" She didn't want this weekend to end.

"I'm going to take a rain check on that. I've got to go pick up Hunter. Get some rest. I'll see you in the morning."

She leaned back, keeping a little space between them. "Thanks for the getaway. It was good. Really good." She hoped he thought so too, because she just put herself all out there.

❖ Chapter Twenty-One ❖

Water bubbled around Brooke as she languished lazily in the hot tub. After Mike had left she couldn't stop thinking about him. She'd been unexpectedly anxious to see him the next day when he'd come to take her to work, since her car was still at the office. She could've easily walked the short distance, but seeing him had far more appeal. She'd replayed the weekend over and over in her mind all night and the lack of sleep had made for a long workday. Exhausted, she even skipped out on the Monday-night yoga class at Happy Balance.

Tonight the weather had been perfect for a relaxing escape in the hot tub, and she was glad she'd decided to put all her chores aside for a little me-time.

The reflection from the setting sun colored a rainbow across the deck.

"Rainbow, good luck," she said, feeling the immediate wash of happiness. It would be a perfect evening, after all. The wine wouldn't hurt either. She took a sip, breathed in a deep breath, and relaxed, then put the Blackstrap Manassas CD in the player and sank down into the bubbling water.

Stitches was curled up on the deck within eyesight. It was nice to have absolutely nothing better to do.

Brooke closed her eyes and listened to the music, then tipped the wine bottle, letting the deep-red liquid gurgle into her glass for a second time. One of her farmers had given her the vintage when she'd told him she was leaving. It was a nice gesture even if she was more of a beer kind of girl. She couldn't tell the difference between good and bad wine. It had even been her experience that the cheaper the wine was, the more she liked it.

Her thoughts kept racing back to her time with Mike. Especially now, because somewhere along the way her guard had dropped and she was having feelings for him that she wasn't ready to have.

The sun dipped lower in the sky and it must

have been close to seven because the lights had just come on in the garden. Stitches barked, and at first Brooke thought she was barking at the lights, but then she noticed the dog focused on the back gate.

Brooke sloshed water over the side of the hot tub as she moved to the other side to try to get a view.

Stitches stomped her paws, giving it her all, but no matter how much yipping and stomping she did, she didn't look too menacing.

Brooke's cell phone danced and vibrated across the deck just out of reach. She dried her hand on a thick towel at the edge of the hot tub and leaned out to answer it. "Hello."

"Hi, Brooke."

His masculine voice warmed her immediately. "Hi, yourself."

"Whatcha doin'?"

"Sippin' wine in the hot tub," she sang out in tune to the song that filled the air.

"Wine? Alone? Either you have a problem, or I'm interrupting. I'm not sure which I hope it is."

"You're not interrupting, but I'm getting a pretty good buzz."

"Is the gate unlocked?"

"Sure . . ." Before she could finish the sentence she realized the call had ended and her heart began to pound.

She quickly pulled the scrunchie from her hair.

It tumbled past her shoulders, the ends licking the bubbling water.

Brooke threw the scrunchie across the deck. Stitches ran after it and brought it back to her. "Hell of a time for you to become a retriever."

Mike walked through the back gate. Even from a distance he was easy on the eyes. He wore a white dress shirt with the sleeves turned up, tucked into khaki shorts, and Top-Siders with no socks. For a working guy, he sure did sport a good tan.

Stitches spotted Mike and dropped the scrunchie to run to him. Like an instant traitor, Stitches did her happy dance, spin, and a handshake.

Mike patted Stitches on the head, and then kept moving toward the deck.

His gaze caught Brooke's immediately. It wasn't dark yet, but it would be soon.

Nervous energy made her breath quicken and her lips tug into an awkward smile. She swallowed hard as he took the three steps to the gazebo part of the deck and kicked off his shoes.

"You should've brought your swimsuit." Her voice shook nervously. He looked incredible. "The water's great."

Mike squatted by the hot tub and picked up her wine glass.

Her eyes locked on his.

He swirled the red liquid with finesse and then took a long sip from the glass. He lifted the glass toward her with a nod. "That CD playing. I recognize that music."

"It's the one you gave me, Blackstrap Manassas."

He smiled. That dimple accenting his cheek. "Were you thinking about me?"

She tried to look away, but even as awkward as the moment felt, she couldn't. "Maybe." Her voice was almost a whisper.

"I've been thinking about you too." He stood and pulled the wallet from his pocket and unclipped the phone from his hip, dropping them both on the towel she'd dried her hands on just moments ago.

Brooke's muscles tensed. Was he really going to—

His blue eyes held hers hostage and if she weren't in the hot tub and hot already, she knew she would be now. Sure as heck he was going to do it.

Mike leaned down and sat on the edge of the hot tub, dangling both of his legs into the water. But he didn't stop there. He stripped off his shirt and tossed it next to his things, then slid down into the water next to her.

The sheer size of him coupled by the quick entry caused the water to splash up to her chin.

Brooke's mouth fell open, nearly choking on the gulp of water she'd swallowed in surprise of his quick and unexpected move.

Mike slipped the expensive watch from his wrist and laid it next to the cell phone.

Brooke was speechless.

Mike wrapped his arms around her, gliding her easily through the water into his space.

"I couldn't stop thinking about you," he said in a hushed tone.

She didn't resist. Oh, who was she fooling? She didn't *want* to resist this.

Mike slowly pulled her closer and placed his mouth over hers.

The warmth of his kisses coursed through her body. Her eyelashes fluttered against Mike's cheek. She smiled as they kissed, unashamed of being caught peeking, because he was too.

He pulled away first, resting his cheek on top of her head. "I've been dying to do that."

They sat in the bubbling water inches apart, neither saying a word for what seemed like a long time. She pressed the button, sending the water into a churn to mask the pounding of her heart.

"I want you, Brooke." He breathed the words into her hair.

She didn't reply, she couldn't . . . she didn't have the air left to eke out a word. She moved from his side, shifting toward him in the hot bubbling water. Becoming the aggressor, she kissed him full on the mouth, her tongue teasing his, softly nibbling his bottom lip.

What had gotten into her? She was questioning herself, but her body wasn't slowing down. Only separated by the thin wisp of Lycra, a thrill rushed through her as her skin brushed against the fabric of his shorts in the warm water.

His hands began a busy trace of her every curve.

The humid steam rising from the water could have as easily been from them as the water. The heat of desire made her bangs fall damp against her forehead.

Mike's face was shiny from the steam. His hand slid along her leg, tickling her. She squirmed as his long fingers teased the edge of her suit.

Brooke gasped, nuzzling in the crook between his neck and shoulder, partly in desire, partly hiding a shy feeling about what was happening in the open outdoors.

They had come too far to turn back.

"Can we go inside?" Mike's voice was urgent.

She wanted him more than anything. Without a word, she climbed out of the hot tub, grabbing a robe from one of the hooks inside the gazebo. Nervous, and still breathless, she tossed a matching robe from the hook his way and led the way inside.

Mike didn't waste a second. A big splash flooded the deck as he leaped out of the water. He pushed his arms into the sleeves of the robe. His shorts were soaking wet and leaving a splashing path as he walked. He pulled the robe tight, then stepped out of his sopping wet shorts before racing to her side.

Brooke couldn't take her eyes off him. He

looked so big, so strong . . . so good. She turned the doorknob and stepped inside, holding the door open for him.

Mike walked up behind her, slowing her to a stop as his hands took hold of her shoulders, and he dropped kisses in the crook of her neck from behind. His big hands worked her neck and shoulders.

The kisses made her want to break into a run to the bedroom or just drop to the floor right there. Too much to take—too much to ignore.

A shiver went through her as the cool air of the house doubled its effect on the wetness of the swimsuit.

His hands and fingers raced over her body.

Wiggling out of the swimsuit wouldn't be sexy, so she left him at the bedside to strip down in the bathroom. When she walked back out, she held the robe in front of her. The room was dark, but the night-light in the hall cast a glow that accented his sharp jawline. She saw him smile when he looked up and saw her.

From the bed, he reached out to her. She moved forward and let him take her into his arms.

Mike tried to pace the arousal that was making him want to get to her sweet spot in a hurry. He took the robe from her hands and ran it across her damp body, rubbing her dry with the soft terry, then guided her back against the bed.

He stretched out next to her, roaming her every curve with his mouth, then settled his cheek against her soft inner thigh.

Brooke pushed her fingers through his thick hair while he kissed his way up to her belly and every sexy curve of her body and back down again. She squirmed, pressing herself up against him.

She reached for him, guiding his face to meet her parting lips, her breaths matching his with each kiss.

Their breathing grew heavier, hearts pounding, as they both moaned in anticipation of what was to come. Mike rolled Brooke over flat on her back, pausing only a moment as he smoothed her hair out on the bed around her, tracing his hand over her face, her lips. He held the arch of her foot in his hand, bending her leg, getting closer to the point that would fill both their needs.

"I need you." He'd fought the feelings, pushed them aside, thinking they couldn't be real, but they were. She made him feel alive again.

She nodded, and mouthed something that never made it into words. Instead, she pulled him back into a kiss.

Her back arched as if she had no control of her body as it danced its own rhythm to his every move.

A perfect beat, and it climbed in intensity, and then in pace.

"Oh, Brooke." He caught a breath midway,

colors splashing across the blackness of his eyes tightly shut.

He held her. Letting her ride the waves of pleasure as long as it would take, and loving the feeling of her letting go.

Breathless and sweating, she relaxed into his arms.

Her head rested in the cradle of his arm. At that moment she knew what it meant to be made love to. "You're unpredictable," she added, "in a very good way."

"Stepping into the hot tub in my clothes seemed like a pretty macho move at the time, but now I don't have anything dry to wear."

That wasn't what she was talking about, but it had been a sexy move. Ever pragmatic, her response was a safe one. "We can toss your shorts in the dryer. That is, as long as the neighbors didn't steal them off the back porch while we were uh—otherwise engaged."

"Not a high-crime area, I checked it out," Mike added.

"Of course you did." They climbed out of bed, wrapping themselves in the robes to head for the deck to rescue Mike's clothes and put them in the dryer.

They sat on the couch in the dark, quiet except for the clang of the metal buttons from his shorts in the dryer.

Brooke spoke first. "Thanks."

"You're welcome."

She groaned. "Not that. Well, thanks for that too, but thanks for being in my life. For trusting me in yours and making me feel safe with you in mine."

"You are very special, Brooke Justice." Mike squeezed his arm around her, resting his chin on top of her head. "Can I stay?"

"You better."

"Thanks." He kissed the top of her head, taking a deep breath in of her scent, exhaling slowly. "I couldn't stop thinking about you tonight. I swear my truck just drove in your direction."

She snuggled in tighter. "I'm glad." She hadn't stopped thinking about him either. She thought about the rainbow she'd seen. This evening was more than perfect. She'd have to move rainbows up a notch on her lucky rating scale if this was the kind of good luck they promised.

The buzzer on the dryer went off, breaking the silence.

"Clothes are dry." Mike squeezed her shoulder tenderly.

"I'll grab them, and meet you back in the bedroom." Brooke got up and headed for the laundry room.

Mike stood. "You ready for dessert?"

"Oh, I've always had a healthy appetite," she said as she walked away.

When she walked back into the bedroom she'd

abandoned the robe and was wearing only a smile. She draped his clothes on the chair next to the bed, then slid beneath the covers. Her body curved against his, leaving no space between them.

Mike wrapped his arms around her, his body reacting immediately to hers. "I think I just became a big fan of dessert."

"Me too," she answered and pulled his hand toward her.

❖ Chapter Twenty-Two ❖

Goto held his breath as he watched Mike Hartman walk around to the side gate of Brooke's house. He pulled his hat down and slipped lower in the seat and looked at the plastic digital clock stuck to the dashboard.

He tugged a pencil from over his ear. He'd stolen the Virginia Lottery pencil after he'd picked his Lucky Six numbers, or maybe they were free for the taking anyway. There'd been a whole cup of them. He took down a few notes in the spiral notebook, and started the car to leave. As he approached the stoplight, he fantasized what it would be like if Mike were in that car just ahead of him.

His heart raced every time he got this close. Fleeting thoughts danced in his mind. Jumping out and shooting him right there in the driver's seat, spraying his guts across that pretty girl's face, wouldn't really get Hartman to suffer enough. He chased those thoughts away. They were dangerous thoughts. Once it was done, it was done. There would be no second chances. He had to get it right the first time. He had every intention of making it slow, and painful, and so bad Mike Hartman would sell his soul to the devil to get out of the situation.

Goto decided it was time for a little road trip down memory lane, but he'd need more gas and he was getting short on cash. He glanced at the fancy sports car in front of Hartman's girlfriend's house. There was bound to be some cash in the console of that sweet ride.

He turned around and headed back to her neighborhood. He parked about three doors down in front of a house that was for sale. The street was quiet. The only thing he heard was his own breathing as he made his way down the street and up her driveway. Knowing Hartman was in the house with her made the deed all that more exciting.

Goto slid his hand under the door handle and readied himself for a quick escape in case the car had an alarm. One click and the door opened. He scooped a handful of change from the console. Perfect! As he eased back out, he noticed a beach chair in the back of the car. He could use some furniture of his own. He slid the brightly colored chair out, taking it too.

With his spoils, he got back in the car and headed to his favorite landmark. He'd driven by once, but that was weeks ago and things looked different with the new growth of spring. He was beginning to think he had taken a wrong turn, when suddenly he saw the familiar street sign. Now large homes lined the once rural road. He'd been surprised to see the little cottage was still there. He'd figured they'd have torn it down after all this time. Just one more sign that this was meant to be.

A grin spread across his face. It was like coming home. He pulled into the dirt lane to his favorite spot.

There it was.

He sat there breathing heavily and sweating like he'd been running for miles. Then he laughed until he sobbed. As quickly as he lost control, he regained it. Goto slowly exited the car to walk the perimeter of the house. He ran a hand along the siding, feeling the old connection. He'd scarred this place.

Sticks cracked under his feet, and the humidity hung against him heavy like a wet blanket.

The house looked as if it had probably been empty since the last time he was here. Plywood and boards crossed the windows and doors. He took the steps one at a time, pausing on each one and breathing in each memory.

He wrapped his hands around the porch column.

Memories flooded back. A small circle of faded yellow plastic hung from the bottom. He smiled. Police tape. Crime scene. His crime. He was the mastermind, the artist behind it all.

He closed his eyes and laid his cheek against the column. His bony white fingers stroked the gritty pole like it was the long hair on a woman. She had been so pretty. He took in a deep breath trying to remember all the details of that day. He could almost remember how she smelled. Sweet. Fruity. Her hair was so soft. He could taste the saltiness of the tears that were on her face.

He moved from the column to the handrail, gripping it with both hands. Squeezing as hard as he could, his arms shook.

It had almost been a perfect day. It had almost been the perfect crime.

The little house where he'd killed Mike's wife was boarded up now. It had possibilities. On payday he'd had every intention of filling up his gas tank and making the drive back out here again, but the money from the console of that fancy car had made it all possible tonight. A scouting trip. Location. Location. Location. And timing is everything.

Goto gave himself a nod for good thinking.

The next morning Goto pulled into the parking lot for his meeting with the parole officer with two minutes to spare.

He walked into the building and signed in, giving the receptionist a warm, polite smile. The kind of smile that girls thought meant you were a good Christian boy. It fooled them every time. Women see what they want to believe, but he saw the evil in his soul every time he looked at himself in the mirror.

After the meeting with his parole officer he cruised back to paradise. Frank Goto felt like king for a day sitting in the beach chair in the middle of the little house he'd killed Jackie Hartman in and he reveled in the details of that night all those years ago.

What a kick. Goto loved that all these years and he still held the power. Not many could say that. This plan was going to hit Mike Hartman where it hurt the most.

Goto got up and took a thick marker from the windowsill. He removed the cap, and inhaled the pungent chemical compound. They said that it, like gasoline or glue, would kill your brain cells.

On the opposite wall he'd marked off a calendar and the timeline for his plan. He marked off another day with joy. The countdown. Mike was wearing an expiration date, and he didn't even know it.

The thick dark ink spread across the old plaster wall, picking up cobwebs and dust from all the years this place had been shut down. He closed his eyes and the picture practically drew itself. For he didn't know how long, he let the picture take on a life of its own as night turned into morning.

He let out a breath and stepped back to take it all in.

A slash of satisfaction filled him. He had a plan. A good plan.

In celebration, Goto decided to hike to the market. No sense wasting gas, and the walk would do him good. Physical shape was as important as mental sharpness. He walked along the ditch on the side of the narrow road, then along the shoulder to the store. Work wasn't going to fit into his plan today. He dropped coins into the pay phone outside of the store. No one was in the pizza shop yet, so he left a message that he'd be out sick today. It was easier to lie to a voicemail than to a real person anyway.

Goto treated himself to a forty of malt liquor and bought a bag of ice to keep it cool. In the parking lot he dumped out part of the ice and slipped the forty down in the center. On the walk back he tried to find any weak spots in his plan. There wasn't much more time.

He spent the better part of the morning prying the boards off the back windows of the little cottage. Light poured in, casting a glow against the mural on the living room walls.

He surveyed his surroundings. This place was home. It was where he belonged. He didn't need

Pizza Boy for a crash spot now that he had this place.

Goto put his celebratory drink in the kitchen sink and tucked newspaper around it to help keep it cool until tonight. Then he grabbed his keys off a hook by the back door and headed for his car.

He dragged a hefty-looking dead branch from across the path that had kept it hidden from the road. He pulled his car out from the cover of the briars and overgrown vegetation, and headed back to town. Pizza Boy would be done with his shift. He should be able to catch him at the apartment and let him know he was moving out.

Goto sat on the couch writing in his notebook.

Pizza Boy walked in and shut the door behind him. "You okay? You called in sick today."

"I'm fine. You didn't blow my cover, did ya?"

"No way," said Pizza Boy. "I got your back. Blood brothers and all." Pizza Boy pulled up his sleeve to show his tattoo—the one that Goto had etched into his skin with a mechanical pencil and a mixture of soot and shampoo. It was an exact match in placement and style to the one on Goto.

"You're cool, dude." Goody Two-shoes kid would shit a brick when he realized what was on his arm. The image that would tie him to Goto and the dirty deed to top off all his life works—forever.

Pizza Boy beamed.

"Got bad news for you though." Goto pulled himself up off the couch, and plunged his hands deep into his pockets.

"What's that?"

"I found another place. I'm moving out. It's a fixer-upper but it'll give me more space to work on my art."

The kid had whined. Goto hated whiners.

Goto made one last trip to put his bags of belongings in the car, along with a few changes of clothes that were Pizza Boy's. They were the same size, after all. He took the cooler that they'd used for a coffee table and stuffed more than his share of the food into it. He'd need the cooler for ice, since he didn't have a refrigerator at the new place.

Part of him would miss Pizza Boy. But the kid had served his purpose. Too bad for him.

Goto pushed the thought from his head. He whistled through his teeth and sang "Jesus Loves the Little Children" the whole drive back, popping the Jesus air freshener to keep it swinging to his beat. That felt good.

He pulled the car off the road nearly a mile before the driveway to the house. The old logging site pallets made it easy to drive into the brush. It was the best spot to tuck away the car. He dragged the birch back across the outlet, covering his tracks in.

He couldn't take a chance trampling the grass at

his house by using the driveway. Someone might notice he'd taken occupancy. He'd only have to keep the secret for a few weeks. When it was all said and done, he'd torch the place. That ought to make headlines.

A place of his own. It was meant to be. It took him two trips to walk all of his new stuff to the house, but he didn't mind.

Sweat dripped down the side of his face as he hauled the heavy cooler on the last trip to the house for the night.

Suddenly he needed to spread out—no sense living like he was still isolated to a cell. After being in prison he needed to keep moving. The feeling of being in one place for any length of time sent him into a tailspin.

He grabbed the pillow and blanket and set them up in the bedroom, then moved the beach chair next to the window in the living room and set a box next to it like an end table. He put his food in the cupboards and then slid the cooler where a refrigerator once sat.

Hell, this was a lot better than prison. It was perfect, really. Only a few miles or so in either direction and he could get to the guy responsible for putting his ass in jail.

That sweet little yoga girl had been his first ticket to freedom with the place to crash and extra money. Funny how, in a way, she was funding the murder of her very own best friend. Small world.

Helluva small world. But then, he didn't have this place back at the time. He loved this place. It was still the perfect location. Yeah, this was a better plan. Everything happens for a reason.

He'd sworn if he could just make parole, he wouldn't kill another woman. He burst into a raucous laugh. "Goto Hell."

He wasn't worried about being out of practice anymore either. It was like riding a bike. He'd already proved that today. Sorry, Pizza Boy.

He walked out the back door and around to the front porch. That door was still nailed shut to keep up appearances. He sat on the step and leaned against the post.

She died right here. Mike's pretty bride. She'd been a spirited one. Had she not tried to fight so hard, it wouldn't have ended up the way it had. He might even have let her go.

The headlines had been sweeter than he'd ever imagined. Coast to coast they'd named him the Goto Hell killer.

Goto smacked at a mosquito. It was starting to get dark, and those little buggers were buzzing around like crazy. He walked back around the house and went into the living room. He glanced at the wall. With only the glow from the moon he could still make out the papers tacked on the wall.

His notebook was nearly full with notes and options, and he had begun pulling some of his best ideas from the pages of notes and scripting them with care on the opposite wall of the living room. He called that wall the pathway to hell.

He'd sprung for an eight-pack of poster paints at the dollar store. Small containers of paint and brushes lay sprawled across one of the windowsills.

He'd come up with the idea of painting the gates of hell around the front door. Painting an arch that looked just like stone had been a labor of love. The gray stones looked so real that they almost felt cold to the touch.

When he finally brought Brooke here, he'd open that door. Pull the plywood from the other side, and set her right in the middle, like an offering.

GOTO HELL topped the archway in perfect lettering, red with yellow flame borders, over the arch dripping with fiery red flames that looked so real they seemed to give off heat.

He stood under the archway and pictured his master plan. His best ideas were coming together under that arch. Inspired, that's how that made him feel. Inspired and powerful. He was the devil. No. He could teach the devil a thing or two.

He'd use Brooke to lure Hartman in, to torture him, to crumble every last bit of hope, before he killed him. It had been a long planning stage, but he'd use that to his advantage.

It was too bad that he might not be able to make good on the promise to himself that if he made parole he wouldn't kill another woman. But then the devil was known to lie.

194

❖ Chapter Twenty-Three ❖

Mike woke up to a pressing feeling in his chest. He glanced at the clock and swallowed hard. The room seemed to be closing in on him and he tried desperately to regain a sense of where he was and what was happening to him.

His body was sweaty, and he could barely take a breath. The ceiling fan swirled above him, but it wasn't helping. He laid there as long as he could, but the feeling wasn't passing. In fact, it was getting worse.

He looked at Brooke lying next to him. She was beautiful under just the soft glow of the moonlight that snuck through the curtains. He slid his arm out from under her, shook it to get the blood flowing again, and then eased his legs from between the sheets. He rolled away from her, careful not to jostle her or the bed. He didn't know if she was a light sleeper.

Planting both feet on the rug, he reached for his clothes on the chair next to the bed. Stitches slept, curled in a tight ball on the chair. She lifted her chin, but settled right back. Thank god.

He hated to do it, but he had to get out of there, if even for just a minute. The overwhelming guilt and worry consumed him.

He moved down the hall, out to the living room

before he dared breathe or make a noise. He slid on his shorts, and sat on the couch, lowering his head to his hands.

He needed to leave. How mad would she be when she realized he'd left? He went to the kitchen and put the coffee filter and coffee in the pot, and pushed the button. Maybe he just needed to relax, to shake it off. He leaned against the cool granite countertop as the coffee began to drip into the pot below, but he couldn't relax. He grabbed his shirt, and things, and headed for the front door.

He stood on the front porch, but after a moment, there was no going back inside. He pulled the front door closed and locked it behind him. *No turning back now.*

He sprinted to his truck, half-tempted to push it to the edge of the driveway, but the master bedroom was in the back so instead he just prayed she wouldn't hear it. He pulled out to the street, glancing behind him. No lights in the house. He rubbed his chin with his hand.

Lights reflected in his rearview mirror. Someone else must be having a sleepless night too. The person pulled up behind him at the stoplight heading out of the neighborhood. Poor sucker. Mike drove in complete silence.

He'd started it, for god's sake. He'd made the first move. He'd even *asked* if he could stay. He had feelings for her, there was no doubt in his mind about that, but somehow, lying there in the quiet, all he could think of was what if something happened to her too.

He drove, unsure of his destination until he got there. The truck seemed to navigate itself, passing the old farm and heading to the end of the street where he and Jackie had once lived.

Mike slowed and turned down the overgrown driveway in front of the house where he'd lived with Jackie. He hadn't been here since . . . well, years. He continued until his headlights glowed across the front porch of the boarded-up house. A cottage really. Just one bedroom, a living room, kitchen, and bath. All of just over eight hundred square feet. He could still picture it. That night. The night his whole life changed. The night hers ended. Silent tears dripped down his left cheek. They'd only been married a few months. She was so beautiful. Her long hair had shone in the moonlight. It was too late. She was already gone by the time he'd reached her.

Mike leaned across the steering wheel.

"It's been so long, Jackie, but I can still feel it like it was yesterday." His breath caught, and he looked up. "I'm so sorry I wasn't there. I still think I'll wake up and find out it was all just a dream, but that never happens. I miss you. You know that, right?"

Something caught his eye. Jackie? Did something just move? He focused on the darkness that cloaked the house. He wanted so desperately for her to appear. "I'm so sorry I couldn't protect you."

Mike sat in silence. His mind rolled through old memories of Jackie and new ones with Brooke. He'd fought those feelings for Brooke when they were apart, but every time he saw her there was that connection. He needed her. She made him feel happy again. But now the guilt over what had happened to Jackie that had driven him to a successful career and awards in the Marines was going to ruin any chance with Brooke. Would she forgive him for leaving tonight? He should have told her about Jackie himself. If he had, would he be feeling this now?

"Jackie, I met someone," he said out loud. "Just like the day I first laid eyes on you, there was something the minute I saw her."

He pictured Brooke marching up to the house and coming on like she owned the farm that day. He liked that about her. Confident, borderline bossy, but in a cute way. As caring as she was feisty, her quirks like those lucky signs and her love of that little dog just made her more unforgettable. Tough on the outside, but fragile when you got close. A walking contradiction. She was definitely unique. Being near her made him feel something he hadn't expected—love?

"I think I could fall in love with her."

Saying it out loud, even if it was just to Jackie's

memory, confirmed what he'd been avoiding. "I am. I already am." He'd been so busy trying to avoid the attraction that he hadn't even allowed himself to consider he already had.

Mike took in a deep breath. "Jackie. I hope you forgive me for not being able to protect you, and I hope you understand my feelings for Brooke. I'm alive again for the first time."

He pushed the shifter into reverse, and turned his truck around. It was time he let go of the past and allow himself to love again. With Brooke was where he needed to be.

The gravel crunched under the weight of his tires. He glanced in the rearview mirror as he pulled back onto the pavement and left the old memories behind. He took a double-glance.

Was someone standing at the back of the house? He pushed his foot on the brake. The red lights illuminated where he'd just been.

He must be losing it, or maybe it was Jackie saying good-bye too. He needed to believe that. He shook the thought off, and headed for home.

How would he ever apologize to Brooke for sneaking out on an otherwise perfect evening? He'd start with the truth.

❖ Chapter Twenty-Four ❖

When Brooke's body clock tripped at six in the morning, she wasn't sure if last night had been one delicious dream or reality. Her body ached in a way that reminded her just how good the evening had been. No. It hadn't been a dream.

The happy feeling engulfed her mood this morning, but facing him the morning after made her stomach swirl. She lay still for a few minutes before opening her eyes. She took in a breath and tried to regain focus from the fog of the deepest sleep she'd had in months. She rolled over toward Mike, but faced an empty bed. Her heart suddenly felt as empty as the chair that had held his clothes just a few hours ago.

Deflated, she shuffled out to the kitchen. The smell of fresh coffee met her as she walked down the hall. Maybe there was an explanation. *There I go jumping to conclusions again.* She padded into the kitchen wearing a smile, but he wasn't in the kitchen either. She reached her hand toward the coffee pot. The carafe was hot. She walked through the living room, then walked to the front window and looked outside. His truck was gone.

He made coffee before he left? "What the hell?" She went back into the kitchen looking for a note, or a sign of some kind, but there wasn't one.

"What kind of guy does that? Didn't even say good-bye?" Her jaw set and she bit down on the inside of her cheek so hard she almost drew blood. Anger flooded her good sense. "I knew better than to let my guard down."

A million thoughts went through her head. Mostly the told-ya-so kind of self-reprimanding ones. She balanced a cup of coffee in one hand as she pushed the door open to let Stitches out to make her morning rounds.

Brooke hoped she'd come back as a dog in her next life. If she did, she'd pee right on Mike's shoe.

The phone jingled and she snagged it on the second ring. "Hello," she snapped.

"Sorry."

His voice made her tense right up like she'd poked her finger in a light socket. "Why are you apologizing? Because you ruined a perfect night? Or because you make a terrible cup of coffee?"

"You're mad," he said.

She let out an exasperated huff. "You think?"

"I needed some air."

"Well, excuse me, but weren't you the one who came traipsing over uninvited?" He was wounded. She got that, but that didn't give him a free pass to trample on her heart.

"Guilty."

"I don't recall even inviting you."

"I know. I'm sorry."

"I agree." She took in a deep breath. She wasn't going to let anyone treat her this way. Last night had seemed like something special, but he sure fixed that in a hurry. "I thought there was something special going on here, but clearly I was wrong."

"No, there was, there is. I just needed some space to sort it out. It was unexpected. It has been a long time since . . . well—I just didn't expect to feel so many things."

"Well, you should have thought about that *before* you came over and sparked it all up," Brooke said, but her anger was met with silence. What? Did he think she was just going to say all's forgiven? Forget that. She wasn't about to play this game. "I have to go. I've got better things to do."

"Wait."

She heard him and even thought to hang up anyway, but pulled the receiver back to her ear. "What?"

"I want to explain."

"I don't want to understand. I don't even want to like you today."

"Brooke, please, you're making a big deal—"

"Damn right it's a big deal. You asked to stay, reeled my ass right in like I was special. You knew how cautious I was after what I went through. You tricked me, and then snuck away before I woke up with not so much as a 'kiss my ass good-bye.'"

"I made coffee."

"Well, it sucked."

"I don't want this to change anything."

She rolled her eyes. "Too late for that, buddy." She clicked the End button. There was something less than satisfying about hanging up a cell phone. She dumped the entire pot of coffee into the sink. "Jerk." Her teeth gnashed. Jerk wasn't even bad enough. "Asshole."

Brooke slammed her way through her morning routine, getting dressed and ready for the day in record time. Even Stitches steered clear of her foul mood. She got to the office early too, running the only red light in town and pushing the speed limit the whole way. Her anger and adrenaline made her act irrational behind the wheel, something she was working on, but then this morning had been anything but normal.

At the office, Brooke whisked right past her coworkers without so much as a hello. She asked her administrative assistant, Victoria, to hold her calls, closing the door behind her. *Screw that open-door policy.* She grabbed the project plans for the Summer Break Livestock Show and began reviewing them.

When she retreated from the office to grab some coffee a couple hours later, she laughed when she saw the eight huge bouquets of flowers on Victoria's desk. "Goodness, girl. You must have a winner on the hook," Brooke said. "Sorry if I was short with you earlier."

"That's okay. But as for the winner, actually, no I don't." Victoria pointed a finger toward her boss. "You do."

"I do what?"

"Have a winner."

Brooke looked confused. "What are you talking about?"

Victoria smiled. "The flowers started coming at the top of the hour right after you closed your door. They've been arriving every fifteen minutes since."

"For me?" She looked surprised. "Are you kidding?"

"No, and look—there's another one now." She looked at her watch, tapping the face. "Right on schedule."

Brooke took the basket of wildflowers from the delivery boy while Victoria signed off on the delivery. She pulled the card and read it aloud.

Please forgive me.
I'm wild about you.—Mike

"Wildflowers. Cheesy." Brooke resisted the urge to smile. It was cute, but it didn't change what happened.

Victoria nodded. "They all have cards."

Brooke plucked each card from its bouquet and walked back into her office. The first one was the most honest.

I screwed up. I know it.
I don't want the past to ruin a future
with you.
Please let me explain.—Mike

The rest were silly, but sweet. Each one was as dopey as the last.

Victoria followed her into the office with another one. "He must have done something really bad."

"At least the florist in town will love me."

"Oh yeah. You'll be Teddy Hardy's favorite new resident after this." Victoria shoved the bouquet in Brooke's direction. "I'm running out of room out there. Maybe you should call him."

"He should be calling me."

"He has." Victoria pushed a stack of pink "While You Were Out" slips toward her. "You told me to hold your calls. The calls are coming as frequently as the deliveries."

Fanning through the stack of messages, Brooke said, "Fine. Put him through next time."

"Yes, ma'am." Victoria walked back out to the front office.

No sooner had Brooke sat down, than the call rang through. She held her breath. She wanted to stay mad, but the Southern girl in her had thank-you already in the queue. She squashed that thought. It was really hard to be mad surrounded by flowers and silly cards.

"Brooke Justice," she answered, even though she knew full well who was on the line.

"I am so sorry, Brooke. I screwed up."

"Yes. You did."

"I'm sorry."

"Can't argue with you there." She softened once she heard his voice, though.

"I didn't mean to hurt you. I got scared."

"Too late." But part of her was as scared as he was. "Before I discovered you were gone, I was lying there still as could be trying to be sure I didn't wake you while I tried to figure out how to handle the morning. It was wonderful, but it was too soon."

"I'm sorry."

"Don't be. We'll get over it. I wouldn't trade your friendship for anything. It was a mistake."

"No. Brooke, it wasn't a mistake. That's just it. That's not what I want. I freaked out. I don't know why. You're not the first woman I've been with since my wife died, but you *are* the first one who's mattered. It was different. I—"

"I'm sorry about your wife."

"I should have told you about it myself, but it's been something I've kept tucked away for eight years. Last night . . . my feelings . . . I just got scared."

"Of me?"

"Of caring," he said.

"I was scared too."

"Can we put this behind us and start over?"

"I can't. We should probably put some distance between us for a while."

"I want to see you."

"That's not a good idea," she said as she toyed with a purple hyacinth.

Victoria tapped on her office door lightly and peeked in.

"Mike . . . hang on a sec." Brooke pulled the phone to her shoulder and motioned her in. Victoria walked in with another bouquet and quietly placed it on Brooke's desk with the others. "When are these flowers going to stop? It looks like a hospital in here."

"I guess I made my point, huh?"

"Yes, I got it. There must be ten or twelve bouquets in here."

"Just a few more to go."

"How many did you send?" She took count of the flowers framing the room.

"My lucky number is fifteen. You're into the luck thing, so I thought I should go with that."

He was playing dirty now. "Are you making fun of me?"

"Nope. I'm just not taking any chances. I'm sorry about last night. Not about last night, but this morning. Really. You've got to forgive me—please. We both have scars to heal. We can do that together. Give it a chance."

"I just got a huge pot of marigolds."

"I know they're your favorite. I remembered. I figured if you were still mad after all those flowers and cards, I'd have to pull out an extra-special something to get your attention."

"You've got it." She slid a finger in the flap of the card of the last bouquet that had arrived. She read the card to herself. Her nose tickled like it always did right before she cried. She cursed herself for even considering forgiving him.

Your grandpa would have loved me!
You can't deny Grandpa, can you?—Mike

Mike sounded concerned. "What? Hey? Are you laughing or crying?"

Brooke stuck the card in the corner of her monitor. "I'm laughing. I just got the Grandpa note. How did you get all of this arranged so quickly? Do you have florists on retainer? You must break hearts all the time."

"No I don't. I can't even tell you the last time I ordered flowers. I've been a busy guy trying to undo my mess."

"I see that. I'll tell you this. I don't know if my grandpa would have loved you, but Grandma would have been a goner for you. She was a hopeless romantic."

"Well, there you go. Aren't you even curious to know why fifteen is my lucky number?"

"Why *is* fifteen your lucky number?" Brooke asked.

"I got your case on the fifteenth of the month . . . bye."

She hung up the phone and flipped the calendar. Sure enough, he was right. Was fifteen a lucky number for her now too? It was a one and a five. Sure enough. Good luck.

❖ Chapter Twenty-Five ❖

Brooke met Jenny at Vinnie's Bar-B-Q-rino. The new restaurant was a play on the old seventies sitcom *Welcome Back, Kotter*, and all the meals were named after the characters from the show. You couldn't get a better bagel or New York–style deli meal anywhere in town, and he'd nailed Southern barbecue too. Not an easy thing for a Northerner to do, but it sure was winning him points with the locals.

The owner swore his uncle had worked on the show back in the day. No one believed him, but he made a mean barbecue in a yummy Carolina style so they let him ride with it. The place had been getting rave reviews. The old premise and seventies music to match seemed to appeal to all demographics. Just inside the restaurant one wall was reserved for graffiti. A crate of paint pens lured customers to partake as they waited for a coveted booth in the busy place. Some folks just wrote their names; others actually did some pretty good artwork and tags.

Jenny picked out turquoise, orange, and white markers and got down to business tagging the HAPPY BALANCE logo while they waited.

"That looks good," Brooke said, admiring Jenny's handiwork.

"Thanks. Nothing compared to some of the art, though. I should have done this at my place. It looks cool."

"Except where some jerk painted that eerie devil scene with the flames." Brooke pointed Jenny toward the other end of the wall. "Look at it. It's freaking me out."

"Me too, a little. And I don't get freaked out easy. Those flames look so real they made me look twice."

"Justice. Party of two." Brooke took the paint pens from Jenny and capped them as they headed toward the waitress. "You can add to it next time."

Once they were seated, Brooke departed from the small talk. "I'm dying to know how things are going with you and Rick. I've barely seen you lately. I'm hoping that means things are going great."

"He's amazing," Jenny said. "A man's man, but such a nice guy."

"Of course he is. Aren't all cowboys with white hats the good ones?"

"I don't know, but Mike's the one you need to be thinking about."

"I've got updates on that front." Brooke pulled the menu in front of her, but closed it almost instantly, knowing she'd order the Epstein. There just wasn't anything better than *arroz con habichuelas*, the Puerto Rican red beans-and-rice dish, served with a toasted bagel on the side for the Jewish part of that character. "For the record, Mike and I have cooled things."

"What? You haven't even got hot yet. You can't cool it already."

"Actually it got hot and cold in a matter of hours." Brooke gave Jenny the short version of the hot tub scene and the extreme exit, leaving out the details of the weekend when she'd crawled into his bed. "I knew better. I don't know what the heck I was thinking."

"Why? Because he freaked out? His wife died. No, wait. I take that back. She didn't just die. She was murdered. Give him a break."

Brooke should've known Jenny wouldn't see it the way she did. "That was eight years ago.

"Oh, come on. He said he was sorry. What guy buys out nearly the whole flower supply of the county and puts that much effort into a forgiveness plan? You've got to give him a break, girl. He's sorry."

Brooke shook her head. "Sorry won't mend a broken heart, and that's all I'm heading for with that guy. Look. It was too soon anyway. I let my guard down and look what happened—I'm just going to wind up getting hurt."

"But y'all are good together," Jenny said.

"He might be a widower, but I think he's probably not over her. I can't compete with that."

"Fine." Jenny pushed the napkin and silverware across the table. "I wouldn't try to tell you what to do. That would be a waste of time, because we all know how hardheaded you are. Just don't forget that we all have baggage. You might try to put yourself in his position before you ruin it."

Brooke took pause at Jenny's reaction. It wasn't often she went all serious on her. She may have a point. She just wasn't ready to hear it. "Quit worrying about me. I want to know about you. What's going on with you and Rick?"

A smile played across Jenny's lips. "He's the perfect guy for me. He loves kids, makes me laugh. He's just like me, except with boy parts. We've been having so much fun. It's good. It's easy."

The waitress walked up to take their order, saving Brooke from the details that Jenny loved to embellish until she made Brooke blush.

Brooke placed her order, then stared out the window as Jenny held a leisurely conversation with the waitress about how things were cooked and made a decision.

When the waitress walked away, Brooke leaned

across the table. "I wish I had your carefree way about life. I envy you for that. You keep it so . . ."

Jenny tucked the menu behind the condiment tray on the table. "So what?"

". . . simple."

Jenny plopped back in the booth. "Trust me. It looks better from over there. Things in my life are anything but simple."

"I thought you just said everything was going so well."

"Oh, it is. The problem is on my end. I'm late."

"You mean *late* late?" Brooke's eyes went wide.

"Yep." Jenny said, popping the *p* for effect. "I can't believe it either."

"Well, you couldn't be that far along. I mean you and Rick haven't been together that long. Or maybe it's a false alarm."

Jenny shook her head. "More complicated than that."

"Oh." Brooke sat back in the booth. "Not Rick?"

Jenny nodded.

"What are you going to do?"

"I'll make sure first. I've got a doctor's appointment tomorrow."

"I can't believe it, Jenny. Rick's so perfect for you. Wouldn't that just be your luck? You finally meet Mr. Right and the timing is all off."

"If it's meant to be, it will, no matter what I do. You can't mess up destiny. If I'm pregnant it's from that stupid night with Jim. I can't believe we had unprotected booty-call sex."

"Jim? Jim, your ex-husband, Jim? Jenny. Really?"

"Well, I'm not the type to just sleep around, and it just kind of happened after his mom's birthday. We were both nostalgic after all the stupid pictures and memories his mom was stirring up. We even laughed about it the next morning. Too much good wine can make anyone make a mistake."

"Apparently." She knew that all too well, though it hadn't felt like a mistake at the time.

"I didn't mean you and Mike."

"Well, if the shoe fits . . . so have you mentioned it to Jim yet?"

"Yeah. I called him. I knew what his thoughts were about it already, not that I'd want him involved anyway. I told him that if it turned out I was pregnant, he'd be off the hook."

"You don't need him. He couldn't even raise a dog."

"I know," Jenny said. "Pitiful, isn't it?"

"So what about Rick?"

"I'll tell him, then break it off. What else can I do?"

"Have you considered all your options?"

Jenny leaned forward. "Brooke. You know how much I want children. There's no way I would ever end a pregnancy. No matter what."

"Sorry. I was just thinking that if you and Rick

are perfect, you could have babies together. That wasn't helpful, was it?" Brooke felt horrible for saying it without thinking first. "Just know I'm there for you no matter what you do."

The waitress delivered their sweet iced teas. Brooke toasted Jenny. "To going with the flow. Let the man upstairs take us where we need to go."

Brooke raised her glass to Jenny's. "We're going to be old maids at this rate," Brooke said. "I'm fine with that. Are you?"

"I never thought I'd be raising a child alone. But I can do it."

"You know I'll help."

"You'll be a great aunt."

Brooke's phone buzzed in her purse next to her. She grabbed it and lifted it with the face turned to Jenny. It read "Mike Hartman."

"Answer it." Jenny encouraged her. "Quick, and be nice."

Brooke hesitated, but then picked up. It was a brief conversation, and Brooke wasn't doing much of the talking. "It's probably good timing anyway. We could use some time apart."

Jenny shot her a look.

Brooke leered back. "No, you don't need to call while you're gone. We'll catch up when you get back in town." She said good-bye and closed the phone, tucking it in her purse.

"What did he want, and why did you go all 'space is good' on him?"

"He's going to be out of town." Brooke pressed her lips together. "Montana. Who the heck goes to Montana? Running for the hills, if I had to guess."

"Oh, he is not. What did he say?"

"He said he's got a case out in Montana. Some guy he was in the military with. I didn't ask for all the details."

"Well, there you go. It's for work. Promise me you'll just let it ride until he gets back in town. You'll have a whole new perspective by then. Trust me." Jenny folded her arms across her belly, even though it was still flat and taut. "You have to forgive him, you know."

"I don't have to, but I probably will. Besides, it's good timing. It'll give you and me time to make plans for the unexpected addition. That's way more important."

"Oh, great. Maybe I should call and beg him to stay," Jenny teased. "You know I'm not much on the whole planning thing."

"That's why you need me." Brooke pulled a tablet out of her purse and started jotting things down. "I saw the cutest nursery on HGTV the other day. Never thought I'd have the chance to use those ideas, but I'll pull them down off the Internet. I guess it's way too early to know if it's going to be a boy or a girl."

Jenny said, "Lord, I'm in trouble."

❖ Chapter Twenty-Six ❖

Mike had been away for exactly three days to the hour since Brooke took his phone call at the restaurant with Jenny, but it felt longer. Brooke picked up the stack of florist cards. She hadn't been able to toss them. It might have been a desperate attempt to make up, but it was kind of working. She'd kept them all. Carrying them to the couch, she tucked her feet up underneath her and read through each one again, one by one—all fifteen of them.

He had an imagination. She had to give him that. He hadn't wasted any time apologizing, either. He must have already been on the task before she crawled out of bed that morning. What a way to mess up a perfect night, and it had been perfect. Every single moment of it—up to that point.

She wished she could forgive him, but that would mean putting her heart in danger's way. Everyone had baggage. She could fill a luggage cart by herself, but she couldn't put her heart through that again.

The guilt Mike felt for his loss had to have been terrible. She'd kicked Keith to the curb, had considered dumping that baggage a treat, in fact. But even now, as imperfect as the relationship had ended up . . . losing him would still have been awful. She'd never really lost anyone close, a lucky thing for a girl her age. Even her grand-parents were still alive. She knocked on wood, just in case.

Any loss is horrible, but the way Mike had lost Jackie . . . Murder was the kind of thing that you think only happens to someone else. There wasn't any guarantee that things would have turned out differently if Mike had been there, or that he wouldn't have ended up dead too.

That sent a wave of fear through her. Things could have been so different. She might never have met him. She missed him. He hadn't called, but then she'd told him not to. He was giving her exactly what she'd asked for. Time.

Someone pounded on the front door. She wasn't expecting anyone. Brooke leaped from the couch, grabbing her phone to dial 911.

"Open up," called Jenny from the porch.

Brooke flung the door open, relieved at the familiar sound of Jenny's voice. "Jenny? What's the . . . ?"

Jenny and Rick stood on her porch holding hands with big grins on their faces. Jenny pulled a huge hat from behind her back and plopped it on her head.

"What the heck is going on? Are you two drunk at this hour? It's barely lunchtime!"

"Only punch-drunk. Can we come in?" Jenny pushed through with Rick in tow.

"Sure." Brooke stepped aside. "Hey, Rick."

"Hey, girl." Rick gave her a quick hug, and then let Jenny pull him into the living room. She bounced onto the sofa and tugged Rick down next to her.

Brooke caught up with them and sat on the edge of the coffee table in front of the two googly-eyed fools. "What is going on?"

Jenny started. "We're parents."

Brooke knew she wasn't hiding her surprise very well. Surely Jenny wouldn't have lied to Rick, or would she? She really did want a family and going it alone would be hard. *Oh, girl, what have you done?* Brooke tried to sound calm. "Parents?"

Rick looked proud as he announced, "He's even already got a name. Hillcrest Joyful Kixx."

"You what?" *Joyful what? That would be one hell of a name. And I thought stars made up crazy names. This one would take the cake.*

"Yeah," Jenny said. "He's one of the horses that Cody Tuggle's mom owns. We bought interest in him together and we're going to have the biggest daggone Kentucky Derby party you've ever seen right here in Adams Grove."

"Shouldn't be too hard to impress me with it since I've never *been* to a Kentucky Derby party." Brooke pointed at the monstrosity of a hat on her best friend's head. "And if that hat is part of it, I'm not sure I'm in."

"Yes." Jenny tugged part of the wide brim down and posed, then giggled like a schoolgirl. "This hat is totally part of it. Hillcrest Joyful Kixx will be running the Derby and we'll be throwing a big party to celebrate it." Jenny squealed. "Can you believe it? I'm so excited. Isn't this a neat surprise?"

"Surprised would be an understatement." It was great to see Jenny so happy, but it seemed kind of a frivolous idea when she was just getting Happy Balance off the ground, and possibly a family too. Jenny hadn't known Rick all that long. He seemed great, but then so had Keith in the beginning. "This. Well. This . . . *is* a surprise." She turned to Jenny. "You don't know anything about horses."

"I'm not training the darn thing. We just own part of him. But I'm going to learn. We went to Colonial Downs and I swear I fell in love with the whole thing. It's all good. Plus, you know stuff. You'll help me too."

Brooke was afraid to say anything so she just gave Jenny "the look."

"Yes. Oh, I know what you're thinking. Quit worrying," Jenny said.

Rick threw his arm across the back of the couch around Jenny. "We were meant for each other. I don't care whose child she's carrying, or what happened before I was in the picture. All I know is that I love this lady, and I'll love this child too.

We'll just have a little head start on things. I knew that day she sidled up to me at the fair she was different."

What was she supposed to say to all of this?

"No secrets between us." Jenny turned and smiled at Rick.

"Congratulations." Brooke leaned across to hug Jenny. "I guess you were right. It doesn't matter what we do. We can't mess up what's supposed to be." She wished that had been true when it came to her and Mike.

"I have a favor to ask you." Jenny looked hesitant.

"Why the look? I'd do anything for you. You know that."

"I need you to help me plan this party," Jenny said. "You're so much better at details than I am."

"Jenny, I don't know anything about the Kentucky Derby." It was just like Jenny to want to have a huge theme party, but not to plan it. Well, that was what she loved about Jenny. Somehow she did always seem to keep things light and fun. She sure wished a little of that would rub off on her.

Rick jumped in. "I want to have the party on my farm, and I want to invite all our friends. I'm hoping you can work some magic to make it look suitable. I've already arranged for a giant whopper of a screen so we can air the race."

"That ought to set you back a penny," Brooke said.

"Money's no object," Rick said. "We want this to be a celebration to remember."

It would be perfect timing to get her mind off Mike. "I'd be happy to help. Do you have a date for it?"

"The Derby is the first weekend in May," Rick said.

"May is in just a couple weeks," Brooke said. "I'll have to do some research. From the looks of things Jenny only knows about the hats." Brooke shook her head. "Let me go on record that I'm not a fan of the one you've picked out there."

The brim of the hat bounced as Jenny nodded. "Rick said I look cute. That's all that matters."

"Oh, goodness. I could get a toothache from all this sweet going on between the two of you," Brooke said. "This is going to be interesting."

"There's something else." Jenny chewed on the left side of her lip.

Brooke knew that look.

"I've got that big spa gig in Tennessee this month. I won't be back until the party."

Brooke remembered the annual event. "So how are we going to do all of this?"

"I can help some from there, and Rick said he'll help, but I'm going to need you to really kind of do more than help. I hate to ask, but . . ."

It would take every spare moment. Exactly what she needed. By the time they had the party, maybe she would have all but forgotten Mike

Hartman. "Not a problem. Consider it done," Brooke said. "I'm thrilled to do it."

"Thanks. You are the best friend." Jenny's eyes glistened. "I'll owe you."

"You'd do it for me, but then you're such an awful planner I'd never ask you to," Brooke said.

"True."

Brooke pulled up the calendar on her computer. "Okay. Great. I'll start a plan. When do you head out?"

"Tomorrow."

"Okay, so we'll use e-mail to communicate. Do you have a list of the guests?"

"Not yet. We came straight from the lake after Rick got the news that the deal was officially done, but I'll get it together tonight."

"How many guests?" Brooke asked.

Jenny said, "A hundred-ish."

Rick spoke up. "Probably closer to a hundred and fifty."

"This is going to be a heck of a party," Brooke said.

Rick put a hand between the women. "Whoa, there. Do you two think you could work out these details over some pizza? I'm starving."

"Perfect. I'm starved too," Brooke said. "Let's move the party-planning session to the pizzeria."

"No pizza for me," admitted Jenny. "I feel queasy all the time now, but I'm not going to stand in the way of you two and pizza."

They headed out to Rick's truck. The last time Brooke had been in this truck she'd been about as giddy as Jenny was today—on the way back from that trip with Mike.

Rick drove them to the little pizza shop just out of town on Route 58.

When they walked inside Jenny stalled. "Oh, no," she said as she clasped her hand to her mouth, trying to keep from gagging.

Rick laughed. "This is going to be a fun ride with you, Miss Dramatic."

"I can't help it. The smells make me so sick. It's weird, because I usually love the smell of pizza." She wrinkled her nose, and dropped her hand to her stomach.

"Want to go somewhere else?" asked Brooke.

Jenny swallowed and shook her head. "No. I think this is just the way it's going to be for a while." She turned to Rick and tugged on his sleeve. "Can you see if they have ginger ale?"

He dropped a kiss on the top of her head. "You got it, babe."

While he went to the counter and got the drinks, Brooke and Jenny sat in the booth by the front window. The list Brooke had started was already pretty long, and had boxes ready to be checked next to several of the items.

Rick came back with the drinks and a menu.

They picked out a pizza, and Rick went to place the order while Brooke and Jenny googled

"Kentucky Derby parties." "Mint juleps?" Brooke looked at her best friend. "Have you ever had one?"

Jenny shook her head. "No, and I think I'm glad I'm pregnant and won't have to start now."

Brooke's fingers flew across the tablet as she researched the drink. "Oh, it says here you use spearmint. I was thinking like peppermint."

"Still doesn't sound good to me," Jenny said.

"Oh, but look here." She twisted the screen toward Jenny. "Spearmint is good luck. We are so doing the spearmint."

"Of course we are," Jenny said. "You wouldn't risk the whole day without it."

❖ Chapter Twenty-Seven ❖

Goto looked up from the topping station. He froze mid-sprinkle, cheese spilling in a clump on the pie he was in the process of topping. He swished the cheese, scattering it, then realized he'd completely forgotten the order in that split second. He ripped down the slip of paper and tried to refocus.

He'd recognized the women immediately, and he didn't need them to see him. He pretended to cough so hard he choked. The guy at the register ran to his aid, patting him on the back.

"I'm okay, man." Goto sputtered out the words. "Let me just go get some water. I'll be back in a few minutes."

"That's cool. Take your time. I've got it."

Goto threw up a hand and nodded, then slipped away. He made one more loud coughing sound for good measure, then ducked into the storage room that opened up to the front of the restaurant near the restrooms.

He ran to the door, unlocked it, and twisted the knob, opening it just enough to get a better look.

Leaning in, he listened to them talk. Now he knew why he hadn't been able to track Mike Hartman down for the last week. He was out of town, but by the sounds of it he'd be back in town just in time for a big party they were planning.

Elation ran through his veins. It was perfect. He loved a public challenge. He'd crash that party then whisk Brooke away right under their noses and put the rest of his plan into action.

That was the final piece he'd needed.

Goto heard footsteps coming through the back hall. He closed and locked the door, then pretended he'd been getting napkins. With an armful of napkins he nearly ran into his coworker as he rounded the corner.

"You okay?" he asked Goto.

"Yeah. Figured I'd put myself to good use back here. I'm fine as wine, my good friend." Goto couldn't help but bounce when he walked. Everything was falling into place, and more dramatically than he'd ever dreamed.

❖ Chapter Twenty-Eight ❖

Jenny took a long sip of the ginger ale and then grabbed Brooke's arm as they looked at ideas for the party on the computer screen. "I love that hat, but it would look better on you."

"Do I really have to wear one of those?"

"Absolutely. You'll make a gorgeous Southern belle. Mike's going to go gaga."

"Is he on the invite list?"

"Of course."

Brooke scrolled down the page. "Why do you keep bringing him up?"

"Face it. You were really happy spending time with him. You were like the old you. I liked seeing you that way."

She'd felt that way too. "He's taken," she said, hoping Jenny would drop the subject.

"No, he's not."

"Yes, he is. Jackie might be dead but she's very much alive in his heart. If he hasn't gotten over it by now, he won't. That's more baggage than even I can handle."

Jenny gave her an accusing look. "Maybe he's your dream guy from that log cabin fantasy of yours. You've been talking about that forever."

"I wish I'd never told you about that. It was

just a silly fantasy. Besides, Mike could live in a tree fort for all I know."

"A tree fort. Is that another one of your fantasies?" teased Jenny. "You got a little Tarzan fantasy you've been keeping from me?"

"Shut up." She elbowed Jenny. "Look at this setup. We could go with the pewter for the mint juleps but I think these glasses are much prettier. We could even probably get them personalized as a keepsake for folks to take home."

"I like that. By the way, Rick drove me by where Mike is having his new house built. It's no tree fort."

"Shush." Brooke shot Jenny a look. "I don't want to know."

"Quit shushing me. You have to admit it would be fun to be married to friends."

"Please stop it. It's not going to happen. I can't even think about Mike like that anymore." Brooke's attention moved to the landscape out the window. "Look. Rainbow, good luck!" She pointed toward the horizon.

Jenny looked in that direction. "See, a lucky sign. You have to give Mike another chance. He could be your dream guy."

"I'm not going there. I'm glad you found yours, though."

"Me too." Jenny watched Rick carry their pizza back to the table.

They brainstormed ideas for the party and Rick

gave them the horse-racing 101 class while they ate.

"It's going to be tight, but we can make it work." Brooke sorted the tasks and then leaned forward to catch Rick's attention. "Okay, partner. We've got a lot to do."

"I'm there. What's first?" he asked.

"Well, one thing you need to do right away is figure out the color scheme. Can you get me the image of what the jockey's going to wear and all?"

"Done."

"It would be great if we could get a few people to say something about the investment, kind of toasting the whole thing. It would set a nice celebratory mood."

"Mike can do that. He's great at that stuff."

Brooke had hoped this would get her mind off Mike, not force her to work with him or involve him. "He's out of town. You might have to come up with someone else." *Please come up with someone else.*

"No. Mike's the guy." Rick pulled his phone from his hip, and dialed Mike's number. It went straight to voicemail. "Hey, man. It's Rick. I hate to leave this on a message, but I'm being forced to do it. That Brooke can be real bossy. Anyway, I'll give you all the details when you get back in town. Hell, you might even think I'm crazy, but I know I'm doing the right thing. Need you to say a few words at the big event." He snapped the phone shut and gave her a "what next?" look.

"Bossy?" Brooke feigned insult.

Rick pulled his shoulders up with a sheepish grin and pushed his phone back on his hip.

"Well, at least it's done. Thank you." Brooke marked the task at one hundred percent. "One down, and a lot to go."

❖ Chapter Twenty-Nine ❖

"Figures." Brooke snatched the sticky note from the dashboard and crumpled it in her hand.

The word *GAS* was nearly invisible to anyone but the one who had written it. She'd scribbled it in cherry lip gloss, the only thing she could put her hands on while driving this morning.

"Great. Now I'm turning into Mother."

When she was a kid her mom's car and purse had scraps of paper taped all over them: *milk and eggs, Dr. Tuesday 1 p.m.,* or a note that read *GAS*. Nothing was worse than the time Mom had picked a group of them up with a note that read *tampons* in thick black marker stuck to the radio. Jenny still teased her about that one. Too bad Mom hadn't been the one to patent the sticky note. They could have made millions. Brooke hated that habit, and yet here she was, the sticky note version of Mom.

The gas gauge was well into the red zone, so close to empty there was no way she'd make it to the Y for her massage appointment without stopping, which would put her further behind.

"Why do I always do this?" She pushed the CD button and tried to unwind to the music as she sped through town toward the gas station.

At the first stoplight, she called to let the massage therapist know she was running late. Because she was a regular, they didn't mind moving her appointment out another forty-five minutes, which was good because it took darn near forty-five minutes to get anywhere from Adams Grove and that was taking some getting used to.

Feeling less rushed, she wheeled into the gas station and popped the fuel latch. While pumping the gas she spotted something on her back glass.

Had it been there for the whole ride or just landed? "Praying mantis, good luck!" She knew it was a stretch, but anything as rare as a praying mantis sighting felt lucky to her. Brooke's rules.

She hooked the hose back onto the pump and clicked the gas cap in place. Receipt in hand, she got back in the car. Then, worried about the praying mantis, she reached under the seat, grabbed her ice scraper and hopped back out to give the little bug some encouragement off her car.

"If you get hurt joyriding on my car, that could be bad luck for me." She slid the scraper under the delicate creature and placed it on the safety of the pump. Feeling good about taking the time to save the insect, she slid back in the car. She leaned against the door to pull her phone off her hip and recheck the time.

The driver's door swung open. Off-balance, she nearly fell out of the car and onto the pavement.

"What the . . ." Her phone fell to the floorboard as she struggled to right herself in the seat, but a strong hand gripped the top of her arm and pulled her from the car and to her feet.

"Keith? What—"

He yanked her tight against his body.

"Stop. That hurt," she seethed, jerking away from him. "What are you doing? I'm in a hurry."

"Make time. I'm still your husband, after all." He grabbed her sleeve.

"Not for long." She tugged her arm away. "Leave me alone," she managed through clenched teeth.

He squeezed her arm tighter. "Get in the passenger seat."

"Who the he—"

"Now." His face was so close to hers that she could feel the moist heat of his stale breath. His skin smelled of sweat. His jaw pulsed and his nostrils flared, sending her cowering back as far as his grip would allow. This wasn't the cool *GQ* man she knew.

"Don't screw with me and don't say another

word," he grunted. "Now . . . get in the passenger seat. We're going to have a little chat."

"You should be talking to my lawyer." She turned to walk back around and get in her car and leave, but Keith raised his hand and when he did, she spotted the gun on his hip. She stopped.

"No more lawyers."

Brooke surveyed the area for help or an escape. The big gas pumps blocked the view of the other customers just a few feet away from her. Their argument hadn't even attracted one onlooker. Brooke started to argue, but the look on Keith's face was so dark she swallowed the words as quickly as they formed and headed to the passenger side of the car.

Keith opened the door and she got in. He leaned in across her.

"What are you doing?"

He buckled the seat belt across her chest. "Don't . . . move." He slammed the door and circled the back of the car.

Brooke unclicked the seat belt and dove for the keys in the ignition. Catching them in the first grab, she stuffed them under the seat and scrambled to exit just as Keith got in the driver's seat. The door lock clicked just as she lifted the handle.

"I said we're going to have a little chat, you and me. It was a statement. Not a question."

"Talk to my attorney. I've already told him you can have whatever you want."

He shook his head.

"Do you hear me? I just want the hell out. You win."

The man at the next pump stepped in front of her car. "You okay, lady?"

Finally. At least someone was curious enough to step in. The good luck from the praying mantis was already paying off.

Keith gave the guy a nod and a smile. "Tell him you're fine."

"My ex," she said through the window with a nod toward Keith. Maybe that would be enough to send a red flag, but no. The man shrugged and walked back to his pickup and continued pumping his fuel.

"I'm not your ex yet," Keith reminded her.

"What the hell has gotten into you?"

"Cute move with the key. Stupid, but cute." He whistled through his teeth. Then he pulled a key from his pocket. He waved it in the air, flaunting it before stuffing it into the switch with a quick twist. The engine rumbled. "Lookee here. Who's smart now?"

"Where did you get a key to my car?"

Keith gunned the engine. He gave her a smug look and laughed.

"You thief. I knew you were in my house. I knew it, and this time I have a witness."

The car rolled through the gas station lot.

She pulled on the door handle, but he clicked it locked again as quick as she could hit the unlock. This was one time she wished she didn't have electric everything on this car. She tried to make eye contact with the man from the pickup truck, but he had his back to them now.

"Don't get clever," he warned as he drove with one hand on the steering wheel and one on the door lock.

She hit the door with her fist out of frustration, then withdrew her hand and rubbed her knuckles. "What do you think you're doing, and why?"

"Why? Because I can." He snickered, looking right proud of himself. "You never did give me enough credit. We had a good thing once."

❖ Chapter Thirty ❖

Mike had resisted the urge to call Brooke as soon as he'd gotten back. The whole reason he'd taken the job in Montana was to give her the space she'd wanted. There was no way he could have honored that wish while in the same town with her. But now that he was back it was harder than ever to do that. He wished he'd arranged to pick up Hunter from the kennel tonight. The apartment was just too quiet.

He checked the data on Keith Farrell and didn't

see anything concerning. There were no issues logged in the security system either. That was probably behind them now.

He looked out the window wishing he could catch a glimpse of her.

Things had moved so quickly with her, but even after the cooling-off period, he wanted to see her more than ever. How would he even know if she felt the same way?

The mail had stacked up while he was gone but by the end of the day he had everything caught up. He grabbed his keys and headed to the filling station just out of town and got gas. He parked on the side of the building and went inside to pick up a couple things. As he walked out of the store, he saw Brooke's car. His heart raced, and he couldn't stop the smile that spread across his face.

But just as he walked toward the car, he noticed the man standing to her side.

Keith.

He raced to his car to call the sheriff, but before he could get into the car, they'd sped out of the lot.

❖ Chapter Thirty-One ❖

Brooke held her breath as Keith eased into traffic. Two green lights put him on the interstate in a hurry and Brooke was regretting getting in the car with him. Trace Adkins badonkadonked from the CD, matching the beat of Brooke's heart. Keith ejected the CD, pushed the button to lower the window, and sent it reeling across the highway like a tiny UFO.

"That was my favorite CD."

"I hate that country noise."

"So next time use the off button, how 'bout it?" She threw a hand up in frustration. "You've made your point. You're smart. Smarter than me. You win. Now stop this car and let me out. I'm already running late for an appointment."

"You're gonna be late all right, and if anyone will be rubbing your back tonight . . . it will be me, baby."

Her mouth dropped open. "How did you know where I was going? Why can't you stay out of my business?"

He grinned and winked. "Doesn't matter how, what matters is that I do know. I'll rub you for free. It'll be the rub of your life."

"You're disgusting. I wouldn't let you touch me if I was dying and needed CPR."

"Might be the last rub of your life then. Suit yourself."

"Let me out now. You're creeping me out. Stop. Right here. I'm not kidding." Keith didn't say another word as they continued south on the interstate.

He flipped on the radio and switched to the static of an AM sports radio station and cranked up the volume. The loud banter of overexcited testosterone and static made it hard to think clearly.

She put a hand up to her right ear, trying to muffle the noise. "Turn it down. I can't think."

"You don't need to think. You have no control now."

No control? Like hell.

Keith sat stiff and straight, his eyes focused on the road ahead like he was programmed for a mission. Her options were limited. She couldn't jump from a moving car, that's for sure. He was exceeding the speed limit. She prayed for blue lights and sirens. Where was a cop when you needed one?

She pulled her hands up over her ears and settled back in the seat.

Finally, he turned off the radio. She was grateful for the peace at first, but the silence became worse than the noise. This was out of character, even for Keith.

"Where are we going?" she asked, trying to sound calm.

"You'll know soon enough."

"I need to get home to Stitches. Please turn around."

"You love that dog more than you ever loved me," hissed Keith.

"We're not having this conversation again. This is stupid."

"Stupid? I'm not stupid. And I didn't do anything to that moppy-lookin' little piece of shit dog of yours."

"At least she never cheated on me. She deserves my love. Can't say that for you."

His hand came from the wheel to her throat, pushing her head against the passenger window, nearly choking her. "Take that back."

There was fury in his voice. Her eyes went wide, realizing the strength in his grip. She scrambled and he let loose, his hand settling back on the steering wheel.

She rubbed her throat and chin, and opened her mouth wide to make sure he hadn't broken her jaw with the forceful move.

"All you ever do is work. I've been watching."

Not doing a very good job of it then. She held her tongue. There was no sense battling with him.

His voice was steadier now. "I know you miss me."

"What the heck are you talking about?"

"You shouldn't have left me."

"Keith, you were gone way before I ever left. You have no idea what I'm doing with my time, so shut up."

"You have no idea how much I know. Would it scare you that I know every move you've made for the past two months?"

"Don't play head games with me. I'm not falling for it."

He shrugged.

"You're turning into some kind of stalker. You need to just leave me alone, but thanks for the confession too. I'll use it against you in court. Count on it."

Keith smirked. "I'll do whatever I like, thank you very much. And get away with it too. Don't you love how the judge feels so sorry for me being shit on by a bitch like you? I have them all believing you're the one who abandoned me." The smirk turned into an all-out laugh. "The way I see it, I win either way. I'll either get you back, or if I play my cards right, I might even get some alimony from you. Now wouldn't that be a hoot?"

"I somehow doubt that a man with your income and skills is going to get alimony from me. You make more money than I do."

"Not if I quit my job. Maybe I'll get fired and just start doing car restorations. That would be fun."

"You practically make your own hours now. That's just stupid, and so is any inkling that we'll ever have something again. We are not getting back together. That will never happen."

Without looking her way, he pointed an accusing finger at her. "I don't care what you say. I didn't think there was anyone else, but you wouldn't be so damn adamant about not reconciling if there wasn't. Who is it?"

"That's ridiculous. I'm not like you. I never

cheated on you. I don't *need* anyone. I can make it just fine by myself—better in fact." It made her nervous that he wouldn't look at her. "You don't even know what marriage is about. What do you care?" she answered sharply. Maybe praying mantises weren't lucky after all. She looked to the sky. It was just getting dark. She prayed for a shooting star.

"I'm taking you back."

"What? Back where?"

"You never listen." Keith slammed the steering wheel. "I tried to make it easy for you. I figured you'd come back when you cooled down. We're not getting a divorce."

"Are you on something? You're delusional. What is wrong with you? You're already getting it all!"

"There's nothing wrong with me. You're the problem. You don't get it." He licked his lips nervously. "I bought that log cabin you always talked about. I'm taking you there now."

"You always hated that idea. You leave my dreams out of your plans. What in the world makes you think I want to go anywhere with you? Take me home!" she demanded.

"Aren't you listening? I *am* taking you home. I'm taking you to our new home. It'll work. You'll see."

"I don't want to be with you. I don't want to be with anybody. I already have a home. Stop the damn car and let . . . me . . . out." She lifted repeatedly on the door handle.

"No," he roared, the word vibrating through the car like a missile.

Brooke choked on a quick intake of air.

"Damn it, Brooke. Why do you always blow things out of proportion? You think everything is all about you?" He smacked the rearview mirror, sending her crystal horseshoe and lucky Indian beads flying. She slumped in the seat, trying to avoid the air assault.

"It is not . . . always about you. Damn it. I'm in control now," he growled. "You hear me?"

He glared at her. "Do you hear me?"

She flinched in response to his booming voice. "Yes, yes. I hear you." She shook beads from her shirt and lap, scrambling for a way to react. "You're acting crazy, and you're scaring me." How could she get control of this situation? He was bigger, madder, out of control, but she was smart. Think, Brooke, think. She lowered her voice, trying to sound calm. "Will you please take me home?"

"This is the way home now, Princess."

"It is not."

He didn't answer.

"You can't do this."

"Who's going to stop me?" He took his eyes off the road and looked her right in the face. "Tell me, Brooke. Who? Who do you see stopping me?"

Their eyes locked. He was right. She didn't have any control.

He mashed the accelerator, and never bothered to take his eyes off her.

"Stop. You're going to crash into those cars in front of us!"

"Don't tell me what to do. Not one more word out of you. Not one." He jerked the wheel and whipped around a light-colored Mazda.

"I hate you," she muttered through gritted teeth.

He jerked the steering wheel, swerving from the left lane to the right shoulder of the interstate. "Fine. Forget it. Have it your way."

She clutched the door and braced herself as they careened toward the embankment. There wouldn't be much protection in her fiberglass car. The way he'd swerved across the lanes someone might think a tire had blown out. Maybe someone would stop to help, or better, call the police.

The car slid through the damp grass and stopped just off the road.

He turned off the headlights. "Get. Out. Of. The. Car."

Words swam around just out of reach.

"NOW!"

The cars that were ahead of them were out of sight now. Traffic seemed to have disappeared with Keith's sanity. "Please don't. It . . . it doesn't have to be like this." Her only hope now was to get back to a public place where someone might be able to help her. How she wished she'd realized now how crazy Keith was. Why had she been so hard to convince he might put her in real danger? If she'd taken it more seriously before, this may not have happened, but now . . . that was looking pretty foolish. "Let's go somewhere and talk."

"We are somewhere, and I'm tired of your talking. Yap, yap, yap, nothing but nonsense." He snatched the keys from the ignition and bailed out of the car.

She unclicked her seat belt and lurched forward, grabbing for the keys she'd stuck under the seat earlier at the gas station. Some miracle or maybe the praying mantis after all, allowed her to grab them on the first sweep. She threw her body across the console toward the driver's seat and pushed the key into the ignition, turning it. The motor roared, but she heard the key unlocking the door behind her.

Brooke grabbed the steering wheel. Sprawled across the leather bucket seats she pulled herself to get behind the wheel, but Keith opened the door and grabbed her foot. He tugged her with such force, she slammed against the shifter, moving it into neutral. The car began to roll down the slope of the shoulder.

"Stop it, Brooke."

She kicked, but his hold on her was stronger. There was a loud snap. Agony flared through her body.

"Damn it, girl," he grunted as he dragged her out of the car by the leg.

Her butt slammed the ground and the empty car continued to roll down the emergency lane.

Keith lifted her to her feet and shoved her forward. She screamed out. The pain in her foot and ankle stole the air from her lungs.

"Why did you have to make things worse? I love you. I bought you that stupid Lincoln-Log house you always wanted so bad."

"Buying a house is not love." She winced. "My ankle. Can't you see I'm hurt?" She lifted her foot in the air and dropped her head back, praying for relief.

"We were going to have a nice reunion. I had it all planned. Even bought that champagne you like. But no, you had to ruin it." He glared in her direction. "Damn you. I'm not giving you up."

She was no match for Keith's strength. She wasn't going to outrun him on this bad ankle either. She needed to be in survivor mode. Outwit. Outsmart. Outlast. His breathing was loud, and he kept cussing under his breath.

"You're right. It was good once." She spoke slowly. Trying to appear calm, she swept a bead of sweat from her lip. Glittery spots spun in her line of sight. *Don't pass out.* Between the pain and the fear, she didn't know which was worse, but she couldn't pass out. She had to fight back. *Breathe.* "We can fix this. Give me another chance."

❖ Chapter Thirty-Two ❖

Brooke stood on her good leg like a flamingo, wishing the throbbing in her ankle would dull. The charade might work. She swallowed hard and continued. "Keith. We loved each other. It shouldn't be like this."

"You're not going to make me look like a fool. Not twice. It ends here."

Brooke watched the dark cloud veil his normally bright brown eyes. "You're scaring me."

"You should be scared. You ruined everything. I gave us a second chance and you blew it." He shoved her forward.

She limped, trying to minimize the pain, but then she tripped over a branch and hit the ground on all fours.

"Damn you," he sneered, dragging her to her feet by her arm. "Quit stalling."

"I'm hurt." She wasn't sure where the injuries were anymore. The pain spiked up her leg to her neck and she felt the warm trickle of blood down her shin. Keith pushed and prodded her. She slid in the slick grass. Finally, the ground leveled as they reached the tree line at the bottom of the slope. Brooke leaned back against a tall pine, pausing to catch her breath. She squeezed at the stitch in her side.

In one swoop Keith lifted her with one strong arm, scraping her back along the rough bark of the tree, balancing her crotch on his knee. Her feet dangled above the ground.

Something glistened in the moonlight. *He has a knife?*

"Heeeeeeelp! Let me go." Brooke wiggled, trying to throw herself off-balance from where he had her perched.

He pushed the back of his hand against her mouth; her teeth sliced her lip. She tasted the salty blood. Pulling back just a little, she bit into the fleshy mound of his hand. Then screamed for help again.

"Damn." He pulled back. "You bit me, you bitch." He waved the knife in front of her face, resting the hand with the sharp blade on the tree just above her head. "Shut . . . up," Keith enunciated each word.

"No-oo-oo." Her eyes followed the blade.

"QUI-ET! SH—SHH." His hot breath sent a spray of spit across her face. He shook her. The bark scraped her shoulder and she felt the sting of blood oozing through her blouse.

"Please," Brooke squeaked out, barely able to swallow. "You've made your point. You were right," she panted. "I messed up."

"Now you're talking."

"I was j-j-just jealous," she lied in desperation. *Outsmart.*

Keith flashed a smile. For an instant she fel hope, but then he pushed his knee up harde against her crotch. Pinned tight, she couldn' move. Keith laughed. The sound echoed throug her brain. A sound she would never forget.

"You must really think I'm a fool to believ you want me back now."

"Isn't that what you want?"

"Oh, don't you worry about what I want. I'l have what I want." He flipped the knife betwee the buttons of her blouse, revealing her lacy bra.

Brooke turned her face away, squeezing he eyes tight.

He bent toward her. His teeth scraped a lin down the inside of her neck. The bristle of hi chin burned her skin. He bit down on the stretch elastic of her bra strap and tugged. Snap. Sh flinched as the elastic stung her skin.

He straightened his knee, and she crumbled t his feet in the unexpected release, striking he head on something on the way down. A shar pain. The sky seemed to spin. She tensed, waitin for another strike. He loomed above her.

Brooke scrambled along the ground. Some thing dug into her leg as she tried to get to he feet. If he was going to kill her she wasn't goin to make it easy. Her fingers trembled as sh wrapped her hands around a small branch. Sh took a breath and lunged forward.

He leaped back, cursing her. She grabbed for

branch to stand, but he seized her by the shirt and then wrapped her hair in his hand with a twist, tugging her backside against him. "Where d'ya think you're going?"

His breath burned hot on her ear. Her shoulders lifted, protecting herself from his words. She felt him hard against her. *Relax. Don't tempt him in this state of adrenaline, or he is going to kill you.*

He pulled her closer, nuzzling her neck and leaving a damp trail behind. Was he crying or sweating? "You're hurting me," she whispered. "My hair—please . . ."

He eased his grip. "I never wanted to. I love you." He pulled his hands away and she dropped to the ground. She landed on her stomach, all the air evacuating her diaphragm, leaving her gasping for oxygen against the screaming pain in her chest. She lifted her eyes and saw the tear run down his face. *Outlast.*

He swept the tear away and kicked her once in the shoulder before turning away.

"Ow." She rolled away. The knife lay on the ground just to her right. She wrapped her hands around it. The handle slipped in her sweaty palm. She stood, concealing the knife by holding it tight against her leg. "Then don't. Please, don't hurt me." Tears slid down her cheeks, pooling in the crease of her mouth. "Let me go. I promise I won't tell." Her eyes pleaded, her voice small compared to the girl who was fighting so hard just minutes before.

"I don't know." His free hand stroked nervously through his thin hair. "I need to think." He passed a hand over his mouth and eyes and hung his head

Outlast. She lunged forward. The sharp blade plunged into his flesh. It was her only chance to outrun him. She didn't even stop to see his reaction but ran as hard and fast as she could on the one good ankle, back in the direction of the car. She slipped, but clawed at the ground to right herself. He called her name from behind her. Getting closer.

She ducked behind some brush. She lay on the ground, tucking herself into a small area, hopefully hidden. Afraid to lift her head, she pulled her knees in tighter and fought the urge to run again. He was close. *Help me, God.* Bracing herself for the worst, she pulled her arms up, shielding her face and covering her ears. She waited.

Only the whoosh of her own blood and pulse hummed under her palms, and then the sound of a heavy thud against the ground vibrated beneath her.

"Brooke." A warm hand landed on her shoulder. She squeezed her eyes closed tighter, tensing for a blow, but nothing happened. She heard her name a second time. It didn't sound crazed or angry, but the words weren't clear. Then a light. *Is this the light you see when you die?*

Someone knelt beside her. She cowered, still, praying there'd be no more pain. Light washed over her. She held her breath.

"Brooke. It's me, Mike." He pulled her closer. "Brooke, look at me. You're safe."

She shivered and clung to the warmth of the safety he offered. It was a long moment before she dared open her eyes.

❖ Chapter Thirty-Three ❖

"Talk to me. Are you hurt?" Mike tipped her face toward him.

She opened her eyes, but she seemed confused. "I think so," she answered in barely a whisper. "It was him."

He swept his penlight over her, then pulled a handkerchief from his pocket and folded it into a tight, thick square. "Here." He placed it over the gash on her forehead. "Hold that tight."

She held it in place, but her hand shook.

Keith was unconscious a few feet away, cuffed ankle to wrist. The reflex instincts from the special ops maneuvers had come in handy. One swift move and Keith, who probably outweighed him by a good fifty pounds, had gone down. "You're safe now, Brooke."

"He was going to kill me." She seemed unable to shift her focus off her ex-husband lying there in a heap. "He could have."

"But he didn't. I've got you. You're going to be fine." He ran his hand across her back in an effort to slow her breathing down. "I've got you." His heart clenched at the sight of her.

"Why?"

He turned her face away from Keith. "Don't try to make sense of it." But he knew how that question could consume you. He'd been there, and even though he'd been in life-and-death situations, and done his share of rescues, an unexpected burst of emotion had overcome him when he'd seen Keith grab Brooke at the gas station. He wasn't even sure what had turned his attention to the gas pumps, but he had and in that instant it was like someone had just delivered a shock from a defibrillator to his heart.

His heart raced, maxing out just like the car as he sped to catch them. Watching and praying, he didn't even bother with a safe distance. He knew he needed to be close enough to step in. If he hadn't gotten caught behind that tanker truck he'd have been there even sooner. Thank goodness Keith had left the car along the side of the road. If he hadn't, he'd have lost them completely, and Brooke would have been in an even more dangerous position.

He watched her for a moment, wishing he could erase it for her. This kind of stuff didn't go away so easy, though.

"I won't ever let him bother you again," he said, realizing at that instant that he was about to break his number one rule: Don't let it get personal. What he was feeling didn't feel a bit like business, and he damn sure couldn't bear the thought of losing her.

It wasn't about the rescue. This time it was about the girl.

It had taken every ounce of his strength not to kill the sorry bastard. He had the skill to do it swiftly, and he could have done it and left with no one knowing the better. But he'd called Sheriff Calvin instead to get them involved as soon as he'd seen trouble brewing. Maybe he'd done it to keep himself from killing the guy.

Brooke sobbed in his arms, gulping loudly for air.

He leaned his head down against hers. "You're safe." He stroked her cheek and held her for a moment, then hit redial on his phone and gave Sheriff Calvin his location and the update. He snapped the phone shut. "Medics are on the way."

She tipped her tear-stained face up toward his, her lips trembling. "Thank you."

Mike leaned in, trying to warm her with his own body. She looked fragile. Her face was dirty beneath a tangle of hair and mascara stained her cheeks. Something touched him bone deep that wouldn't allow him to take his eyes off her.

Sirens suddenly filled the heavy evening air.

Unable to resist the pull, he took her soft, swollen lips into his in a kiss.

For a fraction of a second she struggled in his

arms. He began to pull away, controlling his own need at that moment, but as he retreated, she returned the kiss and relaxed into the safety of his arms. The kiss went on until the sound of footsteps made them pull apart.

Equipment rattled as rescue workers flooded the area.

A woman EMT wrapped a white sheet around Brooke's body, covering where her clothes had ripped. Mike knew it was more an emotional barrier than for the exposed skin. They strapped Brooke to a gurney and made their way back up the embankment to the ambulance.

Mike spotted Sheriff Calvin over by the emergency vehicles that now lined the highway. Blue lights flashed, bouncing off each other like a disco.

Sheriff Calvin watched as one of his men re-cuffed Keith for transport.

Keith spat on the ground, cursing and complaining the whole time. "Y'all think you're so smart. This is not over. It was just a little domestic. We're married. She'll never press charges." The officers pushed Keith down into the backseat of the police car. "You're wasting your time. I'm telling you. She loves me."

"Sure she does," Sheriff Calvin said as he headed toward Mike. He handed his cuffs back and shook his hand. "Good job."

Mike nodded toward the police car. "All by the book, right?"

"Oh, yeah. No loopholes. He's toast."

"Good deal."

The sheriff shook his head. "Makes you wonder how people get to that point in a relationship. She's filed several reports, but we've never been able to help her. Glad she got you involved."

Mike extended his hand. "Thanks for the support. I wasn't sure if an investigator was going to be welcomed into your community."

"I'll admit I was a skeptic at first. I wasn't sure how I felt about some civilian coming in here and hanging out a shingle, but I'm always happy for good help. And any friend of Von gets an instant checkmark in my book." He nodded toward the ambulance. "I just talked to the medics. She's pretty banged up. They're taking her in to check for broken bones, and make sure there's no internal damage."

Mike's focus was across the way, where Brooke was being lifted into the ambulance. "I'm going to check on her one last time." He didn't bother to wait for a comment from the sheriff, breaking into a jog. By the time he got to the ambulance, they were getting ready to close the door.

"Can I have one second?" he asked the EMT.

"Sure." The EMT pulled the door back open and Mike leaned into the back of the unit. "Hey, Brooke. I'll check in on you, okay?"

She nodded. Tears stained her cheeks, and a contusion had already started blooming on her cheek, making her appear even more fragile under the bright lights. Still pretty though.

"Thank you for being here," she said through the tears.

Mike patted her leg. "If you'd locked the car when you got in, I would have gotten him in the parking lot."

"If only." She looked confused and beautiful even with the bruising. "How did you get here?"

"Good timing. I'm pretty good at some things."

She attempted a smile, but winced. Her hand went to her bloody lip. "Better at this than farm management or new relationships?"

"I am." He laughed. "Promise me, from now on when you get in the car, you'll lock the car door. I can't take another scare like that again." He paused. She probably wasn't up to a lecture but the near tragedy had him feeling like he needed to give it. "So simple you can't believe someone would need to remind you, huh?"

"Get in the car. Lock the car." Her voice felt weak.

He gave her shaking hand a little squeeze through the sheet. "You're going to be fine; it's over."

"I thought I was going to die."

"But you didn't. You fought back. We'll talk later. Right now you need to get checked out."

"I was lucky."

Mike stepped back as the paramedics prepared

the unit to depart. He didn't know how long he'd been standing there, but Sheriff Calvin had come while he was.

A deputy carried a purse and handed it over to the sheriff.

Mike acknowledged the bag. "Brooke's?"

"Yeah."

"Her phone in there?"

Sheriff Calvin flipped it open and looked back up, rolling his eyes. He held the purse open toward Mike, displaying the disarray. "God. Who could tell? Enter at your own risk." The sheriff pushed the purse in Mike's direction.

Mike pushed through pens, and twenties and fives, and pulled out the phone. He thumbed through a few screens as Sheriff Calvin looked on. Mike glanced through the entries in Brooke's phone. It was password protected, but like half the numeric passwords on these things, a simple one-two-three-four got him right in. "Shame, shame, Miss Brooke, you know better." He read through the calendar. Was there anything this girl didn't plan? The name and phone number of the locksmith, every appointment and personal plan down to the quarter hour, even reminders to get gas, yoga, and coffee breaks. Keith had known her every planned move, and it looked like she pretty much planned everything.

He scrolled through the entries and then stopped at the one that must have thrown Keith over the edge. It simply read, "Investigator-Keith—I'M DONE."

"That's what I thought. Thanks, man," Mike said as he handed the phone back.

Sheriff Calvin took the phone and dropped it into the purse. "No problem. I need to get back to the station."

"You bet." Mike hiked back to his truck, and got in, the adrenaline still kicking so hard that he slammed the door. The ambulance still hadn't left the scene, and he just couldn't bring himself to leave until he saw the ambulance pull away. Kind of like how his mom had always said to wait until his date was safely inside the house before he drove off. Some lessons just never left.

Something in him had sparked when Brooke had shown up at Kasey's place.

He'd tried to stick to business and ignore that feeling, but instead he'd found himself asking her out. Even as he'd tried to talk himself out of the dinner with her, it was like the more he resisted the more she was like a magnet to his pull because he'd run into her over and over again around town. The feelings he'd been prepared to never feel again were itching at him.

Von had lost his wife and he'd found love again. Mike still remembered the day he'd gotten the news about Von getting remarried. It not only felt like a betrayal of the grounds on which their friendship had been built, but it had been downright hard to even like Riley at first because it felt like a betrayal to the memory of Von's wife and his own. The bond that he and Von had from losing their wives in separate but so similar ways—so tragic, brutal—had left him broken beyond repair, but somehow Von had risen above it. That had made him feel so lonely.

Yesterday he thought the rest of his life would be a solo act, but right now he wasn't sure of what he'd been so sure about.

❖ Chapter Thirty-Four ❖

Brooke shielded her eyes from the harsh hospital lighting. Her forehead had received three stitches. It took ten to close the gash on her leg where she'd fallen on that branch. They'd dug so deep to extract pieces of the stick, she wondered if they'd mistaken the bone for foreign matter.

Her ankle wasn't broken, just sprained. The snap she'd heard must have been the leather strap on her shoe and that had left a nice slice across the front of her ankle. She thought she might prefer a broken ankle to ruining those brand-new shoes. At least insurance would cover the broken ankle. Those shoes had been a total splurge—a waste in a small town like Adams Grove where no one could appreciate them but her. It wasn't likely she could replace those.

Brooke pulled the thin hospital blanket up to her chin. It felt like she'd already been here for hours, and all she really wanted was to get home into her own bed. She closed her eyes, but the room was so bright she couldn't sleep.

She opened her eyes and repositioned herself on the pillow, closing her eyes until she heard someone clear his throat at the doorway.

When she looked up, the blue-eyed man in the black ball cap filled the doorway like he could have stepped right off a movie screen.

"Come to play doctor?" she asked.

Mike broke into a broad smile. "Hardly."

"Darn. I was hoping you could sign me out of this place. I just want to go home." She pulled herself up and grappled with the gown. "Thank you *so* much for being there tonight."

Mike stepped into the room. "Just doin' my job, ma'am." He was overplaying the Southern gentleman, but it was cute.

"Yeah. I know, the whole big bucks thing, but I'm pretty sure what you did tonight far exceeded what I was paying for."

"You scared me."

"I was pretty scared too."

Mike looked away for a second. "Are they letting you out of here tonight?"

"I'm sure they will," Brooke said. "I got a few stitches, and the ankle is just a sprain. I did ruin a brand-new pair of shoes. That's kind of heart breaking, but other than that, I'm fine. Thanks to you. How did you know? I thought you were still out of town."

"I got back last night. I wanted to see you so badly." Mike shifted from one leg to the other. "When I saw your car at the gas station, I was excited to bump into you because giving you space was the hardest thing I've had to do in a long time. Then I saw Keith. I had a bad feeling. That's why I followed you. You know the rest. You won't need to worry about Keith again."

"He's not . . ."

"Oh, no. Very much alive, but very much in custody and up the creek without a paddle." His brow arched. "So, would you mind if I stopped by your house, and checked on you?"

"Not at all." She felt the sides of her mouth tug at the thought. *Be cool.*

"Good. I'll do that then." He leaned back, looking toward the hall. "Brooke. I really am sorry that my fears have messed things up. I hate that I did that, but I can't change it. God, how I wish I could take back that part of that night."

"I know."

"Let me give you a ride home."

"Thank you, but I have no idea when they'll be back. I don't want you to get stuck waiting around if they decide to not let me go."

"I don't mind. I can wait."

Was he talking about tonight at the hospital, o[r] something more? "No. Really. I'm fine."

"Well, then I guess I'll be on my way. Call me [if] you need me."

"I will," she said as he walked away. *Who sai[d] good guys don't wear black hats?*

❖ Chapter Thirty-Five ❖

Brooke sipped a cup of coffee in her offic[e] reviewing her proposal for changes to the annua[l] Farm Day in Adams Grove. She was excited t[o] raise the bar on the well-attended event with som[e] of the ideas she'd used in Virginia Beach. Hope[-] fully, her boss would like the recommendation[s] and approve the budget and plan so she could ge[t] to work on it. Setting up a function like tha[t] took time.

Victoria poked her head in the office. "Yo[u] have a visitor."

"I'm not expecting anyone," Brooke said.

Her assistant slipped into the office and sai[d] quietly, "It's Mike—"

Before Victoria could finish her sentence, Mik[e] strolled in.

"What are you doing here?" she asked.

"I wanted to see where you work. I couldn'[t] picture you behind a desk."

"Uh-huh, maybe you're really here checking o[n]

me." Brooke rolled her eyes and slumped forward on her desk.

"I told you I was going to check on you."

"I know. Sorry, it's just that everyone is checking on me. People I haven't spoken to in years are calling. I'm not so fragile that I'm going to have some kind of meltdown or something." She lifted her head and shook back her bangs.

"Want to grab something to eat?"

"I can't. I have too much to get through here." Brooke patted the top of three stacks of folders neatly piled across her desk. "Can I get a rain check?"

"Of course."

Brooke's phone rang. "Sorry. I've got to get that."

"I'll let you get back to work." He turned and headed out the door.

She watched as he left, then picked up the phone, but to her delight it wasn't the auctioneer she was expecting, it was Jenny.

Jenny's voice was frantic. "I can't believe you didn't call me. Are you okay?"

"How did you hear about it?" *News sure traveled fast around here, but across state lines was a new one.*

"I just talked to Rick. I can't believe I heard about something that was a matter of life and death from him and not you!"

"I'm sorry. I'm fine. I promise."

"I can't believe it. No. I take that back. I totally believe it. How did you get away?"

"Mike showed up."

"I told you he was a guy worth keeping around Am I right? He's not just another pretty face, tha one."

"I'm paying him for that, remember?" Some times Jenny's energy was downright exhausting "Guys. That's all you ever think about?"

"Guilty as charged. It wouldn't kill you to thinl about them once in a while. And while you're a it, think about forgiving this one okay? No crim there, honey." Jenny laughed so loud Brook had to pull the phone away from her ear. "Get it' *No crime.* An investigator?"

"Yes, I got it. Not funny, and yes, maybe yo were right." She pushed the paperwork to th side, and laid her head on the desk.

"Well, don't come crying to me when you'r lonely. I doubt a guy like Mike will be single fo long. You better quit messing around. I have class to teach, but I needed to hear your voice fo myself. Don't let anything happen to you. I'll b home on party day. Love you."

"Take care." She hung up the phone, wishin she could have just one day to be like Jenn where she didn't worry over anything. Jenny wa Brooke's complete opposite: no plans, no worries and she let her mood or current interests lead th way. That's how she went from banker to yog instructor. She just up and decided one day that banking wasn't for her and did something about it. Her outwardly chaotic appeal seemed to somehow work for her, though. She'd landed high-paying gigs at swanky resorts a few times a year. She considered them vacations, even if they were very good-paying jobs.

Brooke picked up her pen and drummed it on the desk to bring herself back to the work in front of her. The room fell out of focus for a moment. She took a deep breath. She'd been on raw nerves since the incident. The spinning room was the first indication another anxiety attack was coming on.

How would she feel safe? Usually her instincts were good, but this thing with Keith and then the feeling someone was watching her every move was making her doubt her good judgment.

The workday felt long and Brooke's ankle throbbed so badly that she'd had one of the guys at work give her a ride home. She stripped out of her work attire and stepped into the tub, daydreaming about the log cabin she'd always thought she'd live in. *How could Keith grasp at that straw?* A little too damn late, but he must have been listening somewhere along the way. She had to give him that. Home never would have been with Keith. The regrets around ending the marriage and the failure of that relationship were gone. She was just thankful things hadn't turned out worse.

She closed her eyes and let her mind wander to a more relaxing place, the one with the faceless stranger in her recurring log cabin fantasy. The shape of the house came into focus. Big logs and heavy timber made up a strong structure. Stonework, textured and glistening in hues of rust and gray climbed the side. She could always see herself so clearly. She was smiling and relaxed, but her partner was always a blur. The faceless stranger felt warm, safe, and definitely tall, and someday she hoped he'd show himself.

This time the man in her dream no longer felt like a stranger. Brown hair. Steel-blue eyes. Wide shoulders. For the first time, she recognized him. He looked just like Mike.

The sexy investigator was still having a very physical effect on her. That he invaded her private fantasy was personally disturbing, but it felt too good to push him out. She let her hands slip along her body beneath the warm, silky, bubbled water. Her thoughts lingered on the muscular arms around her that night he rescued her. Even more so, their night together. Her heart beat a little faster. Her body reacted to the memory of his kiss. His lips were strong, but soft on hers. That kiss. And in his arms. Warm. Gentle. Safe.

She opened her eyes with a start. "No. Stop. This is not going to happen."

The water splashed as she flailed, trying to sit upright to escape the dream and get back to reality. "That was nuts," she said to Stitches, who was sitting next to the tub. Brooke's wet hand dripped over the side. The tiny Westie lapped droplets of water from her palm. "Stitches, what was I thinking?"

Stitches barked in response.

"I know. I'm crazy, aren't I?"

Stitches barked again and ran to the door. Stitches wasn't having a conversation with her, someone was knocking at the front door.

"Why won't everyone just leave me alone?" She stepped out of the tub, grabbed for the robe on the back of the door, and did a one-footed *Flashdance* quickstep on the fluffy bath rug to shake the water from her legs.

"Coming," she yelled. "Hang on." She half ran, half hopped, pulling on the robe on her way to the door.

She peeked out the peephole.

Mike?

Her stomach did a flip. "I'm not dressed," she said through the closed door. What's he doing here?

"I won't stay long."

"I just got out of the tub. I look a mess. Can you wait?"

"I only have a minute. Can you open the door?"

Brooke groaned. What choice did she have? He did save her life. She ran her hand through her hair trying to give it a quick fluff, and tightened the robe around her otherwise naked and damp body. She pulled the door open with a forced smile. "Hi."

He looked like he was searching for what to say. "So how's the ankle?"

"Sore, like most everything else on me." She hung on to the door, half behind it.

He shifted in the awkward silence of the moment. "Brought you something. Can I come in?"

"Uh. Yeah. Sorry. Sure." Probably the bill. Maybe that's why he'd stopped by this morning and she'd shooed him out before he could give it to her. She stepped from behind the door and opened it. "Yes, come in."

He raised a kraft-paper bag as he stepped inside. Not just a grocery bag, though. Leather-braided handles on grocery bag paper with cattle brands along the edge.

"A present for me?"

He moved toward the couch in the living room. "Well, not really a present."

"Oh." Brooke tugged on the robe again. "I like the bag."

Very aware of her own nakedness under the robe, she leaned on the arm of the couch rather than chancing sitting and giving him a peep show.

He lifted something from the bag with a smile.

"Soup?" she questioned in surprise. "You brought me a can of soup?"

He looked at the red-and-white-labeled can and then back at her. "Well, not just any soup. Chicken noodle."

She faked a smile of appreciation. Was this really what he'd come by for? This was definitely a first.

"It has healing properties. Oh, and . . ." he dug back in the bag, pulled out a cobalt-blue bottle, and held it up by the neck in the same hand that palmed the soup can. "Chicken soup and water. My mom always said this combo will cure anything. You were so busy at work I thought I'd make sure you ate dinner."

His mom? How sweet. She raised a hand over her mouth to hide her smile. She didn't want to hurt his feelings, but the gift was kind of funny. In spite of herself, tears threatened to spill over at the sweet, goofy gesture. "Well, then I'm going to be in good shape in no time, aren't I?" She accepted the soup and water and hobbled to the kitchen with them. This was the first time a guy had brought her soup. Flowers, sure, but soup, never. She wondered if she should eat it from a vase. "Can I get you anything?"

"No. I promised I wouldn't stay long."

This couldn't have waited? "Do you always keep your promises?"

"Yes, ma'am."

She gave him a quick nod. "Me too."

"You promise to let me know if there's anything

I can do for you?" He arched a brow, challenging her.

"Yes, but I'm okay." His look told her she wasn't being too convincing. "Okay, well, maybe I'm feeling a little cautious, you know . . . not safe. Maybe safe isn't the word. I kind of feel like Keith's still watching me, even though I know he can't be."

"He's definitely not watching you unless it's in his dreams. I checked in with Calvin. Keith isn't going anywhere for a while, and when he does we'll know."

"Thanks. That does make me feel better." She limped back into the living room and sat down on the couch.

"Good. What else can I do to cheer you up and put that smile back on your face?"

"I'm fine." She forced an extra-wide grin. "See?"

"Not convinced."

"Don't worry. I won't let him win. No man is worth that."

"We aren't all alike." He nudged the big paper sack with the toe of his shoe. "There's something else in there."

"More?" After the soup and water, she had no idea what to expect. She opened the bag, and then her mouth dropped open. "My shoes? How?"

"I had the strap fixed."

"From the accident? They're fixed?" She pulled

them to her chest and this time the smile was genuine. "How did you get them?"

Mike nodded. "I'm good."

"No way." She examined the straps; sure enough, they were like brand-new. "I saw one of the cops throw them in a trash bag."

"That wasn't a trash bag. They put all the stuff from the crime scene in paper bags."

"Crime scene. That makes it sound worse."

"It was pretty bad."

She held his gaze and took in a breath. "I know."

"I don't have a one-rescue-per-night limit. That's why I get paid—"

"—the big bucks," they both said at the same time.

Brooke laughed. "I can't believe this. How'd you get them fixed so fast? No one does anything fast in this town."

"One of my Marine buddies comes from a long line of boot makers in Texas. He married a Virginia girl about a year ago and they opened a shop up in Richmond. It took all of about ten minutes to put them back in shape. He was done before I finished my coffee."

"A boot maker messing around with New York designer shoes? I bet that's a first."

"Careful now. He's not just any boot maker. This guy's family has made custom boots for the last three presidents. He could probably teach that high-dollar girly shoemaker a thing or two."

She held the snarky comments. It wasn't the time to tease. "I don't know how to thank you. You are too nice."

"Well, I didn't want you to think I didn't understand the relationship between a girl and her shoes."

"Your wife? She loved shoes?"

"Yeah. She probably had a hundred pairs of them I had to get rid of. Funny thing is, I never much paid attention to them, but they obviously meant something to her."

She could almost picture the memory in his mind.

"I bet those memories are precious," she said softly.

"It's been a long time since I allowed myself to remember them. But it's okay . . . now."

She lifted the shoes. "Thanks for sharing that with me. That means a lot to me that you would."

"Things are easy with you." He shrugged modestly. "Anyway, I just hoped this might make you feel better. Something little I could do. Not business."

"Better? Are you kidding? I'm cured!" She jumped from the couch with shoes in hand and arms splayed for a hug.

Mike stood and looked down on her. "You're a short shit without those shoes on, aren't you?"

She slapped at him with the strappy heels. "Didn't anyone ever tell you great things come in small packages?" She lifted a hand to her hip, causing her robe to gape, which she pulled closed immediately.

"Get better soon, will ya?" His hands slid from her arms to her waist.

"Yeah, I will," she said quietly up at him. He towered over her. She could feel a dampness that had nothing to do with the tub.

He dropped a playful kiss on her nose, but pulled away quickly and was halfway to the door before she realized he had moved on.

Do you have to leave? She found herself wishing silently. *Please, please stay.* She raced to catch up with him at the door, leaning easily against it, watching him walk against the dusk. Those tall, sturdy legs took him to his black truck in just a few strides. "Don't be a stranger."

Mike didn't turn around. "I'll be back," he called over his shoulder.

"Soon?"

"Count on it."

"I will," she said, still wishing he'd turn around and come back now.

"Take care of you," he called from the door of his pickup, then slid behind the wheel.

Brooke put the shoes down and picked up Stitches. Raising the dog's paw in one of her hands, they waved good-bye.

She stepped back inside and said to Stitches. "Soon? Not a woman on earth knows what that measurement of time means."

❖ Chapter Thirty-Six ❖

Brooke pushed up the sleeves of her black sweater as she walked to answer the front door. She hoped she was dressed appropriately. What do you wear to plan a party with your best friend's boyfriend while she's out of town? People were going to talk. She knew it.

She pulled the front door open and started laughing. "We look like twins!" There he stood wearing a black shirt and khakis. "At least you're on time. Jenny is always late."

"Raring to go. You say 'cake' and I'm Ricky on the spot." Rick hooked his arm. "Madam."

Brooke slipped her arm through his and pulled the door closed behind her as they headed to the truck. He slowed down. "You're sure you're up to this, right?"

"Absolutely," she said.

"Good. So, where are we off to?" Rick asked as he held the door for Brooke.

She clicked the seat belt into place. "You're in luck," she said, as he climbed behind the wheel. "Because of our short timeline, we only have two bakeries that do theme cakes that can accommodate us. We have appointments with both."

"Where to first?"

"To the oceanfront. Susie T's Bakery on Atlantic. Our appointment is at ten. We should be right on time."

Rick started the diesel truck, and they rumbled out of the driveway.

Brooke pulled out a pink piece of paper from her purse, tracing a manicured nail down the list. "After we get done at Susie T's, we'll stop by the florist and pay the deposits. I think we've got everything picked out from our phone call, but I want to see what you think. Then we'll have time for a quick lunch before we meet with the folks at A Cake to Remember."

"Jenny wasn't kidding. You really are into planning. Do I have time to stop and get fuel?"

"Do you need to stop?"

He laughed. "No. I just wondered if it would screw up your whole system."

"Real funny. I'm flexible."

"Sure you are." He gave her a sideways glance, and she knew he was right to be skeptical.

She was relieved when he merged into the HOV lane to make good time down to the beach.

When they walked into Susie T's Bakery, Rick's eyes lit up. Like a kid in a candy shop, he rubbed his hands together and took in a breath. "I hope this is what heaven smells like."

"Susie T," a short, heavyset, smiling woman, swished into the front wearing a crisp white apron with bright-pink rickrack and a swirling *S* on the pocket. "You must be Brooke and Rick. I'm Susie." She reached toward Rick to shake his hand. "Congratulations on the racehorse. I've never done a Kentucky Derby cake."

"Thanks." Brooke jumped in. "We're on a tight schedule. The derby is the first weekend in May."

"I have some samples ready for you. Follow me." The woman scurried through two swinging doors, motioning them to follow her. Three round tables were set with white tablecloths and silver-tiered trays adorned the middle of each table in a small dining area. "I do a lot of weddings too." The woman motioned them to take a seat and then rushed through another set of doors.

"This is awesome," Brooke whispered to Rick.

"Nice." He picked up a fork and pretended he was going to pound on the table. "Cake. Cake. Cake," he mouthed to Brooke.

Susie breezed back into the room carrying two platters covered with silver domes. She placed them in the center on the raised display. "Okay. So before we get started, how many guests are we talking? That'll help me know how big a cake we'll have."

"About a hundred and fifty. Max."

"Okay. And do you have an idea of the style of cake you'd like?"

Rick looked dumbfounded. "Big?"

Susie laughed. "You know, stacked tiers, or

raised tiers with columns between—kind of like a wedding cake—or those topsy-turvy cakes that are kind of contemporary? Square layers or round layers? Or one giant sheet cake? Some folks like those or some people even prefer mini-cakes, like a cupcake size for each individual. Lot more work, but it's quite trendy right now."

"Holy shit," said Rick. "I thought cake was the easy part."

"Told you there was a lot to do." Brooke cleared her throat and jumped in to rescue him. "Jenny is set on letting Rick have his way with the flavors, but as for style the only thing she specifically asked was that it not be topsy-turvy layers. She doesn't like that look."

Susie pulled the silver dome from a platter, revealing an assortment of cake slivers.

"If I knew I'd get to do this, I might have done more than buy a horse with a girl. We'll be back when I ask her to marry me," teased Rick.

An hour later they had a theme, colors, and the whole cake planned out.

Brooke liked what she saw and Rick seemed like he was pretty happy too. "Rick, I think if we're happy with this, we can cancel the meeting at the other shop. Can we seal a deal right here and now?"

"Works for me."

Rick and Brooke practically skipped out of

Susie T's Bakery happy with the cake, and the extra free time they'd just earned back.

"I don't know if it's Susie or the sugar from all that cake we just ate, but I'm tickled pink with this decision," Brooke said.

"This party planning is a piece of cake," Rick said as he climbed behind the wheel.

❖ Chapter Thirty-Seven ❖

Brooke was pleased with all she and Rick had accomplished today. She'd asked Rick to stop at a convenience store so she could grab a local paper while they were in Virginia Beach. She missed the big, thick, newsy paper. The paper in Adams Grove was only four to six pages long and most of that was news that was already two weeks old.

Once she'd e-mailed Jenny the updated project plan and reordered the remaining tasks, she settled on the sofa with a glass of iced tea and the newspaper. Stitches jumped up on the couch and nestled with Brooke as she read under the light of the lamp.

She poured through her favorite sections. The "Beacon" was the little section of the paper that came out only a couple times a week, but she always recognized a few people that she'd connected with over the years. It made her a little homesick, but she was starting to prefer Adams Grove. It was becoming more like home every day.

Saving the news for last, she opened the front page and the headline caught her eye. She set down her tea and sat straight up.

GOTO HELL MURDERER RELEASED:
Franklin Gotorow Paroled After 8 Years

She shifted to her knees on the couch and folded the paper back. He'd been out of jail for nearly two months. There was no way Mike knew about this. How could they let someone like that out of prison?

If his reaction was worse than hers, Goto would be the one who needed to worry.

She pulled the article up on her computer and got ready to e-mail it to Mike, but really, was that the kind of news you blasted through an e-mail? A phone call would be better. Maybe he already knew. Her heart ached at the notion that creep would be out on the streets, and how that would make Mike feel. She walked over to the desk and pulled out a pair of scissors. She snipped out the article and tucked it aside so she could give it to Mike.

How do you even start a conversation to break that news to someone?

The story weighed heavy on her mind. At nine

o'clock she picked up the phone and called Mike.

"Everything okay?" he answered with a tone of urgency.

"Yes." She felt bad for waiting until so late to call now. She'd worried him for no reason. But her heart warmed a little to know that there was someone out there who did. "I've got something I need to tell you."

There was a pause, then Mike said, "Okay. I'm listening."

"I was in Virginia Beach today with Rick." Her throat felt dry. "I picked up a newspaper while we were there and I was just reading it tonight. Mike, there was an article about the guy who killed your wife in the paper."

"What kind of article?"

"You might already know. I didn't . . ." She wished she wasn't the one giving him this news. Didn't victims get notified when people got out of jail? It seemed only fair, but then he'd done his time. "Goto is out of prison. He made parole a couple of months ago. Mike, he's living in Virginia."

She heard the slam. It could have been the desk or it could have been the wall, but the cursing that followed was a mixture of angst, fury, and pain. "Are you sure?"

She pressed both hands over her eyes, wishing she could block out what he must be feeling right now. "I . . . I just thought you should know."

"Damn right I should know. Which paper?"

"The *Pilot*."

His voice was steady, almost eerily so. "I'll get it online. Thanks for letting me know. Does Rick know?"

"I don't know. I wanted to talk to you first."

There was a cold edge in his voice. "I'll call him. I gotta run."

"Yeah. I understand. Mike. I'm sorry." But he'd already hung up.

❖ Chapter Thirty-Eight ❖

Brooke and Mike hadn't seen much of each other all week. She missed him, and she hoped it was just a matter of circumstance—them both being busy—and not that it had something to do with the information about Goto. She knew that hurt him, and whatever glitch there was in the system that should have alerted them as victim family members, it didn't change the fact that Rick and Mike were probably both reliving those painful memories.

We both have scars to heal. His words were still clear. Hers were easier to overcome.

She hoped he was okay, because she needed him. Thinking about him was making it impossible to concentrate on work.

The phone rang, breaking the semi-trance she'd fallen into.

It was her attorney. He had the signed divorce papers from Keith.

Finally. Brooke glanced at the time in the bottom right hand of her computer screen. 5:46 p.m. She gloried briefly in the moment. Tears tickled her eyelashes and her mood buoyed. There had been times when she'd wondered if she'd live to see this day.

That terrible night had triggered events in her favor. What a relief. Keith's attorney had talked him into signing the papers to help with the pending charges against him for abducting her that night. He'd spend only a few days in jail with a prolonged probation and counseling, but the end to this mistake was at least in sight, and she wouldn't have to worry about him bothering her anymore. That part of her life would be behind her as soon as her attorney could get a court date.

She picked up the phone to call Jenny and then placed it back down. If Jenny were in town, this would be their night to do dinner. Maybe she'd call her at seven during their regular get-together time like a virtual girls' night.

Brooke cleared her desk, and jotted a couple items on a grocery list while her computer took its own sweet time to shut down. Finally, the fan silenced and she slid the warm machine into her briefcase. She hiked her purse and laptop over her shoulder, and she was on her way.

Brooke stopped at Spratt's Market in town.

square. With her basket nearly full, she drew a line through the last thing on her list. She stopped and pulled out a bouquet of fresh flowers with lots of daisies in it. She laid them across her purse in the front of the cart, and headed for the cashier.

She pulled the plastic sacks over her wrists and headed for her car parallel-parked along the curb just outside. Just as she tried to twist and shuffle the bags and her keys, a man in a red baseball cap stepped up next to her.

"Let me help you with that." He smiled. "You've got your hands full."

She hesitated, but only for a moment. "That's really nice of you. Thanks." She handed off two of the slippery plastic bags, freeing her hand to unlock the car. "I appreciate the help."

Brooke opened the car door, then turned when she heard her name called from down the street. She spun to look over her other shoulder. It was Connor Buckham, waving and walking in her direction.

The man shoved the bags onto the seat of the car, but when she turned back around to say thanks, he was already gone.

"Hey, girl," Connor said.

"Good to see you. It's been a while," Brooke said.

"Who was that guy?"

"Good Samaritan. He offered to hold my stuff while I was trying to get into the car. Wasn't that nice?" Brooke leaned in and placed her remaining bags on the passenger seat, and then stood by the open door. "Oh, and here's some news you'll appreciate."

"Good news, I hope."

"Great news. Keith signed the divorce papers."

"I know you're thankful for that," Connor said. "I take it you got good service from our new investigator."

"Mike? Absolutely. Thank you so much for the connection. I can't thank you enough."

"Glad to hear it. He seems to be a good addition to the town." Connor checked his watch. "I've got to run. Got to pick up some chops before Spratt's closes. That's one of the bad things about little towns like ours. Streets roll right up on you if you're not careful."

"That's for sure," Brooke said.

She headed home feeling a little lonely with Jenny out of town. She made a salad, then went out on the deck to call her. She sat with her feet up in the oversize teak chair and dialed Jenny. "Hey, girl. It's our dinner night, so I'm surprising you with a virtual dinner night. Can you talk?"

Jenny's voice exploded over the line. "Yes! It's so good to hear from you. I'm missing y'all and all the fun."

"Planning a party that big is work, Jenny. It's fun for me, but I know it would not be fun for you."

"Whatever. I can't wait to get home. I'm just sick about this thing with that Goto guy out of jail. Rick is five kinds of mad. How are things going with you and Mike?"

"Been quiet since the news. Same as Rick. Jenny, the pain in his voice when he heard . . . It was gut-wrenching." She could still feel that twist in her gut. "I think he pounded a hole in his wall."

"Can you blame him?"

"Not really, but I'm a little worried. I haven't spoken to him since. What's Rick saying?"

"He's not talking about it either."

"Makes me worry." *Mike, why won't you let me help you? I'd be there for you too.*

❖ Chapter Thirty-Nine ❖

Somehow Brooke's lawyer was able to snag an opening on the docket for the divorce hearing. She'd been so nervous that something would go wrong that she hadn't even been able to drink her coffee this morning, but now she was pushing through the revolving door of the Virginia Beach Courthouse with a huge smile of satisfaction on her face. She'd waited so long for this. To have the divorce papers in her hand felt powerful.

She nodded to two men making their way up the walk. "Good afternoon." She flashed a bright smile.

They nodded in return. Their eyes followed her as they half-continued their conversation, and she saw one of them trip as he misjudged the curb.

She shook her hair from her face as she hopped off the curb, clipping along toward her car parked in the far corner of the packed lot.

Brooke hummed a little tune to the sound of her heels clicking the pavement, accenting the beats by patting the papers in her hand against her stockinged leg. She felt like skipping through the parking lot, but she didn't want to push her luck and re-sprain her ankle, which would totally ruin her day.

The crepe myrtles in each of the median barriers bobbed in bright shocks of pink. The pavement was littered with the papery flowers that had shaken free from the trees in the storm overnight. Finally, she reached her car. Checking her reflection in the window as she opened the unlocked door, she ran her hand through her hair, then scattered the bangs. There was no taming a hairdo in Virginia humidity, and this spring was dishing up some Indian summer weather. Her hair felt like it was getting bigger by the minute.

She was wearing her favorite Kasper suit. Her *lucky suit,* and it had proved itself again. The soft pink made her lips and cheeks look rosy and her green eyes even greener. She even had on her favorite lucky shoes, pink-and-gray snakeskin pumps. They were old, but the luck hadn't worn out and she wasn't about to retire them until it had. She hadn't taken any chances, right down to wearing her lucky underwear, because one can never be too lucky.

Since Keith was still on probation and had finally signed the papers days ago, having the court decision in hand put Brooke on top of the world. The nightmare was officially over.

A cardinal skipped between branches in one of the trees in the median. "Cardinal, good luck!" she said out loud. "I love that." She tossed her purse into the passenger seat, and slid in clutching the papers in her hand. She kissed them and looked to the sky, then hugged them to her chest.

"Thank you, thank you, and thank you!" She let the papers fall to the passenger seat and started the engine. The air-conditioning blew across her face, drying her bangs.

After all this time, she could finally put it behind her. She picked up the divorce papers again, scanning over what she'd already memorized. "I am going to frame you," she promised the divorce papers. "I'm going to get you the nicest mats and frames that I can find and hang you right up on a wall, where I can smile every time I look at you." She reached back and pulled her briefcase up.

As she slid the papers inside, a rap on the window startled her. She whirled around, just as the car door flew open. She yelped and her heart pounded as fast as a horse on race day.

A flood of relief washed over her as she recognized the intruder, who had casually positioned himself in her car doorjamb.

"You scared the pudding out of me!" she said swatting at Mike's pant leg. "How could you? Her heart was still pounding like crazy.

"Excuse me. You should be more careful You've already forgotten everything I taught you? What did I tell you about locking your car door?" Mike's remark was made in fun, but th serious undertones did not go unnoticed.

"Get in the car. Lock the car," she recited.

Somehow, Mike seemed to appear out o nowhere at the oddest times and today he ha perfect timing to share her good news.

"I know, I know, but that's not fair. You snuc up!" She silently reprimanded herself for forget ting the most simple of caution points. *Get in th car. Lock the car.* Simple as pressing a butto "What are you doing here in Virginia Beac today, anyway?"

"I had to be in court this morning, and I didn sneak. I walked right up and opened the door." H leaned down on one knee, and all six feet thre inches of him took up the space of the open doo

"How are you doing?" she asked. "I've been s worried about you since the news." She watche the cloud replace the smile in his eyes.

"I'm fine. Dealing with it," he said.

Brooke could almost see his gears switch. H

had no intention of talking about that with her. "I saw you trip that guy back there, by the way."

"I didn't trip anybody."

"Not physically, but it was your fault. That guy was staring at you when he tripped up the curb."

"Hey, that's what he gets for staring. I'm innocent." She laughed, shutting down the engine of the car. Mike always smelled good. He looked good, too, in a pair of khakis and a blue dress shirt. "I'm so happy I could just bust. Can you believe my divorce is really final? I swear I should have you pinch me so I know that it's real."

Her smile was irresistible. Mike caught her lips in an unplanned kiss. She was about the only good thing in his life right now, but that didn't change what he knew he had to do.

"Wow. What a day," she said, pressing her fingers to her lips then smiling.

He released her. "I love it when you smile."

"You are part of the reason for this big silly grin. I really appreciate everything you've done for me," she said. "I'm lucky to have you in my life."

"Just think, if you had decided not to hire me before Keith tried that little stunt, no telling what would've happened. We may have never crossed paths again." *And maybe I wouldn't be in this position right now.*

Brooke put her hand up. "Enough about me. More importantly, how are you doing?"

"Want to talk about that over coffee?" Mike

289

asked with hope. Perhaps he'd be able to talk to her in person.

"I'm due back at the office." She checked her watch. "In fact, I'm running late. Can I get a rain check?"

"Those rain checks are stacking up. You just give me a yell when things settle down for you. Oh, and remember—get in the car, lock the car. No exceptions."

"Yes, sir." She gave him a wink.

"I'm not kidding, Brooke. Be careful." She had no idea how worried he was about her right now. With Goto out and about there was just no telling what might happen. The system might think that guy was ready to be in society, but Mike knew that monster wasn't rehabilitated. No way. Not someone that damn sick.

She smiled like all was good in her little world. "You'd think I'd have already learned that the hard way."

Mike stood to his full height, and stepped back from the car.

Brooke met his gaze. "Thanks for sharing my celebration. It's good to see you today." She held her hand to shade her eyes to look at him as he stepped away from the car out into the sun.

"Drive careful." He stepped up on the landscaped median as she revved up the engine on the Corvette and pulled slowly out of the parking lot.

Mike made a motion with his hand for her to lock the door. She shrugged her shoulders, pushed the button to lock the doors, and signaled an okay sign.

Mike gave her the thumbs-up sign and waved her off.

With Mike still in her rearview mirror, she grabbed her cell phone and punched Jenny's number on speed dial. She picked up on the second ring.

"You're the second to know," Brooke said. "It's a done deal. Keith didn't get a thing!"

"Oh, Brooke, that's great. You must be so relieved. Wait a sec. Why am I not the *first* to know?"

"Mike caught me in the parking lot at the courthouse."

"Of course he did. That guy shows up everywhere. He better not try to take my best friend status. I'll kick his ass," said Jenny.

"Not a chance. You and I know so much about each other. We *have* to be best friends. We have too much blackmail material on each other."

"Brooke, darling, I hate to dash your self-esteem, but you've never done anything that scandalous that was worth blackmailing."

"Be nice. This is my day. Don't be raining on it."

"You're right. Sorry. Congratulations. Good riddance to Keith. Now you have no excuses to not get serious with Mike," Jenny said.

"It wouldn't be so awful to be alone for a while." But in her heart she knew she didn't mean that.

"You've been alone for too long already. Let go, girl. You can't always be in control of everything. No risk, no fun."

"Aren't I a little old to be sowing wild oats?" Brooke asked.

"God, I hope not, because I'm not that far behind you. But then I have my Mr. Right."

"I know. I'm so tickled about you and Rick, but Jenny, you're a hopeless romantic."

"Guilty."

"How's Rick handling the news about Goto?" Brooke asked.

"He still doesn't want to talk about it, so I'm trying to be patient and understanding. How about Mike? What did he say?"

"Same. He avoided the question, but I could see it in his eyes when I asked. Kind of wish I hadn't brought it up." She glanced at her watch again. "I have to dial into a meeting in a few minutes. I gotta run. I just wanted to share the news."

"Thanks for calling to let me know, but the next time Mike tries to take my spot as number one info-getting friend, kick his ass to the curb for me, would ya?"

"Later, bye." Brooke smiled as she realized she'd picked that saying up from Mike. It was good to see him. Really good.

❖ Chapter Forty ❖

The next morning Brooke's phone rang bright and early. The name on the display put an instant smile on her face.

"Have your feet hit the ground from the divorce decree yet?" Mike asked.

His voice sounded good. "A hello would be nice," she said.

"Hello. Have your feet hit the ground yet?"

"As a matter of fact, I'm still pretty much floating around. It feels great to officially close that chapter of my life."

"I bet."

"I've been thinking about framing those divorce papers. Do you think it would be tacky to hang them on my office wall?"

"You might check with Martha Stewart or some other notable about that. I wouldn't know."

Brooke eyed her diploma and several awards on her office wall. "I don't know. I think this might look pretty good. Hell, it means more to me than my diploma and awards do!" She cocked her head and considered it. "I'm thinking Martha would be all for this."

"Got enough energy left for dinner tonight? I wanted to see you."

"Sure." She wished she hadn't answered so quickly.

"Great. Nothing fancy. I thought we'd run up to the diner. That work for you?"

"Yes. They've got the best fried chicken around."

"Deal. I'll pick you up at your place at five thirty."

"I'll be ready."

He pulled into her driveway and she was at the truck before he could get out. "Thanks for the unexpected call."

"You're welcome," he said.

His mood seemed stoic. "Are you okay?"

"I'm fine."

"Fine?" She looked for a sign of a smile but there wasn't one. "You don't sound so fine."

He gave her a half smile but he was trying too hard. It took just a few minutes to get over to the diner on Main Street. They placed their orders at the counter then took their drinks to a corner booth.

"How's the party going for Rick and Jenny?" Mike asked.

"Right on schedule."

"Cracking the whip, I hear."

She wondered if Rick had complained. "Maybe just a little, but with Jenny out of town there's a lot to do. Careful or we'll recruit you to help too."

The waitress slid their dinners in front of them.

and Mike kept the talk to safe subjects like the weather. That made her nervous.

Mike put his fork down. "This has been kind of hard for me, Brooke."

"What's wrong? Did something happen?"

He looked toward the ceiling. His lips pressed in a thin line. "I'm not going to be able to see you."

She dropped her fork with a loud clang. "Excuse me," she said to the folks at the next table. She picked up her fork and leaned forward. "You what?"

"I'm sorry. I can't put you in danger like that. If something happened to you . . . Brooke, I know what it's like to lose someone I love to a creep like Goto. I can't risk it again. He might be out, but that guy isn't healed. He's a killer. He'll kill again."

"You love me?"

"It doesn't matter. You just being around me puts you at risk. I won't do it."

She reached over and took his hand in hers. Not long ago he'd given her the best night of her life, then he'd freaked out and begged for a second chance, and now that the divorce was final and things seemed like they'd gotten back on track she was still going to lose. Would she ever catch a break?

"You can't do this, Mike. We'll be fine. He wouldn't dare risk coming around you. He'd be the number one suspect if anything happened."

"That kind of man doesn't give a shit about that."

She pushed her plate to the edge of the table. "Mike. We can do this. Together."

"You're not hearing me. This guy is dangerous. I'm putting you in danger."

"You are not putting me in danger," she said. Her voice had gotten a little loud and people around them were staring.

Mike pulled a wad of money out of his front pocket and dropped a couple twenties on the table. "Come on. Let's go."

She walked out behind him, and opened the door to the truck.

"Are you okay?" she asked again before climbing in. "I'm not letting you lose me because of him. What's the difference if I'm dead or not if we're not together?"

He slid behind the steering wheel. "No. I'm not okay. And you are at risk. I'm sorry if it hurts you, but I wanted you to at least understand why I can't see you. I will not put you in danger. It's not up for debate."

She stood there. "What makes you think you get to even decide?"

"I just did. It's for the best."

"For who? For you? Well, I think it's lame, and I'm tired of you ping-ponging my heart around. Just for the record, I'm in love with you too." She slammed the door and started walking home. It wasn't that far and there was not enough space in that truck cab for the two of them.

She muttered every curse word and told him off six ways to Sunday under her breath every step of the way home. She heard him roll up behind her. She wasn't getting in that truck; she didn't care if he did follow her. He wouldn't change her mind this time.

When she got to her house she saw him go to the end of the street and turn around.

She went inside and didn't set the alarm. Just for good measure. "Just who the hell do you think you are telling me what we're going to do?"

She watched him pull away, then a familiar car caught her attention just down the street in front of the Parkers' house. They'd left on vacation earlier in the week. That prickly feeling crawled up her arms. She hadn't had that in a while.

Mike drove right past the vehicle, but something wouldn't let her let go so easy. She stood there watching from the window, and then someone popped up in the driver's seat.

Her heart seized for a moment in time. Her eyes stayed glued to the car. Her heart pounded so hard it felt like it was in her throat.

She set the alarm and watched the car go on by; the driver stopped at the next mailbox and slid a flyer behind the flag, then did the same at the next house.

She heaved a sigh of relief. "I must be paranoid." But just in case, she twisted the deadbolt too. Mike must have *all* of her emotions out of whack.

❖ Chapter Forty-One ❖

Goto had ducked low in the seat of the blue Pontiac as Mike's truck passed by.

He had to be a lot more careful now that his cover had been blown. When he'd stopped in to see Wheelie and he told him that there'd been a write-up in the paper about him being paroled, Goto's heart had fallen. They'd been so careful. If the victims' families realized that alert hadn't gone out, they could trace it back to Wheelie's second cousin. She'd been in that job long enough that no one even took a second look at her work. But now . . . if they started getting nosy . . . that could cause a string of problems. His wasn't the only file that had pointed victim contacts to members of Wheelie's friends and family.

After all they'd done to be sure the alert didn't go out, he hadn't moved fast enough. It could ruin everything. But he and Wheelie made a plan, and now he had to be careful, but that would all change soon. Very soon.

Goto peered over the edge of the window. Mike didn't pull into her driveway; instead he drove to the end of the street and then turned around. When Hartman's truck rumbled by, he figured the coast was clear.

He hadn't considered the lady of the house might be staring right at him when he slid back up in the driver's seat.

He had to be careful. This was no time to get lazy. There was already so much invested in this plan. He had the location and everything figured out. He couldn't blow it now.

Goto gathered his composure, and rolled toward the next house on the block. He leaned low across the passenger seat and put a pizza flyer on the mailbox. He stayed low in the seat for a two-count, and then lifted just as slowly as before. It would look like this was exactly what he had been doing when he popped up before her eyes earlier. He idled to the next mailbox and did the same. The perfect cover.

Who woulda thought the flyers would come in so handy? The huge stack would allow him to continue the charade as long as necessary. He'd never had any intention of really distributing them. He'd been collecting an extra thirty bucks a week for it, even though he'd been dumping them in the trash. Being employed was a condition of his parole, so he was willing to be flexible and volunteer for just about anything to keep the shitty job. The last thing he wanted was to end up with one of those tracking devices around his ankle or in a group residence under watchful eyes. Either would blow the plans he'd so carefully made.

The lame job had turned out to be a blessing in disguise. Goto continued tucking flyers in mailboxes all the way down the street in case she was still watching him from a window. When he got to the back of the neighborhood he pulled into the playground. He didn't want to risk passing her house again until she was asleep. It would do no good to have her on the lookout for him.

He stretched across the front seat and flipped open the spiral tablet to the list of lottery numbers, pulled a calculator out of his shirt pocket, and did some calculations, trying to come up with the winning numbers. Algorithms covered the side of the page, representing the trend of the last dozen winning series. He sucked on the end of the pencil and then jotted down his predictions for later. He shoved a hand in his pocket and pulled out a wad of money and slapped it on the dash. Nine bucks and some change, and he still needed gas.

There could be money still in her fancy-schmancy-ass car. It wouldn't hurt to take a look. Hell, he was already in the neighborhood.

The streetlights had come on a long while ago. He flicked his lighter to see the digital numbers on the stick-on clock. Almost 10:50 p.m. She'd be fast asleep.

Goto drove slowly toward Brooke's house and parked a few doors down. He stepped out of the car and clicked the door shut. No dogs barked.

The coast was clear. He made his way closer to her car, pausing near the bushes along the sidewalk to reevaluate the situation. Still quiet. He walked toward the car and pulled on the handle. It opened easily. He pressed the button on the inside jamb to dim the inside lights.

He spotted the coins and a crumpled bill in the console. "Jackpot!" He quickly scooped most of the change and the bill into his pocket. You'd think she'd have learned after he'd stolen the money last time.

He shut the door and ran back to his car, then got the hell out of there.

Adrenaline was a familiar friend. He hooted and spanked the steering wheel. He hadn't lost his knack at all.

He drove up the street to the nearest convenience store. Sitting in his car under the bright lights, he pulled out the contents of his pocket to see how much more than nine dollars he had now.

He smoothed out the bill he'd heisted from the console. "Hot damn. A five." He slapped the steering wheel. "I knew my luck was changing." Then he counted out the change. There was a lot of change. Mostly quarters. "Three dollars and ten, twenty, thirty, thirty-five, sixty, and eighty-five cents." He smiled wide. "Eight eighty-five. Not bad for a minute's work."

He walked into the store and bought his lottery

ticket, and prepaid for ten dollars in gas. Goto licked his lips.

He looked up, surveying his surroundings. Mike Hartman passed by in his truck. Goto turned the key, but the car didn't start. It just cranked. "Don't conk out on me now, you piece-of-crap car." He tried again, and on the third crank it finally caught and fired up.

Goto pulled onto the road and sped up to catch Mike. He followed him for a good mile and a half. He wondered where he was headed. They stopped at a light just out of town.

He messed with the radio station, waiting for the light to turn, when a loud rap scared the living daylights out of him.

Mike Hartman stood there, a Maglite in his hand resting on the window jamb. He could just as easily slam him in the head. He moved toward the passenger seat. Shit. He'd gotten sloppy.

Mike leaned into the car, and took Goto by the collar. "I'm telling you this once. Don't give me a reason to kill you. All that it'll take is for me to see you in this town again." He shoved Goto back against the console. "And if you're going to tail someone, do a better job of it."

Goto sat there wondering why the guy hadn't killed him right then and there.

Mike slammed the truck door and peeled rubber through the red light.

The light turned, but Goto still felt a little green

in the gills after the confrontation. Wheelie would kick his ass for making such a stupid mistake. He headed back to Wheelie's garage. He'd have to get him to expedite things. It was his only chance to save the plan.

❖ Chapter Forty-Two ❖

Rick had proven to be the best assistant party coordinator Brooke could have asked for. Still feeling like she'd been destroyed by the bomb Mike had dropped on her last night, Brooke sat at her desk checking off tasks on the Hillcrest Joyful Kixx party plan. Jenny had called last night to let her know that she'd bought the perfect hat as a gift for her. If that hat Jenny had picked out for herself was any indication, Brooke feared it couldn't be good. But then again, right now nothing felt like it would turn out well.

Satisfied that they'd be on time, with less than a week to go, she printed out a fresh copy of the remaining tasks and e-mailed Rick an updated copy. Brooke topped off her cup of coffee and pulled up the online newspaper before getting down to the day's appointments.

"GOTO HELL Murderer Found Dead" was the headline that met her eyes. Her hand shook as she scrolled down the computer screen to the story below.

Adams Grove, Va.—A 39-year-old man died Wednesday night in a fire at Sergio's Pizza in Adams Grove, according to the Holland County coroner.

It took firefighters more than four hours to control the blaze at the popular restaurant. Sergio's Pizza went up in smoke just after closing Wednesday evening. A passerby called 911 when they saw flames in the back of the shop.

The Holland County fire chief said the fire started in one of the restaurant's wood-fired brick pizza ovens, and it appeared the victim was trying to put out the fire when he collapsed.

Firefighters had a tough time containing the fire in the old structure, but nearby buildings escaped damage.

The victim was pronounced dead at the scene, and later identified as Franklin Daniel Gotorow.

Gotorow was convicted of first-degree murder eight years ago for the death of Jackie Hartman, a 23-year-old student, in the GOTO HELL murder, and sentenced to twenty years in jail.

According to parole board records, Gotorow first appeared before the board five years ago, but was denied parole. He went back before the board in January of this year, and was released two months later. The owner said that Gotorow had been a dependable worker and pitched in often before and after hours.

Officials said the fire does not appear to be suspicious.

Brooke took a big sip of coffee to wash down the bad taste in her mouth. She'd always been one to believe once someone served their time, you had to clean the slate. Funny how that seemed so unjust when you knew the parties affected by the hideous deed.

He might not have killed Mike, but he sure had killed what could have been a good relationship between her and Mike. In a way she felt kind of glad that Goto was dead, but that somehow made her feel bad at the same time.

The phone rang, taking her mind off the sad chain of events. It was Rick. He'd just read the article too.

"I understand," she said. He wanted to reschedule their plans for the next day. "Have you contacted Mike?"

"I just texted him. Can you believe the guy was working practically right in our backyards? No one even recognized him."

"Anything I can do?"

"No. Kind of ironic that he died in a fire with the whole hell thing he had going. We all know that's where he'll be rotting too."

"It is. How are you feeling about all of it?"

Rick let out a sigh. "At first I was thrilled. Then I started second-guessing that it could be true. Mike had the same reaction. Hell, he even went down to the coroner's office to see the body."

"I'm sure it's not unusual to feel that way, Rick. What y'all have been through because of that man is just unthinkable."

"Well, he's gone now. There was no mistaking it. Right down to the perfect teeth and tattoo on his arm . . . it was him. He won't ever bother anyone again."

"When you talk to Mike, let him know I asked about him. I know this is a lot to deal with."

"I will," he promised.

Brooke hung up the phone feeling sad for Rick and worried about Mike. She dialed his number. "Please answer," she said, but it went straight to voicemail. She didn't bother to leave a message.

The party was this weekend and Mike had already gotten word back to Rick via text that he'd be there. Funny how guys could just text "I'll be there" and call it a day. She and Jenny were talking hours each day.

When Brooke walked out of her office there was a box in the waiting area.

"That's for you," Victoria said.

"Last time you said that we had flowers on parade."

"You don't have to remind me of that. I still think it's about the most romantic thing a guy has ever done."

"Even if he did have to screw up to initiate the plan." Brooke looked at the return address on the box. "This must be the hat from Jenny."

"For Saturday?"

"I know. Cutting it close, aren't we?"

"You got that right. I've already got my hat. My sister and I made them. They're so cute. I haven't had that much fun with flowers and tulle since I got married."

"Well, brace yourself. With Jenny you never know what to expect." Brooke tugged on the tape. "It better be cute."

"Well, open it," Victoria said, handing her a pair of scissors.

Brooke lunged for the scissors and opened the box. "She'd better not have me wearing orange. I'll kill her."

"You'd look pretty no matter what she sent."

"You have to say that. I'm your boss."

"True," Victoria laughed.

Brooke peeled back layers of lavender tissue paper to find the hat. "It's beautiful." She ran her fingers across delicate beading across the edge of the magenta brim, then lifted it atop her head. "What do you think?"

"I think Jenny may get upstaged. That's gorgeous. I wonder if it's vintage," she said, fingering the soft fabric.

"Probably." Brooke struck a pose. "They might be able to spot me from the NASA space station in this thing, but I have to admit, I like it."

❖ Chapter Forty-Three ❖

Two days later, Derby Day to be exact, Brooke answered the door to Jenny standing there in jeans and a T-shirt. "Not quite the theme party attire I had in mind," Brooke said, then threw her arms around her best friend. "I'm so glad you're home!"

"Me too! I've missed you like crazy."

"How are you feeling? You look wonderful. Positively glowing."

Jenny laughed. "Puking your guts out each morning will do that. Mornings are rough, but I'm getting used to it. Small price to pay for something so amazing."

"I hear ya." Brooke gave Jenny's outfit the once-over. "Please tell me you don't think you're wearing that."

"Oh, don't you worry. I have the perfect outfit in the right colors in my car. I'm going to change as soon as we get to Rick's house. Want to ride with me?"

"No. I'll follow you. I have a feeling you're

going to want to stick around long after the party tonight."

Jenny raised her brow. "You're probably right. I missed Rick so much. We talked every single day, but I couldn't wait to get back to him. I feel like a teenager. Do you think I'm totally nuts?"

"No. I don't." Brooke was dying to tell Jenny what she knew—that today wasn't just Derby Day and the announcement that the two of them had partnered on an investment in one of the Hillcrest horses. Rick was planning that second little surprise announcement—asking Jenny to marry him. It made Brooke a little nervous that things were moving so fast with them, but really there'd not been even one red flag, so all she could do was pray that it was right and the sooner the better in Jenny's situation anyway.

They both drove over to Rick's. Everything was already in place. The old barn had been transformed into a miniature Kentucky Derby. Tall banners with the pattern from the silks that Hillcrest Joyful Kixx's jockey would wear in today's race brightened everything right down to the purple shimmery sand she'd had tinted and sprinkled throughout to match the silks. With a little money and innovation, any place could look wonderful. This party-planner gig had turned out to be a lot of fun. Spending other people's money had a certain appeal too.

They'd borrowed long tables from the local Ruritan Club and covered them in black table cloths. The centerpieces were made of roses, the flower of the Derby. She hadn't been able to resist having Teddy Hardy create miniature garlands of roses like the winner gets as a good luck charm at each table setting.

The big screen that Rick had gotten wasn't just a big screen, it was a trailer that held a movie size screen. Those horses would be large and in charge as they raced across the finish line.

They'd been lucky it had turned out to be such a nice day. Early May was always unpredictable in southern Virginia. It could have been sweater weather, but instead they'd been graced with a perfect sunny day.

The caterer had already set up and Teddy from Floral and Hardy was fussing with the lavish arrangements on the tables.

"I can't believe there isn't anything left for us to do," Jenny said.

"Rick was a great helper, and his open wallet made it nice. We were able to get everything prepared ahead of time and the professionals are putting the last-minute touches in place. All we have to do is grip and grin and hopefully win."

"You're the best friend. Thank you so much for all of your help."

"It was my pleasure. All of it, and I really loved getting to know Rick. I can see why you are so taken by him." And Brooke meant it. She couldn't wait to see Jenny's face when Rick surprised her with the engagement ring later. If that horse ran a winning race it would be one heckuva trifecta for those two.

Brooke and Jenny parked on either side of Rick's truck, and as soon as he spotted them, Rick whisked Jenny right off her feet.

Brooke took a step back, feeling a little in the way.

Rick finally put her down. "Brooke and I have become like brother and sister over the past couple of weeks working on all of this together."

"So I heard," Jenny said.

Rick snuck a knowing look over toward Brooke. "Yep. It's going to be a great party. I can't wait to share all of our news."

"Me too," Jenny said as she reached up and kissed Rick.

"I have to get outside and help finish all the hookups for the race." Rick left by way of the back door and Jenny and Brooke went upstairs so Jenny could get dressed.

Jenny started unpacking her outfit and dressing. "What's the latest with you and Mike?"

"Still off."

"What did you do?" Jenny glared at her. "Tell me you didn't chase him off."

"It wasn't me. I tried to save it this time. He freaked out over Goto being out of jail and said he wouldn't put me in danger." Brooke looked away. "Now the guy is dead, but I haven't heard a word from Mike. I don't know. It's just not meant to be."

A flash of bright red caught her eye as a bird perched on the limb of the blooming crepe myrtle. "Cardinal, good luck. Where were you when I needed you? Maybe cardinals aren't good luck anymore."

"Or maybe they are," Jenny said. "I want this to be a perfect day. For both of us. Oh, dear." Jenny's voice was serious. "Look who's coming up the walk."

"Who?" Brooke ran to the window.

Jenny smiled to Brooke with a look of satisfaction. "I bet Mike's coming up to apologize. That Goto creep is dead. No reason to mess up a good thing now. And you'd better accept that apology, or he'll have to keep you out of danger from me."

"It's too late. It's not going to work. He's batted my emotions around so much over the past few weeks. I just can't deal with it."

"But you love him."

Brooke leveled a stare at Jenny. "I do. I love him. In a more powerful way than I've ever felt love before, but it's not right."

"Sometimes you are so bullheaded," Jenny said. "Wait here. I left my hat in the car. I'm going to go get it."

Brooke waited until Jenny closed the door, then walked over to the window to look for Mike. She didn't see his truck or him. He was probably headed down to the barn. *Thank goodness; maybe he won't stay.*

Mike climbed the stairs to the master bedroom at Rick's. First the whole Goto thing. Now this. What more could happen? Jenny had said Brooke was up there getting ready.

He hesitated for a moment before twisting the knob and going in. She was standing near the window. The wide brim of her bright-pink hat hung low on her shoulders, but her hair fell longer. He knew the texture of her hair, the curve of that hip.

"You look pretty," he said from right behind her.

Brooke spun around. Her eyes met Mike's and her heart dropped an inch. "Hi. I—I didn't hear you come in." She stepped back, putting some space between them. "I've never seen you dressed up. You look—" She shook her head, searching for the right word. "You look so handsome."

He stepped forward. "I'm sorry about the way I acted. It wasn't fair."

Her lips trembled, but she didn't say anything.

"I didn't want to put you in harm's way. I know that I've really messed up with all the back and forth with you, but if anything had happened—" He closed his eyes, and shook his head. When he opened his eyes he looked straight into Brooke's. "How could I have lived knowing that it was my fault?"

She reached for his hand. "Goto's dead. He can't hurt me or you again." A single tear slid down her cheek.

"It's hard to believe it." He took her into his arms and held her. "I'm sorry I hurt you." The warmth he felt with her in his arms was right. He pulled back and took a small flat box from his jacket pocket. "I have something for you." He handed her the slim box.

"For me?" The silver-wrapped box had a single slip of purple ribbon wrapped around it. "Should I open it now?" she asked, just barely over a whisper.

"Please do." He nodded, urging her to open it. "I don't know if you can ever forgive me, but I wanted you to have this."

"I don't deserve you." Her voice shook. What a stupid thing to say. She didn't have him.

"Yeah, you do." Mike shifted his weight to the other leg and took in a deep breath. "Open it."

Brooke removed the delicate silver paper and opened the box. Her hand flew to her chest, and tears filled her eyes. "Oh, Mike . . ." the words trailed as she took in the beauty of the gift. She lifted the delicate antique white- and yellow-gold jeweled hair comb from the box. "Mike, you shouldn't have."

"I wanted you to have it. A special gift, for a very special lady." He gave her a wink.

"This is the comb that we saw in Carolina that day, isn't it?" It was a question, but she knew the answer. "How did you get it? We were together the whole time."

"I went back without you the next day."

"You've had it all this time?" Her hands trembled. Tears welled from the sweetness of the gesture.

"Yep. I pictured you wearing it on our wedding day." Brooke looked stunned.

"My gosh!" Jenny had walked into the room. "He's asking you to marry him." Jenny's mouth dropped wide and she ran to Mike's side. "Are you asking her to marry you? You are!"

"No. Not exactly. Well, not yet. I was thinking just to be together. Give it a try. You know, one step at a time and all that."

Brooke nodded. "Of course. Baby steps. Don't go crazy, Jenny. This is a good restart." Tears spilled over the rim of her eyes. "I love you, Mike. I want to love you but you hurt me. You can't turn me away when things go wrong."

"I'm sorry. I was scared. I couldn't lose you, and then . . . It was stupid. You have to forgive me." He held her gently, his hand on the small of her back. Mike dabbed her eyes. "Don't cry."

She fanned herself to dry the tears as she walked over to the full-length pedestal mirror.

She removed the fancy hat and placed it on the side table, then pulled her hair into a twist and slipped the comb in to secure it. She twisted in the mirror. The delicate pearls, diamonds, and the rubies glistened. It could not have been more perfect. "How's that?" she asked, modeling for him in a twirl.

"Exquisite." Their eyes held for a moment too long.

Jenny cleared her throat. "You can't cover that with your hat. It's too pretty."

"We said hats are mandatory."

"What's a rule if it's not broken a time or two?"

The caterer opened up the buffet. A whole hog—rooter to tooter—was being chopped and sliced by chefs at two different stations. Apple in the mouth and all, because that was just a given in Adams Grove, topped off with mint juleps and other things Derby. Everyone relaxed into the pace, eating, drinking, dancing, and socializing. Kids ran around and played, while the adults talked. Mike had taken her out on the dance floor and she'd been surprised that for a big guy he was really a good dancer. Was there anything that guy couldn't do?

"I need to run and check on some things," she said to Mike.

He feigned major disappointment, then smiled "Don't leave me long."

"Ten minutes max. I promise," she said as she was swept away into the crowd of Rick and Jenny's friends and business acquaintances.

Brooke made sure everything was moving along and then went to the house to catch a short break and a second wind to keep up with all the action.

Jenny took a sip of punch and waved to Rick, who was dancing with an older woman from the church.

Mike walked over to join her and grabbed a mint julep from a passing waiter.

"Don't you ever hurt my best friend again," Jenny warned.

He searched her face for a moment. He needed to say it out loud to someone. "When my wife died I didn't think I would ever love again. Brooke changed all that."

Jenny cocked her head slightly. "She's in love with you."

"I fell for Brooke the day I met her." He stared off as if he were replaying it in his mind. Mike's words trailed off as he shook the ice in his glass nervously. Where was she? She'd said ten minutes max. He glanced at his watch again. It was going on half an hour, and there was that feeling again. The one he got when something was getting ready to go really wrong.

❖ Chapter Forty-Four ❖

Brooke walked out on the front porch to get some air. The excitement of Rick planning to propose to Jenny had been so romantic and then Mike showing up was almost too much to process. With the push of a hundred fifty excited people ready to cheer on Hillcrest Joyful Kixx in the Derby she'd needed just a few minutes to get her thoughts together.

She sat on the porch swing. The sounds coming from the back of the house were comforting, but something didn't feel right. She put her foot on the decking to stop the swing. For a moment she was afraid to even take a breath. The feeling of being watched was familiar, and not in a good way.

She scanned the yard around the porch, but everything looked fine. The celebratory noise from the barn reminded her that this was a happy occasion, and there was no sense spoiling it with some bad vibes.

The phone in the house rang. She ran inside and glanced at the caller ID but it said UNKNOWN.

"Hello? Hello? Is anyone there? Joyner residence." Her greetings were met with silence. She dropped the phone back in its cradle and started to go back out on the front porch. The phone rang again. She took the steps back inside and grabbed it mid-ring.

"Hello."

Someone pulled her backward and a rag went over her face. She kicked her feet, trying to get traction on the slick wooden floor to pull free, but the arm pulled her back farther and lifted her off the ground.

The harder she struggled, the more she seemed to lose ground. Then everything went dark.

❖ Chapter Forty-Five ❖

She was stronger than he'd expected. He hadn't anticipated a struggle. Good thing he had talked through the plan with Wheelie. That guy knew all the ins and outs of everything. He'd received an unexpected lecture about how things in real life weren't like they looked on TV and picked up two or three good tips about making the chloroform mixture. He'd gotten the warning too that it might kill her, but then he'd just have to go to plan B. No problem. He always had a plan B.

There was no way he would have won the struggle she gave him if it had lasted much longer. Good thing he had the help of the chloroform, because she didn't seem willing to give up on her own.

His arms burned from the mixture on the rag and just when he thought he couldn't hold on any longer, she softened in his grip. Still wearing the surgical mask, not as a disguise but to protect himself from the overwhelming fumes of the chloroform, he dropped the towel, thrust his arms under hers, and dragged her quickly toward a truck parked out front.

"Not as quick and easy as it looks in the movies, but it worked." He lifted her into the passenger seat, then slid behind the steering wheel.

He turned the keys that were dangling from the ignition like he knew they would be.

"Country folk are so damn trusting," he muttered under his breath. He didn't know how long she'd be out, so he made quick work of tying her hands together just in case. He wasn't in a hurry. He had a lot to do before tomorrow night and he would be sure to take the time to do it all perfectly according to plan this time.

He turned on the air-conditioning and let the air wash over his face. It was cool against the sweat on his skin. He pulled the truck out of the drive-way slowly so as to not attract any attention from anyone else arriving at the party. The gravel crunched under the tires of the big truck.

He knew exactly where they were going. He had been there before.

❖ Chapter Forty-Six ❖

"Have you seen Brooke?" Mike asked Rick.

"No, not in a while. She's probably checking that list of hers." Rick pulled out his cell phone and pushed redial. "No answer."

The party was in full swing, but he'd wandered through the crowd twice and didn't find her. "I'm worried. It's not like her to disappear."

Jenny cocked her head and gave Mike a look. "Y'all didn't have another fight, did you?"

"No," Mike said. The level of his anxiety rose.

One of the people in earshot said, "I think I heard Brooke tell someone she was going up to the house to do something. That was a while ago, though."

"She probably got sidetracked," Jenny said. "I'll go look for her."

Mike stopped her. "No. It's your party. You're the guest of honor. I'll go." He set his drink down on one of the tables and jogged up to the house.

"Brooke?" He called out as he threw open the back screen door, and stepped into the kitchen.

The telephone was on the floor.

Mike paused. Hearing nothing, he moved quickly through the kitchen to the living room. The front door was ajar, and on the floor nearby was the jeweled comb he'd given to her just hours ago.

He picked it up and held it in his hands.

"No." He dialed her cell phone, but as soon as the line rang he heard the echo of a cell phone ringing on the front porch. He ran outside; there on the porch near the swing—her phone.

Stay calm. There could be an explanation. Gotc is dead. You're just on high alert.

He turned and rushed back to the barn through the groups that stood talking, and climbed on the stage, taking the mic right from the singer's hands.

The band stopped playing.

"Sorry." Everyone's attention turned toward the scuffle on stage. "Sorry. This is an emergency."

Rick and Jenny ran to the stage area.

"Has anyone seen Brooke Justice? Short? Brunette?" Mike lowered the mic as he scanned the crowd, but no one responded.

Mike pulled the mic back up to his mouth "She's the only lady running around here without a hat on."

Heads shook and people mumbled.

"Sorry to interrupt." Mike jumped down.

Rick snagged his arm as he ran by. "What's up?"

"Something's wrong. She's missing."

"I'm sure there's an explanation," Jenny said trying to calm him down.

Mike held the comb out for her to see. "The phone was on the kitchen floor and this was lying next to the front door on the floor."

"She wouldn't have left that behind."

"The front door was open."

"We had that locked. No one was using the house but Brooke and me."

"I know."

"Do you think it's her ex-husband again?" Rick asked.

"Maybe. I'm calling the police. With the pending charges against him they may even still have him in custody. If not, they can run him down faster than I can. I'll get Von on the phone too."

Rick took Jenny's hand into his. "Is her car still here? We were both parked next to Rick's truck out front."

Mike nodded. "Yeah. Her car is still there, but your truck is missing."

"What can we do?" Jenny looked between Mike and Rick.

Mike's lips pulled into a tight line. "Nothing except pray I'm wrong and I'm overreacting."

"Are you thinking—" Rick didn't finish the sentence. He didn't have to. Mike was thinking exactly what he was thinking.

Just outside the front door, Mike noticed the blue rag on the ground. He picked it up and sniffed it. The sweet smell was unmistakable, and although that stuff evaporated quickly, there was still enough there to give him a slight head buzz. Chloroform. Old-school. Just like Goto. This wasn't good.

Mike pulled the front door of the house shut and jogged back to his vehicle, then punched in Sheriff Calvin's number and brought him up-to-date with what he'd just found.

Sheriff Calvin's voice held a tone of concern. "I think she would have mentioned it if she'd heard from that ex of hers. I don't see anything here that she's reported."

"Could you get someone to track him down and see what he's been up to the last couple of days?"

"Absolutely. We're on it. I'll also get an APB out on Rick's truck to see if we can locate that. Let's touch base at the top of the hour and sync up. If not sooner."

"Thanks, Sheriff. I have a couple ideas I'm running down. Just hang tight with me."

"Count on it, buddy."

Rick insisted on going with Mike. The short distance between Rick's and town seemed like miles today. Time was ticking slowly in his state of confusion. Once back at his office, Mike continued his search using the technology he had at his fingertips, which reported no unusual activities for Keith over the last couple of days.

Only fifteen minutes had gone by when Sheriff Calvin got an update from his precinct. They had easily located Keith at his home and he had an airtight alibi. He didn't seem to have any information to help them.

The officers arranged for a detective to keep track of Keith, just in case. Sheriff Calvin was not taking any chances with Brooke's safety.

Mike's phone rang. "Mike here."

"Mike, it's Von."

"What do you have?" He hoped it was something good.

"A text message."

"Great."

"No, not great. It's not from Brooke's number, but it says it's from Brooke."

"Go on . . ." Mike's jaw tightened.

Von read it to Mike. "It says, 'Goto hell. Déjà vu?' "

Mike's text message alert sounded on his phone. "Hang on," he said to Von. He swept his finger over the icons to retrieve the message.

Goto Hell. Déjà vu?

He pulled the phone back up to his ear. "I just got it too."

Rick rounded the corner. "Mike. I just—"

"I got it too," Mike said as he swallowed back the fear that threatened to break him. "Rick got the message too, Von."

Von's voice was rigid. "He has her. Why is he playing this game with us?"

Mike went white. The room spun. Déjà vu? No. "I know where she is."

"I thought the guy was dead. I'm on my way," Von said.

"I knew it was too good to be true," Mike said. "Get here. I need y'all with me on this," he said, looking toward Rick, "because if I find him first I'm going to squeeze the life out of him with my bare hands."

Von's profiling expertise came in handy. He'd quickly pulled the other cases that they'd suspected Goto was guilty of, but had been unable to prove. Then he had their computer system pull data on all the cellmates Goto had spent time with over the past eight years. That was an opportunity for Goto to pick up a new skill or idea that wouldn't have been part of his prior profile. Armed with that data, Mike now had a good idea what else Goto was capable of. As if what he'd done before wasn't bad enough.

Sheriff Calvin gathered his team at the station. Von was on his way, and Mike and Rick had marked out the property information on the diagram in the precinct room.

Mike put Von on the speakerphone as they briefed all team members on the plan and possible scenarios.

"You've been busy. This sounds like a good plan. So my job is to just stall him while you all get into position, right?" Von confirmed.

"Yes. Exactly. No plan is perfect, so I need you

to take the precautions we talked about, just in case. When will you be here?"

Von said, "I should be at your place in fifteen more minutes."

"Perfect. We're all here. Just waiting on you and we can make the move."

"Mike. We'll get her back. She's the pawn. You're the target. Be smart. It's going to be all right."

"It has to be, Von. It has to be."

❖ Chapter Forty-Seven ❖

Brooke struggled to move. Even in her woozy state, she knew something wasn't right.

"You're awake." A low, muted voice came from behind her.

She gulped down breaths as the whisper sent a chill down her neck. She wiggled fingers and toes and seemed to be in one piece but that was all the range of motion she had. The agonizing pain throbbing in her skull made it hard to focus.

Was the voice familiar? Keith? She was too groggy to be sure. She let her eyes close again.

Someone grabbed her shoulder, shaking her back to reality. "Hey, don't doze back off. You want to be awake for this. It's almost show time."

Almost time for what? Where am I? Aside from the two stair steps in front of her, she could only make out trees and overgrown brush through the foggy vision. Why was she tied down? Was she on a stretcher in the ambulance again? Mosquitoes buzzed loudly and itchy bites were already swelling.

None of the pieces fit.

She tried to call out for help, but all that came out was a moan. A puff of air came from behind her, followed by a length of fabric being slung across her face, between her lips, and tied around her neck. The knot pulled at her hair.

Commotion from somewhere in front of her forced her to try to open her eyes again. Voices, maybe one or was it two? She struggled to stay conscious. Aware. Know her surroundings.

The rustling in the bushes stopped and it got very quiet.

For what seemed like a long time, there was nothing.

In the brush about fifty feet in front of her, the crunch of leaves signaled something or someone's approach. Either way, animal or man, it wasn't likely to be a good thing. It was getting dark. It could be a bear. She strained to listen, but the pounding of her heart and the increased rhythm of her breathing was making it hard to make sense of any of it.

She tried to call out, but the cloth in her mouth muffled the noise she made. It wasn't loud enough to summon help. The humidity hung in the air, and as the sky grew darker, the night sounds became louder. And as her mind began to clear, the darkness and deafening chirps and howls only sent her imagination racing.

Just ahead, in a small clearing a large figure stepped out of the shadowy darkness. The fear of the unknown was quickly replaced with hope. The figure moved in the darkness, nearly colo-less against the inky blackness, but she could make out the gait. A man in a Western hat moved slowly in her direction.

Good guy or bad guy?

A gunshot, too close for comfort, nearly sent her out of her skin.

The man in black fell with a thud to the ground.

She screamed, gulping for air and struggling to free her hands or pull up from the porch, but it was useless.

"Scare you?" the muffled voice grunted from the bushes in front of the house.

Brooke shook uncontrollably.

"I got the message," the man yelled toward the house as he began to get up.

Brooke let the breath out that she had been holding. *Mike?* It was his voice, but she'd never seen him in a hat like that. Thank god, he was alive. He'd save her.

"That you, Von?" the voice grumbled from the bushes, followed by a string of expletives.

"It's me, Goto."

The man standing in front of her might have said he was Von, but she knew the shape of his body even in the dark night. And his voice still tickled every nerve ending. There was no doubt it was him.

"Step out here where I can see you."

Mike stepped out of the protection of the trees with his hands in the air, hoping Goto would show himself when he realized he wasn't armed.

"Where's your partner in crime?"

"He's on his way, Goto," Mike called out, praying Goto would buy that he was Von and buy them the time they needed to get everyone in place.

Goto muttered under his breath.

Mike took a hesitant step out into the lane. Playing like he was Von might have been a risky move, but he wasn't putting anyone else in Goto's crosshairs when he knew damn well that he was the target.

Thank god, Rick and Von hadn't given him a hassle about the plan he'd come up with. Not that there'd been much time for bantering around options. They all had the same goal in mind and Sheriff Calvin had his men on board too.

Mike moved into position and now he had a clear view of the whole porch, and his heart nearly stopped when he saw Brooke was there—tied—just like Jackie had been. He prayed to God for the strength to hold it together. Stick to the plan.

Mike tried to keep his voice emotionless. "Why don't you let the girl go? She doesn't have anything to do with this, Goto." Mike stepped back into the cover of the trees. He needed to pull himself together, to keep from running out there and shredding the man limb from limb with his bare hands.

Another shot rang out. The shot whizzed by his right ear, too close for comfort. He dove to the ground.

"Hold it right there, Von," yelled Goto. "What are you doing? Don't move."

Mike threw his hands in the air, trying to get Goto to calm down. "It's cool, man. Quit firing that damn thing. What do you want?"

"Where's Mike?"

Mike prayed Goto wouldn't come too close or he'd see him and the charade would be over. "I told you he's on his way."

"You alone?"

"No. I'm with you and Brooke, damn it. Why don't you let Brooke go?" Mike said.

The laugh was hearty and vile. "Oh, yeah, you'd like that, wouldn't you? That won't be happening."

"Come on, man, let her go. You can put me on the porch and we can wait for Mike together," Mike tried to reason with him, but he knew reasoning with a man like that wasn't going to work. He got up and slowly took four strides forward. So far so good. "What do you say?"

Another shot cracked loudly.

Mike dove for cover in the shadows of the night. That last bullet was close again. Either this bastard was a lousy shot, or Mike was living under a helluva lucky star and he didn't really want to know which. "Okay. I get the message. Go to hell." And those were the words that would send the team into motion.

Sweeping lights filled the lane, filling the darkness with a flood of bright white for a minute. Then an engine shut down and the lights dimmed, making it seem even darker than before.

Goto snickered from the bushes. His excitement scared Brooke even more. He was taking pleasure in this and she wondered if they weren't playing right into his plan.

She prayed Goto wouldn't figure out he was talking to Mike, and she prayed Mike had a foolproof plan or they'd all be dead.

A door slammed.

No. Whoever was getting ready to walk out was surely a dead man.

Voices filled the air, amplified by a loudspeaker. "Police, drop it right there. Freeze."

Two shots fired off from the bushes right next to her, but there was no return fire.

Another car slid across soft dirt to a stop somewhere out of her view.

Suddenly lights came back on from every direction, blinding her and hopefully Goto in the process.

But a flurry of shots came from Goto again.

She spotted Mike in Von's hat run down the side toward the house.

"Who's there?" Goto yelled from the bushes. "Where's Mike?"

"It's me," a voice came from just beyond the tree line.

But Brooke knew she'd seen Mike run to the side of the house. Whatever plan they had going was in full swing, and Goto seemed to be buying it. So far.

The voice that was supposedly Mike's yelled from near the tree line again. "What have you done? You clipped an officer in all that wild shooting. He's not breathing, man. That'll put you away for a long time. Guess you've been missing your buddy, Rabbit, huh?"

"Shut up." Goto stepped out of the bushes, facing off with the man he thought was Mike. "Big deal—you should have come alone and they wouldn't have had to die. They weren't part of my plan. Afraid to fight your own battle?"

"Let me call for help, Goto. You don't want them to die," the man impersonating Mike tried to reason with him.

"What do I care? Just means a bigger hole to bury you all," Goto screamed. "Can't get convicted of killing someone if there ain't no bodies. And they can't convict me since they think I'm dead."

Brooke sensed the panic in Goto's voice.

"Who'd you kill to make us think you died? Who'd you plant your identification on?" The light from the moon reflected from the shiny handgun he held balanced in Goto's direction.

"Doesn't matter. They believe it's me. I'm free. Really free." Goto said. "You might want to drop that gun. I got your girl on the step here. You know I won't have any problem hurting her."

Brooke registered the escalating danger. She'd thought she was in danger with Keith, but now she was in far more danger than she'd ever considered. Mike had been right all along.

Goto swung his flashlight in Brooke's direction.

She shrank back as the light shone brightly in her eyes. She squinted, unable to deflect or hide from the glare.

Goto wiggled the light back and forth across her face, then yelled in Mike's direction. "Say hello to your little friend. She looks kind of scared, don't she?" Goto's laugh was on the verge of hysteria.

"Does that turn you on? It turns me on," said Goto with a grunt.

"Brooke. Stay calm, gal."

"Sorry, she's a little tied up right now." Goto guffawed, and then stepped up on the porch right next to her. "Drop that gun if you want to let her live a little longer."

When the light hit the man Goto thought was Mike, he had his head down. He had disarmed.

Her heart sank. Surely they would die. There was no way for him to rescue her this time. *I love you, Mike.*

"Walk forward."

He challenged Goto. "You come out here."

"I'm calling the shots. But don't worry, this time I'm gonna let you watch it all. You won't have to wonder what happened. You'll know firsthand."

"Your beef is with me. Let her go."

"No, don't you see? I want you to suffer." He leaned over Brooke's body.

He was so close she could feel the heat off his body, and smell the beer on his breath, the stink of his body. Brooke screamed through the cloth of the gag.

He pulled the rag from Brooke's mouth, and then sliced the rope that held her neck to the porch column. She let out a cry and rolled over on the porch, hands and ankles still tied.

Goto screamed out a loud whoop. "I've got years of suffering to repay you for. You are going to watch it all and know it was your fault. I want to strip you of all control just like you did me." Goto stepped to the middle of the porch, and pulled on the plywood that hung across the front door. It fell with a loud clap. He pushed the front door open.

Goto nudged her shoulder with the butt of the semiautomatic rifle. He grabbed Brooke by the roped wrists and dragged her to a standing position. He leaned his face into the back of her shoulder and neck.

She dragged in a stuttered breath as the scrape of Goto's unshaven chin and the heat of his breath against her skin made her sick; the bile rose in her throat.

They needed Goto off the porch. He had to keep from moving in too close too quickly.

Mike had edged his way quietly around the back side of the small house. The boards that once barricaded the back door had been pulled from the house. Goto must have been hiding out here planning this for a while. Mike stayed close to the building to avoid casting a shadow. He moved silently across the overgrown roadbed that circled this house, his home, at one time. His heart was heavy. Breathing and keeping focus was difficult with the past invading his thoughts.

Mike stooped near the edge of the porch. He could see Brooke sniffing back tears. All he needed to do was get Goto in position to the left of the house or surprise and disarm him before then.

Von was holding his own in the role reversal. Goto seemed none the wiser.

Mike's anger grew as Goto ran the butt of that rifle along her body. Brooke's body looked limp and shaky even from this distance.

"Calm down, Goto."

"Calm. Hell." The crazy man's laughter filled the dank air. "Things are just getting good."

The rope around Brooke's ankles tightened as Goto tugged on it and dragged her to the doorway. He positioned her in the middle of the threshold.

"Get down here, you shallow bastard," yelled Von, still pretending to be Mike.

Goto popped a fresh clip in the gun. His breathing was loud and heavy. He stood stone still, then made three quick leaps from the porch down the stairs, eyes focused on his prey.

Von matched Goto step for step, trying to maneuver him away from the house like they'd planned. Mike lunged from his position next to the porch and grabbed Goto's ankle, pulling him off-balance. Mike then jumped to his feet, dragged Goto by the sides of his shirt, and tossed him into a heap.

Goto went down quick and hard, his breath jarring out of him and the gun unloading nearly every bit of ammunition in a sweeping arc across the entire area.

It was just enough commotion for the rest of the team to move into position. Dark uniformed officers moved in from every direction of the house and surrounding area.

Mike and Goto tussled and then there were further gunshots and neither man moved.

"No!" Brooke screamed.

Lights bounced off the house in red, white, and blues like a dizzying Fourth of July display. The first voice Brooke recognized was Sheriff Calvin's.

Blaring sirens were as disorienting as the blinking lights. People scurried around her. Police radio chatter filled the air with so much noise that it created a sensory overload.

"Mike? No!" Brooke broke down into a heap. Gulping for air, and praying.

Rick placed his arm on hers. "Do you know where you are?"

She shook her head.

"The house where Jackie and Mike lived," Rick said. "Stay calm. The medics are here to check you out."

"But Mike. We have to help Mike."

Rick grabbed both of her hands. "Calm down. He's okay."

"Don't leave me," Brooke cried out, but Rick had already run out toward a team of people. "I need Mike. He can't be . . ."

Medics swarmed in and around Brooke. An oxygen mask was placed over her face and they checked her vitals. Her heart rate was frantic as she sobbed in relief over being released and the horror of seeing men die right in front of her. She sobbed, shaking her head and crying, "No . . . no . . . no . . ." between ragged breaths.

A hand caught hers from the left side. When she turned, her eyes went wide as they connected with Mike's. "Mike?"

"I'm right here, Brooke."

She shook her head and tried to pull the pieces together. "Mike? I thought . . . I thought . . . I saw you die."

"Brooke, no. I'm okay. I promise you. I'm so sorry for all of this. I never wanted to put you in harm's way."

"You're alive. You're not . . ." She sobbed, reaching for him.

He held her in his arms. "I thought I was going to lose you."

"Oh, my god. I thought I lost everything."

"I'm right here."

The medics stepped in, informing Mike that they were going to get the stretcher to take Brooke to the hospital to get checked out, and they would bring back the kit to take care of his shoulder, which was bleeding heavily.

Mike nodded.

"I don't want to go to the hospital, Mike. Just take me home. I just want to be near you."

"I love you." He rocked her in his arms, tears in his own eyes. "I love you, Brooke."

They both jerked their heads to attention at the sound of someone yelling, coming toward them, "Hey . . . hey . . . Brooke? Mike?" It was Jenny and Rick.

Rick stooped in front of them and held them both. "I can't believe this."

Jenny reached for Brooke's chin. "Your face looks like it's burned."

Brooke nodded. "I think it's a reaction to whatever he drugged me with. He put something over my face. All I remember is sitting on the porch swing at the farm house, then *bam*, the next thing I knew I was on this porch with one pounding headache. I'm a little dizzy and my head is killing me, but I think I'm in one piece."

Jenny clung to Rick. "He took you in Rick's truck. Oh, Brooke. We were all so worried."

Sheriff Calvin walked over to them. "You don't have to worry about him getting out this time."

"I didn't think I had to worry last time." Rick shook his head in disgust and spat on the ground.

Sheriff Calvin repositioned his hat. "He's dead."

"Dead?" Mike questioned, then looked to Rick and Von.

Sheriff Calvin filled them in on the details he had so far. "We're still pulling the evidence, but it appears it was his own bullet that did it. You should see the walls inside. He painted detailed murals on the walls of his plans. Sick."

Jenny's eyes went wide. "Like the murals painted in my studio."

Rick pulled her close. "Don't even say it. I can't believe he was this close to our lives and we didn't know it."

She shivered in the warm night. "Me either. Brooke, I'm sorry I let him in to our lives. I was so worried about making deals that I didn't even consider he could be bad news. If I hadn't . . ."

Mike shook his head. "Jenny, there's no way you could know. We didn't even know. It's over. That's all that matters."

Rick walked forward and peered into the house. "Sick bastard."

Mike refused to go inside and look. He needed space from all of it. That guy had eaten up his life for more years than he was worth. He wouldn't give him another second.

Rick walked back over and wrapped Jenny into his arms. "We'll paint over those murals in the locker rooms tomorrow. Don't even think about it."

Sheriff Calvin walked up. "My guys will help with that painting. I think I can speak for everyone that the sooner we wipe away any memory of this—the better."

"Thanks, man." Rick sucked in a breath then asked, "Any idea where my truck is?"

"It's in the tree line just up the road. One of my guys just called it in," said Sheriff Calvin.

After a quick debrief of each of them with the sheriff, Rick stood and slapped the dirt off his jeans. "Can we catch a ride with you, Sheriff? I think these two need to be alone."

Mike held Brooke. "Are you sure you won't let the hospital check you out?"

"I'm okay. Just take me home."

"I'll take you home with me then. I'm not ready to let you out of my sight. Is that okay with you?"

"More than anything."

❖ Chapter Forty-Eight ❖

Mike tooted the horn and exchanged a wave with Sheriff Calvin and Rick, who were standing by the car talking.

Brooke slumped back against the seat. "What a day."

"What a month. I'm just thankful you're here with me now," he said, resting his hand on her leg.

"Me too."

A couple miles down Route 58 and a left turn, then Mike was driving down a heavily treed asphalt driveway.

"Where are we?" she asked.

"Almost home."

She smiled. That sounded nice.

As the truck approached the lighted area around the house, Brooke had to blink twice to believe her eyes. It was like she was living her fantasy. This was the log cabin of her dreams. The same style, the same colors, the same lights. She shook her head, hoping like hell she wasn't dead or dreaming all of this. "A log cabin? Is this where you live?"

"You don't like it?"

Brooke was so shocked she could barely pull the thought together. "No. That's not it at all. Did Jenny tell you about my fantasy?"

"No." He slowed to a stop. "But I hope like heck I'm part of it."

Brooke eyed him cautiously. "So, do you live here or not?"

"I don't live here yet, but I don't think you need to be climbing the stairs to my apartment and I don't want anyone interrupting us. We had the power turned on so the guys could finish the kitchen installation. The last thing on the list. I haven't finished moving everything in, but it'll do for tonight. Besides, Hunter is here and I need to check on him. I asked Jenny to stop by and take care of Stitches for you."

"Thank you, Mike."

"Come on, let's get inside. I'll start a fire." Mike headed up the stairs ahead of her and opened the door.

"It's not cold out," she said.

"I know. We'll crank up the air-conditioning if we have to."

Brooke walked in, nearly fainting from the déjà vu, but in a good way this time. She could have told him how it was decorated. In fact, she kind of wished she had, because there was no way he'd believe her if she told him now. It was spot-on with her fantasy.

Mike disappeared down the hall. When he came back in the room, he pointed her in that direction. "I have a hot bath running for you, and left something out for you to put on."

"Thanks." She knew the way, she thought to herself. She had made this walk a hundred times in her dreams. Sure enough, as she followed the light down the hall, there was the claw-foot tub filling with water. She took the quickest bath of her life. She couldn't even relax and enjoy it. She was too excited to get back in Mike's arms. She needed to be in his arms. She climbed out of the tub and dried off, then she slipped into one of Mike's shirts that he'd left out for her, rolling the sleeves a couple turns until her hands peeked through the cuffs. The men's socks were big, but warm and soft on her feet. She turned this way and that in the mirror. She looked far from sexy, but she didn't even care at this point.

Mike's hair was still wet from his shower. He looked up from the snap and crackle of the hot blaze of the fire he had just built. The fire sent a warm gold glow around the room. His gaze met hers.

She shook a hand through the damp waves of her hair. "This was not exactly the look I planned to make you fall in love with me someday."

"You have never looked more beautiful to me." He motioned her to come to him. She padded softly across the floor to where he was on one bended knee in front of the fire. He took her hands in his, and from the kneeling position in front of her asked, "Brooke, will you be my bride?"

"I will. Forever. It's what I want more than anything," she said.

He smiled, and grabbed her hands, holding them in his.

She loved the way the lines formed around his eyes when he smiled.

He wrapped his arms around her, pulling her in. Kissing her. They were lost in the emotion of the day and the possibilities of their future together.

"Do you love me as much as I love you?" she asked.

"Even more." He stood and extended a hand to her. "Come with me?"

"Anywhere."

He led her to his bedroom. The strong colors and manliness of the room suited him. She could feel him in the space. He laid her back on the big bed, unbuttoning his own shirt from her tiny frame, letting the soft fabric fall to the sides. He let a hand fall to her foot, squeezing the arch in his palm. "Sexy socks."

"Warm," she said.

"I don't think you're going to need them."

"Me either."

He rolled the sock off her foot and let his hand under the arch of her foot bend her knee toward her chest. He kissed the inside of her knee softly.

"That tickles."

"That wasn't what I was going for." His hand caressed her leg. His eyes closed, as he enjoyed the journey and the softness of her skin. He reached forward and rubbed the outline of her bottom lip with his thumb. He let his palm trace a path from her chin to her flat tummy and then pulled himself alongside of her.

"I love you," she said in barely a whisper.

He let his mouth drop full on to hers and the hunger in the kiss matched the emotion of the day. He pressed his body full against her, leaving not a space between them.

She wrapped a leg around his body, needing to be closer to him.

He made a trail of soft kisses down her smooth skin.

She closed her eyes and gave in to him.

"I don't want to ever let go," she whispered.

"Don't." He hugged her close. "You're my angel."

She kissed him. "I'll always be yours."

They lay still, breathing in the silence and each other.

She nearly stopped breathing. There on his right shoulder, just like in her dream, was the tattoo. She hadn't noticed it before. The blues, the yellows all the same as in that dream. She could make it out now though, it was of the log cabin. She lifted up on an elbow and blinked, to be sure she wasn't imagining it.

"Are you staring at me?"

"When did you get that tattoo?"

"Oh, that? I've had it for years. It's partly why I wanted this house," he said. "Only tattoo I ever got. I was young."

"I love it."

He lowered his mouth to her ear and whispered. "I love you." He climbed from the bed.

She watched as he padded toward the door. Her fantasy was coming true before her eyes, nearly every small detail.

She flopped back into the pillows. "I'm the luckiest girl in the world."

Mike must have heard her, because he leaned back into the doorway. "Not as lucky as me."

❖ Chapter Forty-Nine ❖

Mike leaned across his desk, reviewing notes from a case. Now that he'd moved into the house and was only using the space as an office, it was nice to just leave the door propped open during the day.

A tick-click-clicking sound came from down the hall. He got ready to get up and see where the noise was coming from when Stitches pranced through the doorway.

"What are you doing here?" He didn't hear or see Brooke behind her. "Where's your mama?"

Hunter came bounding out from where he'd been sleeping in his kennel.

The two dogs danced in the middle of the office for a moment, then Stitches went to Mike, and tapped him on his leg to get her head patted like she always did. When he reached down to pet her, he noticed a small blue envelope with his name on it hanging on a ribbon around her neck.

"What did you bring me, girl?" He tugged on one end of the bow, and lifted the dog into his lap. She rewarded him with two soft kisses on his cheek, and Hunter pawed for attention. "Thanks for the sweet kisses. Let's read this together. What do you say?" Mike opened the envelope and read the short note aloud to the dogs.

Brooke's script was like her, soft and feminine. "Happy one-month anniversary. All my love, B."

Movement from the hall caught his attention.

Brooke stood in the doorway. "One month since I came to my senses. Happy anniversary."

Stitches jumped from Mike's lap at the sound of Brooke's voice, and Hunter just ran in circles around them all.

Mike gave Hunter a command to settle down, then he turned back to Brooke. "Please tell me you're not one of those people who celebrates every little thing by the month, week, and moment? I have to tell you, I struggle with just keeping one birthday straight."

"No-oo. I'm not. Well, not usually anyway. I just love you so much that I couldn't help myself. Things have been so good. Thanks for being in my life."

He pulled her onto his lap and the chair spun to the left. "I love you too." He nodded toward the desk. "Pull open that drawer."

She tugged on the center drawer, revealing neat piles of business cards and rows of pencils.

"Not that one. The one on the left."

She pulled it open. Right on top was a deep-blue velvet box. "For me?"

"Yep."

"I love presents."

"I love giving them to you."

"So you did remember the one-month anniversary?"

"No. This is just an 'I love you' gift."

As she pulled the box out, she noticed another deep-blue box behind it. "Two?"

"The other one is an EBS."

"Is that fancy PI code talk?"

"EBS. Emergency backup spare," he explained.

"I still don't know what that means."

"You will. Open the small one first."

The blue box snapped open with a pop. A row of diamonds on an eternity band with a horseshoe of square-cut rubies glistened. "It's beautiful." She slipped it onto her right ring finger. "What does this mean?"

"Do you like it?"

She wrapped her arms around his neck. "I love it."

"Will you marry me, Brooke Justice?"

"An engagement ring?"

"If you say yes, it is."

"I thought I said yes a month ago. I love you, Mike." She kissed him. "And I love the ring. Of course, I'll marry you."

"And now the ring makes it official. Let's set a date."

"Great."

"So what is the EBS for?"

"Well, I wasn't sure if you would think it was bad luck to have a nontraditional engagemen ring, so I wanted something lucky on hand just to seal the deal." He grabbed the long box and snapped it open in front of her.

A charm bracelet. The bracelet itself appeared to be vintage, but the shiny charms weren't. Hanging from the chain was a clover charm, a lucky horseshoe, a ladybug, a cardinal, a rainbow, a shooting star, the number fifteen, and a high-heeled shoe.

Tears tickled her lashes and nose. Her heart felt like it was about to burst. She couldn't even touch it. "I love it," she mouthed, but the emotion didn't let the words come out; instead tears streamed down her cheeks.

She picked up the bracelet and let it fall across her hand, admiring each charm. Then she looked puzzled. "A shoe?"

"The shoe rescue was a defining moment for us, so I figured it was good luck."

"So it was, and pretty damn romantic too."

"I wanted you to know that I will make sure every day of your life is luckier than the last. I love you, Brooke, every day, always and in all ways."

Choking the words through the emotion she stammered, "This—is—so much more than I ever dreamed. You're the luckiest thing in my life."

acknowledgments

Thank you to the amazing team at Amazon Publishing that has worked so hard to help me bring the Adams Grove series to you, and for believing in me every step of the way.

A big shout-out to Krista McNamara for falling in love with Adams Grove and putting her continuity hat on to help me be sure the story lines continued from book to book in this series without hiccups.

To all of my "writer girl" friends and the members of the Dangerous Darlings Street Team, thank you for always being there and for being brave enough to try mint juleps for the first time. *Mint juleps are not for sissies, by the way!*

Center Point Large Print
600 Brooks Road / PO Box 1
Thorndike, ME 04986-0001 USA

(207) 568-3717

US & Canada:
1 800 929-9108
www.centerpointlargeprint.com